The Cruise

Catherine Cooper is a journalist specialising in travel, hotels and skiing who writes regularly for the *Telegraph* and the *Guardian* among others. She lives near the Pyrenees in the South of France with her family and is a keen skier. Her debut, *The Chalet*, was a top 5 *Sunday Times* bestseller. *The Cruise* is her third novel.

 @catherinecooper

D0250002

By Catherine Cooper

The Chalet
The Chateau
The Cruise

The Cruise

CATHERINE COOPER

HarperCollins*Publishers*

HarperCollins*Publishers*
1 London Bridge Street,
London SE1 9GF

www.harpercollins.co.uk

HarperCollins*Publishers*
1st Floor, Watermarque Building, Ringsend Road
Dublin 4, Ireland

Published by HarperCollins*Publishers* Ltd 2022
2

A catalogue copy of this book is available from the British Library.

ISBN: 9780008497293 (PB)
ISBN: 9780008497309 (E)

Typeset in Sabon by
Palimpsest Book Production Limited, Falkirk, Stirlingshire

Printed and Bound in the UK using
100% renewable electricity at CPI Group (UK) Ltd

For Alex, with love and thanks
for all your support and plot help, and because
this one has a port hole on the cover. xxx

Michael has never been anywhere as grand as this before. He hangs the 'Do Not Disturb' sign on the handle, closes the door of his stateroom and takes it all in.

The bed is enormous. The towel placed on top has been crafted into the shape of a swan. He touches its beak. Clever. The bed linen is crisp white with the discreet blue-and-gold logo of the cruise company, Heracles, on each of the pillows.

There is a basket of fruit on a small table by a gold velvet armchair. Not apples and oranges and everyday pieces like that, but mango, kiwi, papaya and a bright pink fruit which has already been cut in half to expose a strange black and white interior – dragon fruit.

Michael picks up the silver spoon set alongside it on a white, logoed plate with a folded linen napkin. The spoon is pleasingly heavy and hallmarked, he notices, and stamped with the name of the ship – Immanis. He unties the thick, gold and blue velvet ribbon, unwraps the cellophane and

1

takes a scoop of the dragon fruit. He's expecting it to be delicious from the way it looks, but it's strangely tasteless. Ah well. He cuts a slice of mango instead. The juice runs down his hand and he pops it into his mouth. Much better.

He goes into the black marble bathroom and rinses the juice off. There's a walk-in shower as well as an enormous bath and a huge array of toiletries – not only shampoo and shower gel but exfoliators, body lotions and shaving gel. There's also a full-sized bottle of his favourite aftershave which he has been ordering from a perfumier in Morocco since discovering it when he was on holiday there years ago. There's a note underneath on which 'With the compliments of the captain and crew' is written in elaborate cursive.

He picks up the bottle, takes off the cap and inhales the woody scent. It immediately transports him back to memories of dusty squares, souks, leather stalls and hawkers trying to sell camel rides to tourists. He smiles. That was all a very long time ago. But he still orders his aftershave from the same little shop to this day, at least when he can afford it.

He wonders how they knew about the aftershave. He's a bit of a social media addict these days, and comes to the conclusion that he must have mentioned it on his Facebook page at some point. He spends a lot of time on Facebook, looking for competitions to enter. And over the years he's won a lot. Mainly things of no great consequence – a few chocolate bars here or an item of clothing there. A sofa, one time. Sometimes things he can't even use, like a year's supply of dog food. He gave that to a local shelter – they were delighted. Whatever the prize, the thrill of winning is always the same. He lives a quiet life these days – no partner, very few friends, not much of a social life. But he does enjoy his competitions.

The best thing he's ever won is a car. Or at least, that was the best thing he'd won before this trip.

He doesn't remember entering the competition to win the cruise. But he enters so many, especially to try to win holidays, that he's not that surprised.

He's jet-lagged after his long journey, but he knows what will sort him out – a soak in the hot tub on the balcony. Just the thing. He's been looking forward to it since he received the email telling him he'd won, with a link to a virtual tour of the suite he'd be staying in. He loves hot tubs. He can't afford one at home but is forever trying to win one. No luck so far – but this is the next best thing.

He strips off, folding his clothes neatly onto the gold chair, and takes the thick, deep blue robe from the bed to wrap around himself. As he unfolds it, a sign falls out which perkily states 'Want to take me home? I'm available for sale in the gift shop!'

He smiles. He wonders how much a suite like this would cost if he was paying for it. A lot, he is sure. Why would someone with that kind of money steal a robe?

Still, he can see why they might want to – it's about the softest thing he's ever worn. He unties a gold ribbon from the disposable slippers, which are deep blue with the ship's logo in gold. The soles are thick and sumptuous – wearing them is like walking on air.

He takes the mini bottle of champagne from the ice bucket, pops the cork and pours himself a glass. He doesn't generally drink much these days, and certainly never alone. But it seems a shame to let it go to waste, and besides, being here, like this, is in itself a special occasion. One to celebrate, surely.

He pads over to the glass doors and slides them open. It's a beautiful night. Stepping out on to the balcony, he puts his glass down on a small table, folds back the cover on the hot tub and leaves it to one side. He's already put the 'Do not disturb' sign on the door.

He climbs up the wooden steps, puts one foot into the water, and 220 volts shoot through him, stopping his heart almost immediately. He falls face down into the water, where he remains until his bloated body is found by a cleaner two days later.

Prologue

The *Immanis* is eighteen decks high – taller than the Eiffel Tower – and the length of five football pitches. She is five times the size of the *Titanic*, not that anyone wants to think about anything like that right now as they embark, of course. There are twenty-five restaurants on board – one has two Michelin stars – and twenty-two bars, including one which only serves champagne, caviar and oysters. There are six pools, three theatres, two spas and a casino. There's also a water park with slides and surf simulator, a zip wire between two of the funnels, a rollercoaster and a fully kitted out soft play centre, currently the largest anywhere at sea. In short, everything that anyone could wish for on the perfect Caribbean cruise is here.

And the suites! The twenty best suites are each two storeys high with enormous terraces and private plunge pools. Each one comes with its own personal butler who is on hand 24/7 to help with anything that is needed. Anything at all.

All the passengers are very excited – they barely have a care in the world. And why would they? What could possibly go wrong? Cruising is one of the safest forms of transport. Worldwide, nearly thirty million people typically go on a cruise every year. There are very few accidents. Very few. Almost no one thinks about the handful of people who go missing from these trips each year – most of these passengers arriving probably don't even know about them. Naturally, almost no one yet has any idea that someone will go missing on this very trip. Preparations are already being made. Plans are in motion. They have been for a long time.

PART ONE

1

Antonio

New Year's Eve 2021, 12:00
The Caribbean

'Lola! Come on! You're not concentrating!' Jamie, the entertainment director, shouts.

High above the ground, Lola is spinning round and round in her harness, giggling hysterically, the flowing feathers of her costume trailing behind her.

'It's New Year's Eve, Jamie!' she calls. 'Let's have some fun, for once! Wheeeeeeeeee! Wheeeeee!'

Jamie stabs at the iPad that controls the harness and it moves slowly to lower Lola to the ground. She is still twirling, only stopping when the floor comes up to meet her feet.

I try to hide a smirk.

'You're no fun,' Lola grumbles. 'We already know this

routine inside out. Why do we need yet *another* dress rehearsal? There are so many better things we could be doing.' She yawns theatrically. 'Like sleeping, for one.'

Jamie gestures at the iPad again. 'Health and safety, Lola, as you well know. Periodically we have to check the harnesses, and that everything's still all in sync with the app.' He looks her up and down. 'In case you've lost weight. Or put it on. Or—'

'Rude!' she cries good-naturedly. 'How dare you suggest I've put on weight?'

I see him try to stifle a smile. He is trying to be strict but no one can ever resist Lola. Everyone loves her.

'You know very well that I'm not suggesting anything,' he says. 'I just want to keep the Safety Officer off my back, and check that you're not going to come crashing down on some poor unfortunate audience member's head, or be accidentally slammed into the wall or floor. Unless that's what you want, of course.'

Bit unnecessary, the violent imagery, I think. All three of us know these are basically box-ticking exercises.

Lola bites her lip and pulls an exaggerated look of contrition. 'No, Jamie,' she says in a little-girl voice. 'I'm sorry. I don't want that. I'll be good now, I promise.'

He nods. 'Glad to hear it,' he says. 'So, if you're ready to behave *professionally*, Lola, we'll get all the checks out of the way, and then you can go back to sleep or do whatever you want to do. Antonio – you ready too?'

'Yup, ready to go.'

Jamie jabs at the screen, the music starts and our two harnesses rise slowly on either side of the stage as we grip the purple silk drapes which rise with them. I hold the fixed position we take at the beginning of the performance, secured only by one foot and one hand wrapped into the silk, and Lola rises in a mirrored position, only she is twirling her free hand and foot sarcastically, flicking Jamie vees and wiggling her hips from side to side. Jamie sighs and turns away from her. He probably has other things he'd rather do than be here faffing around with the harnesses, but it's his neck on the line if anything goes wrong.

As we reach the top, the music changes and we let go of the silks. The harnesses also drop slightly at the very same moment, as if we are about to fall, which always draws shocked gasps from the audience. In their absence, Lola calls out a silly 'ooooohhhhhh', performs an unscheduled somersault and pulls a stupid face as our two harnesses make us 'fly' to meet in the middle, where we perform our dance, several metres above the stage.

At this point Lola stops messing around and we move in perfect sync, gliding towards, around and away from each other, swooping, turning, looping, meeting each other's eyes and then turning away again. In perfect time with the music, telling its story. In perfect sync with each other.

We have performed this routine so many times it is almost meditative. Hypnotic and mesmerizing for the audience.

The final chords sound, we strike our finishing pose and are then slowly lowered to the ground, where Jamie unclips us.

Lola takes an over-exaggerated bow, collects invisible flowers which are apparently being thrown by an imaginary audience, mouthing 'thank you, thank you' and then asks: 'Happy, Jamie? Are we *safe* enough for you now?'

Jamie prods at the iPad. 'Yep. All done. That wasn't so bad, Lola, was it?'

'It was *brilliant*,' she mocks, 'I have literally never, ever had more fun in my life.'

Jamie ignores her sarcasm. 'Good to hear. See you both later. Don't do anything I wouldn't do in the meantime – the big boss is here for the evening show and I need you both in top form.'

Once Jamie is out of earshot, Lola says: 'God, that guy is tedious.'

'He's just doing his job, Lola – doing his best to keep us safe and healthy. You should be pleased.'

She pouts. 'It's so *boring* though. And speaking of *healthy*, I'm desperate for a smoke – I'm going to get rid of this costume and go outside.' She picks up her bag. 'What are you doing now?'

'I thought I might go to the gym.'

She laughs. 'Rather you than me.'

'What about you? Back to bed like you said to Jamie?'

'Maybe later. I'm meeting Alice for coffee. Stuff we've got to talk about.'

'Stuff? Like what?' I ask. Lola's always saying things like that to wind me up – she knows I hate it when she has secrets from me.

She taps the side of her nose. 'Wouldn't you like to know? Nothing for you to worry about – just girl stuff. See you later, gym boy. Enjoy your workout.'

2

Alice

New Year's Eve 2021, 22:00
The Caribbean

I've been summoned to the captain's table this evening. It'll be my first time since being on board. Apparently, CEO Nico has come for a visit, and he wants to meet me. I'm told he's been desperate to get a three-Michelin-starred chef on *Immanis* for ages, and I have now made that wish come true.

Cute.

I've dressed up for the occasion – it's probably a bit over the top, but I'm in a Vampire's Wife dress I was given by a very rich client as a thank you for a particularly good dinner party I catered. It's about the first time I've been out of chef's scrubs or pyjamas since I joined the ship. I'm looking forward to a night away from the kitchen, eating the best quality food, carefully prepared by my sous chefs and served by fawning waiters. What's not to like? I hope Nico arrives soon; it's a bit awkward making small talk with Leo by myself – he's not exactly known for his conversational skills and neither am I. I'm always more comfortable in the kitchen than at the table.

TopSail is the smartest restaurant on board by far and is at almost the highest point of the ship, accessed by a dedicated glass lift. The sixty-cover dining room (tiny for a ship of this size for that extra exclusive feel) has huge windows which go all the way round and, in a somewhat retro way, revolves.

Tonight I'm also taking the opportunity to check how the restaurant appears from a client's point of view, as I almost never get to do that. Chefs should eat in their own restaurants, but we don't. We never have the time.

'Nico, how lovely to see you,' gushes the hostess, a young woman in a tight, floor-length dress covered in black sequins, as Nico steps through the door. All guests in this restaurant are greeted by name – the staff are sent pictures with their bookings to make sure they get them right. Where possible, there are also a few biographical details so the waiters and hosts can do bespoke schmoozing, plus a list of their foodie likes and dislikes to make sure everything is catered to their personal tastes.

'Your table is ready for you. Captain Leo and Alice are already here,' she tells him. 'Please follow me.'

We stand as Nico arrives at the table and both shake his hand. 'I'm so pleased you could join me for dinner tonight, Leo, Alice,' Nico says. 'I appreciate it. I won't keep you long

14

'– I'm sure you have other people to see. And you should be able to enjoy your New Year's Eve, of course.'

We sit down and a waiter offers us a choice of various types of bread, all freshly baked on site today. I choose walnut and he places it on my side plate with tongs.

Leo smiles politely. 'It's a pleasure to see you, Nico, as always. But I'm afraid I won't be able to linger – I'm back on shift at midnight. The younger ones are more bothered about tonight's party than me, so I'm happy to let one of them have the time off and take my turn keeping the ship on course.'

Nico nods. 'That's very generous of you – I'm sure they appreciate it.'

Leo laughs. 'I doubt it.'

Some amuse-bouches are brought to the table and set in front of us. There's a blob of *wakame* (basically, seaweed by another name, but in a high-end restaurant like this, it is always wakame) on an elaborate spoon adorned with orange fish eggs, a parmesan crisp with cayenne topped with Beluga caviar, and a tiny courgette muffin served inside a freeze-dried and lightly caramelized courgette flower. All of these are my creations, and all ones of which I'm very proud. The waiter describes each one in an impressive amount of detail, as I insist they do. We serve three different amuse-bouches every day of the week, and the menu changes daily, so the servers have a lot to memorize. But it's important. People don't come to a Michelin-starred restaurant just for the food – they come for the entire experience. I sometimes say it's more like a theatrical production than a meal, and pretend I don't see the kitchen staff rolling their eyes. I'm right, though – I know I am.

15

The waiter finishes his spiel, which he does to perfection. I must remember to congratulate him on his next shift.

'This looks delicious, Alice,' Nico says. 'I don't mean to be a fanboy, but I'm not ashamed to say I'm extremely excited to have you on board, and almost as excited to be having dinner with you today. I've eaten several times at your restaurants and I wanted to tell you personally what a pleasure it always is, and how delighted I am that you accepted this post with Heracles. You've already worked wonders with TopSail, and I'm sure you'll put it even more on the map than it already is. If that makes sense.'

'The food has always been excellent on *Immanis*,' he continues, 'but it's really gone up a notch since you arrived. I hope that in the future, we might be the first ever cruise ship to have a three Michelin-starred restaurant. Wouldn't that be something?'

I blush. That would be something. And not something I can promise by any means. 'I'll do my best,' I say vaguely.

Three waiters appear in sync and whisk the used crockery away. The plates are replaced by elaborately and somewhat impractically shaped bowls of squid-ink soup with miso and pork belly.

'I was very pleasantly surprised,' Nico adds, 'that you took the post, to be honest. I never thought we'd get a big name like you on board.'

'Not at all,' I say. 'Who wouldn't want to spend some time in the Caribbean? Makes a change from rainy old London.' It wasn't quite as simple as that, but I don't want to shout about my reasons for wanting to get away, so I quickly move the conversation on.

Nico seems genuinely interested as I witter on about my favourite dishes, interspersed with some name-dropping of a few of the more famous clients I've served. Over the years, I've come to realize that most people are much more interested in hearing about who has eaten my food than about the food itself. However much I am known for my attention to detail when it comes to my dishes, a story about a celebrity ordering a £20,000 bottle of wine or being caught snorting coke in the loos always trumps me droning on about the provenance of my ingredients or the best way to grate truffles.

Once we have cleared our plates, they are again whisked away and replaced with wood pigeon breasts artfully arranged on crisped bok choy.

'And I understand you're staying on during the lay-up?' Nico adds.

'Looking forward to it,' I say. And I really am. I made it a condition of my employment. The lay-up is only two months, but all I'll have to do is cook for a skeleton crew, though I also want to use the time to develop the menus and strategies, and hope this might help me in my quest for a third star for the restaurant. I'll be overseeing meals for about a hundred people instead of several thousand as the ship is renovated, and on the same money too, so it's a pretty good deal for me. And after all that stuff that happened in London, I'm ready for some stress-free downtime.

'Everything is organized for the lay-up, Leo, is it?' Nico asks. 'You've got the required staff to keep it ticking over?'

'Yep – all sorted,' he confirms. 'Way more people wanting to stay on than we could take in the end. You think they'd be ready for a holiday away from the ship by now, but I guess they need the money. Or have nowhere else to go.' There is an awkward pause. 'I'm staying on too, as you know,' Captain Leo adds.

'And I appreciate that,' Nico says. 'I know *Immanis* will be in good hands.'

Dessert is brought out – a fruit salad, chopped into equally sized colourful cubes and delicately sculpted into a tower in a spun-sugar cage, sprinkled with edible glitter. As the two men ooh and ahh over the dessert and how pretty it is, the sparkly dressed hostess appears at the side of our table, her customary smile unusually absent.

'Captain, I'm so sorry to bother you, but I've had a message from the bridge asking you to radio them immediately.' She leans in closer so that the nearby tables can't hear. 'They say someone's gone overboard.'

3

Alice

New Year's Day 2022, 03:00
The Caribbean

I probably wouldn't have known that the ship had turned round and gone back the way it came, if I hadn't been there when Leo got the original call, or if it hadn't been for the general murmurs and gossip among the crew. It's difficult to have much sense of direction when you're on something this huge and can't see land.

But as soon as the lifeboat crews were scrambled, word spread round the workers almost as quickly as norovirus, the dirtiest word on a cruise ship in many senses. And after that, it wasn't long until some of the passengers started noticing that something was up too.

Even from up here on Deck 16, I can just about make

out the lights of the boats which are searching the water beneath. Looking down at them makes me feel queasy. I'm new to being on board, not only compared to most of the crew but also compared to a lot of the passengers, many of whom are veteran cruisers who come year after year – often on the same boat and sometimes even following the same itinerary. While I don't claim to be any kind of physicist, it is still beyond me that something this size can actually float. The sea scares me if I think about it too hard – it's so immense. Vast. Powerful. You fall in, you get swallowed up.

Rick, a junior engineer, is gazing out over the water, watching the lights. He's one of my favourite people that I've met since I joined – he's dry, funny, and reminds me of a brilliant pastry chef I worked with in London. He has a reputation for being a bit of a letch, but I'm too old for him to bother with so I can overlook that. He's not the brightest, admittedly, and neither is he the most popular of the crew, but I've always had a bit of a soft spot for the underdog. It can be lonely out at sea, I find, especially as I haven't been here that long. But I feel like he's my friend, and we have a laugh together.

'If you didn't know they were looking for someone who's either already dead or not even there, you could say the lights on the water were quite pretty,' Rick observes.

I laugh. 'That could be almost poetic, if it wasn't so macabre,' I say. He gives me a strange look.

'Macabre?' he asks.

'Ghoulish. Spooky. Something like that.'

He nods unselfconsciously. 'Right-o.'

'Anyway, what do you mean?' I continue. 'They're either dead or not there? Why would they be spending all this time and effort on a rescue effort if that was the case?'

Rick shrugs. 'The search – it's pointless, isn't it? They sent the boats out on the say-so of some woman who's been in the posh bar chugging champagne all night – hardly the most reliable of witnesses. And if someone *did* fall, there's almost no chance they would have survived. Look how high up we are.'

I look down at the water again and it makes my stomach lurch. It is indeed a long way down.

'Falling from the height of the bar – fifteen storeys – on to water is like falling on to concrete,' he continues. 'Chances are you'll hit the side of the boat at some point on the way down, and unless you land on an awning or something, that's unlikely to be a good thing.'

'Grim,' I agree.

'And even if by some miracle you land in the water alive, the ocean is enormous. The likelihood of you being found and rescued before you drown or die of hypothermia is negligible. Stopping a ship like this isn't like slamming the brakes on in a car. It takes several minutes and travels at least a mile before they can even start turning it round. Plus we're a long way from land. And as well as all that, have a guess how deep the Caribbean is at its deepest.'

'Erm . . . couple of hundred metres?' I venture. I don't really know anything about the sea beyond the occasional episode of *Blue Planet* I've watched when I'm not on shift which is almost never, but 200 metres sounds pretty deep to me.

He smiles. 'You div, Alice. You're way off.' He pauses for dramatic effect. 'More than seven thousand metres.'

'No way!' I am genuinely surprised.

He nods sagely. 'Yep. And that's not even as deep as it goes in other oceans. When you have a minute and the WiFi's working for more than a couple of seconds at a time, you should google the Mariana Trench. I can't remember exactly where it is but it's under the sea somewhere. If you were able to put Everest inside it, the peak would still be two thousand metres below sea level. Imagine that.' He pauses again. 'And then imagine being in a body of water that big, all alone, in the dark, after you've fallen from this height.'

I look down at the water and imagine someone falling into it and sinking, sinking and sinking. Ugh. I shudder. Doesn't bear thinking about.

'How do you know all this stuff anyway?' I ask.

He shrugs. 'It's what comes of a lifetime of having menial jobs where you don't have to talk to people that much. Plenty of time to listen to podcasts about all sorts. I don't read much – next to nothing – but I love listening to stuff.'

We both look at the water in silence together, watching the lights move across the surface, almost as if they're choreographed.

'The other thing to factor in,' he says, breaking the silence, 'is that if someone *did* go over, it's very likely to have been their own choice. The way cruise ships are designed these days, it's almost impossible to go overboard accidentally.' He taps the side of his nose. 'Mark my words, I'm right. One way or another, no one will be found alive. Bet you a mojito in Miami.' He offers his hand and I take it with a smile.

'A mojito in Miami,' I repeat. 'Done. Although betting on something like that feels . . . wrong.' I'm a bit embarrassed to feel my eyes mist as the thought of someone falling into something so deep is horrific. I hope Rick doesn't notice.

He pats me on the shoulder. 'Soft as sugar, you are. Right. Better get back to it. Those broken things won't fix themselves.'

I carry on looking out over the sea, staying where I am. I can't get the thought that someone might be in that dark water all alone, so far below, out of my head.

Many people are already in bed by the time the search begins, but some of those who aren't start to drift out to the decks, attracted like moths to light by the sound of the helicopters. Or perhaps some indiscreet crew members let slip what was going on. It wouldn't surprise me if some of the younger staff were trying to impress some of the more attractive passengers they've had their eye on with a bit of insider gossip, especially now that it's both New Year's Eve and the last night of the cruise. 'Personal liaisons', as HR refers to shagging, are strictly forbidden between crew and guests, but that doesn't mean it doesn't go on. I've only been on board about five minutes in cruising terms, but I've already noticed a lot of it happening, especially among the bar staff. I turn a blind eye though – it's none of my business and I've got enough of my own stuff to deal with.

Antonio appears at my side. He's in black jogging bottoms and his face is almost as grey as his tight T-shirt.

'It's Lola who's gone over,' he says. 'I'm sure it is. I still can't find her and her phone's off.'

23

My stomach lurches. It can't be her they're looking for. Can it? 'Why do you say that?' I ask. 'It's a big ship – she could be anywhere. She's probably turned her phone off because she wants some peace. And you know what the signal's like on here, it's never that good. I saw her at lunch-time and she was fine.' I also saw her later when she wasn't so fine, but I'm not going to tell Antonio about that. She swore me to secrecy. And now . . . I'm not even sure if I trust him. Lola clearly didn't.

'She's always laughing and joking and the life and soul of the party, but no one knows her like I do,' he says. 'She's fragile. If she's . . . if she's . . .' He gulps back a sob and swipes at his eyes.

'I was just talking to Rick about it,' I say. 'He thinks this whole thing is a false alarm. Some woman thought she saw something, but it could well have been nothing at all. I was at dinner with Leo when he was told. If Nico hadn't been there, I wonder if he might have dismissed the whole thing as a stupid rumour.'

He looks at me aghast. 'Who saw something? I didn't know that! Who did they see? Where? Was it a woman? Was it Lola? What did they say?'

Shit. Looks like I've said the wrong thing. 'I've only heard it about sixth hand.' I qualify. 'A woman in Fizz thought she saw someone fall. But they'll all have been pissed as farts. I bet it'll turn out to be nothing – a reflection, or a bird or something.'

Antonio draws his hand across his face. 'Oh God.' He pulls his phone out and jabs at it, stares at it and then rams

24

it back into his pocket. 'Fuck's sake! Why do the stupid phone masts on this fucking boat never work?'

He looks down at the lights of the boats searching. 'How long will they keep looking for?' he asks.

'No idea.' Why is he asking me? He's been on the ships way longer than I have. 'I doubt this happens very often,' I say. 'But . . .' I'm about to tell him I'm sure Lola's fine, because I don't think she's in the water. But *if* someone is in the water, which is almost impossible if you look at the height of the fences and guard rails all around the ship, whoever it is would probably not be fine at all, like Rick said.

I hope no one's in the water. And if they are, I really hope it's not Lola.

'She was . . . she was . . .' Antonio says.

'What?' I ask.

He straightens up. 'I'm going to see if they'll put a tannoy call out for her. I can't stand here doing nothing.'

Swiping at his eyes again, he stalks off. I'm left staring at the water as the sun comes up. By now, most of the passengers have got bored of watching and drifted off to their cabins, so it's just me, a few stragglers and party die-hards left, and some cleaners mopping the decks around them.

The next time I look down at the water, the search boats have gone. A short while later, the ship starts to move again. I brace myself for some kind of announcement about whether anyone was found, but the tannoys stay silent.

It's as if nothing happened at all.

4

Press Association, 1 January 2022

A female crew member is believed to have gone missing from *Immanis*, the world's largest cruise ship, while out at sea in the Bahamas. The alarm was raised after a passenger allegedly saw a person fall past a bar window from an upper deck. The vessel was turned around and two lifeboats from the ship immediately launched a search of the area where it is believed the woman may have gone overboard, along with a team of rescuers sent by the coastguard in a helicopter and a rescue boat. The search was called off after eight hours, when no trace of the woman had been found.

A spokesman from shipping company Heracles, which owns *Immanis*, said: 'We can confirm that a female member of crew went missing on the evening of 31 December. A search-and-rescue operation was launched immediately but sadly the woman has not been found. The search was called off when the chances of finding her alive given the current conditions reached zero. We cannot yet release her name, but our thoughts are, of course, with her family and friends at this very sad time.

'Heracles and *Immanis* both have exemplary safety records and the circumstances of the incident are, as yet, unclear. Heracles is cooperating fully with an investigation by local police as well as launching an internal investigation.'

Almost thirty million people take cruises each year, and an average of a dozen or so people are believed to go missing from cruise ships annually. Official figures are hard to find, but while some are rescued alive, most are not. A significant number are never found.

Following the disembarkation of the passengers, *Immanis* will be 'laid up' (out of service) for two months, for reasons unrelated to the incident.

Ends

PART TWO

5

Alice

Two weeks later, 14 January 2022, 12:00
The Caribbean

Insisting on remaining on board and in employment on *Immanis* for this lay-up was one of the best ideas I ever had. Designing menus for the ship is fun – a totally different challenge from anything I've done before, largely because of the scale. When you're overseeing hundreds of culinary staff preparing 30,000 meals per day in about fifty bars and restaurants and your weekly shopping budget is around a million dollars, it's obviously completely different to planning weekly-changing menus for a fifty-cover restaurant where you can basically import what you want from anywhere in the world (the more pretentious, obscure and expensive the better as far as the clients are concerned) and charge upwards of £200 per head without anyone blinking. But I was ready for a new challenge, as I said in my interview, and had my reasons for wanting to get away, which they didn't ask about and I, obviously, didn't mention.

There's no denying that compared to being executive chef for an entire shipful of passengers, even if I didn't often have that much to do with them in person, overseeing the catering for the small number of crew on board who are keeping it ticking over is a walk in the park. No waiting staff to drill with daily menu ingredients, no worrying about every tiny detail on dishes which can sometimes run into three-figure sums. Crew meals are simple, cheap and cheerful – I could do it with my eyes closed. Plus I still have my sous chef Andreas with me. In all honesty, he does most of the work while I spend my time in TopSail which I have designated my 'development kitchen'; it has a nice sunny terrace and I can work on my tan in between experimenting with various food combinations. It also has the best view and facilities of the kitchens on board – I checked them out before I took the job. You can't cook Michelin-starred food without a Michelin-starred kitchen.

The kitchens on the ship are surprisingly spacious – bigger than some of the ones I worked in in London or Paris. So while I mainly work on development, Andreas oversees most of the cooking for the crew and although the budget isn't anything like we have per head when catering for paying passengers, it's generous enough that we can all eat well, which also helps me maintain my reputation. The crew left on board now is for the most part fairly lowly in rank (except for Captain Leo and Doctor Stuart), but you never know where they might end up in the future. It's important to keep the right people onside.

A buzzer rings, signalling that it's time for dinner, so I head down to the Seasalt dining room. Seasalt isn't as flash as TopSail, but it's my favourite of the larger restaurants on the ship, with huge windows and a shaded terrace which runs along the side so we can sit outside and get some air for a change. The tables are dark varnished wood and each one has a ship's bell above which the passengers can ring to summon a waiter, but obviously I'm not allowing any of that at the moment – buffet service only for simplicity. The other thing that's missing from the terrace is Henry the hawk handler, who would normally be here every day with his giant bird on his gloved hands to scare the gulls away so the punters can eat their meals in peace. Every detail is thought of here, with little left to chance.

When we're at sea, Seasalt is reserved for passengers in suites and some of the higher-grade rooms. But as we currently have the ship to ourselves, we're taking full advantage of the ship's facilities. Normally, we'd be confined to the dingy below sea-level canteen-style dining rooms off the I-95 corridor in the bowels of the ship. The I-95 corridor runs all the way from the bow to the stern (or from the front to the back, to non-ship people like me) and is apparently named after the I-95 highway which goes up and down the east coast of America (so Rick told me, and I have no reason to disbelieve him); I gather it's the same on almost all large ships. Truly, I have learned something new every day since I've joined Heracles, very little of it about food.

There are more people than you might imagine on board, given that the ship isn't currently in service – around a hundred. They're a mixed crew. There's Captain Leo, who I'm guessing is here because he spends his whole life at sea and has nowhere else to go. Some general maintenance staff who are involved in updates and generally tarting up the ship. Safety Officer Bill and his team who are overseeing the new CCTV going in. Engineer Danny and his assistant, my friend Rick. Doctor Stuart – we legally need a doctor on board, thankfully. Phwoar. Head of housekeeping Mara. Several cleaners who clean the ship daily even though there is next to no one here – starting at one end, picking up where they finished off the day before, and then doing the same again once they get to the other end, a little like the crew who paint the Golden Gate Bridge. The cleaners also keep the rooms that we are occupying in order; one great thing about being on board is, beyond doing your job, you barely have to lift a finger. I imagine it's a bit like being at boarding school – not that I would know.

Plus, incongruously, dancer Antonio is here. Heracles doesn't go so far as to provide us with entertainment while we're on lay-up, obviously, but he's decided to take a job as a cleaner to fill the time until the ship starts cruising again. While Lola's disappearance shocked everyone, he has, unsurprisingly, taken it particularly badly.

I didn't know her for that long, but I miss her. She was great fun and we had lots of laughs together. She was a good few years younger than me but somehow seemed both older and younger than her twenty-three years. She kept me filled in on all the gossip and confided in me about some (but not all, I'm sure) of her woes. I think she saw me as a bit of a mother figure; once when she was drunk she told me that she'd never known her own mum.

I'm new to cruising, but while some of the crew said they'd heard of a few cases of people going overboard anecdotally, no one I've spoken to has actually been on a ship where it happened. That said, almost everyone seems to have a friend or friend of a friend who had more direct experience of it, or at least claims they do.

But Antonio staying on *Immanis* seems creepy to me. It's not as if Lola's suddenly going to bob up out of the water, is it? Even though Heracles isn't exactly renowned for its benevolent HR policies, I'm sure, given the circumstances, they'd have let him go without any issues. He's only cleaning, after all – anyone could do it. It doesn't need to be him.

I made the mistake of getting cornered by Antonio when he was drunk the other night and it was a struggle to get away. I'm not sure he should be here at all. I think he's on the verge of a breakdown.

He said we will probably never find out what happened to Lola and even if we think we do, it probably won't be true. He says there will be a cover-up because that's what they do on cruise ships – they don't want people to hear about the bad things that happen. He says he's staying on board so that he can keep an eye on the investigation because Lola doesn't have anyone else to do it for her.

We may not have known each other long, but it was pretty obvious Lola wasn't the most stable of people. Initially, when it became clear she was missing, I thought she'd turn up. Playing some kind of prank, or winding up Antonio or

Jamie. Then, when it became clear that she wasn't going to, I thought she must have had some kind of episode and decided to take her own life. She'd been pretty upset when I'd seen her earlier.

But now I'm starting to wonder if Antonio had something to do with her disappearance after all. Especially after what she told me on New Year's Eve.

Is he protesting too much with the cover-up stuff? Trying to put the blame on someone other than himself?

Then again, as Rick said, on the rare occasion that someone *does* go overboard, it almost always turns out to be a drunken accident or suicide. Not murder. And certainly not on a luxurious ship like this one moored up in the Caribbean.

Unthinkable.

6

14 January 2022, 13:00
The Caribbean

Transcript of police interview

Superintendent Bailey: Interview with Safety Officer Bill Harding, 14 January 2022, 1300 hours. I understand that since our last meeting you have been through the security tapes, as requested?

Bill: Yep.

Superintendent Bailey: Did you find anything which might indicate what happened to the lady in question on 31 December?

Bill: As you know, there's a lot of footage and a lot of cameras, so I've put together the most relevant bits for you. Unfortunately some cameras weren't working when she went missing. The system is old and is being upgraded during this lay-up.

Superintendent Bailey: I see. That is unfortunate. Do you have any suspicion that any of the cameras might have been tampered with?

Bill: It's difficult to know for sure, but there is no specific evidence of that, no.

Superintendent Bailey: Perhaps you can tell me what you did find which might be pertinent.

Bill: Yep. [plays tape] We can see Lola early in the evening in the crew area – that's her – if you zoom like this . . . you can see she looks somewhat agitated and tearful. And then later here, she's in a service stairwell where she doesn't have any business being, heading upwards, towards a point where she could conceivably have jumped to fall past the window where the lady in the bar thought she saw . . . something.

Superintendent Bailey: And did you see her redescend the same stairs?

Bill: No. I've been through the footage for the whole evening and the next morning, and she doesn't come back down.

Superintendent Bailey: I see. Is there another way she could have come down from that point?

Bill: Not easily, not without climbing over railings and similar. You could do it, but it would be awkward and dangerous. I don't see why she would.

Superintendent Bailey: Did you see anyone else behaving in an unusual way in the area in the footage?

Bill: No. There are other people up and down the stairwell all evening, most of whom have a right to be there, some who don't but look like they've popped out for a smoke. We're not allowed to smoke where passengers can see us, so the service stairs are used a lot like that.

Superintendent Bailey: So from the video evidence, which, as you say, is far from complete due to the cameras which weren't working, it looks as though Lola went up to the upper deck but didn't come down? Would that be correct?

Bill: It would.

Superintendent Bailey: But there is no working camera where she is believed to have jumped from?

Bill: No.

Superintendent Bailey: So therefore no way of telling if she fell from there, or, if she did, if anyone else was with her?

Bill: No.

Superintendent Bailey: OK, thank you. Is there any other footage you would like to show me today?

Bill: Yep. We do also have some footage from the bar where the woman thought she saw the person fall [shows footage] It's not very clear, I'm afraid.

Superintendent Bailey: Can I see it again?

Bill: Yep – here you go . . .

Superintendent Bailey: That's it? That white flash? That could be almost anything.

Bill: The cameras are orientated to pick up what's going on inside the bar, not outside. So yeah, I agree, it's not clear at all. It could be a reflection, trick of the light, or something else. I thought you'd want to see it as—

Superintendent Bailey: I understand. It's possible that it shows the missing woman falling, but it's far from clear. Since she remains missing, it is certainly a possibility. I appreciate you collating these clips for me. We will also be reviewing the entire footage ourselves, and will come back to you if we have any further questions. Thank you for your time.

7

Antonio

14 January 2022, 22:00
The Caribbean

It's difficult to think about anything other than Lola as I go about my usual cleaning duties. Everywhere I go on board reminds me of her. The pool deck where she and I did 'surprise' aerial performances at sunset once a week. The three-level 24-hour spa with the warm waterfall Lola would sometimes sneak into in the middle of the night if one of her friends was on the door. The windows of the designer shops with the items she always coveted and would drop heavy hints about if someone on board was a particular fan of hers, which was often. The 'rainforest walk' of tropical trees where there was a 'downpour' every hour, on the hour, to the delight of the kids on board and many of the adults too. She loved it, and would squeal like a delighted child if she was underneath when the deluge began.

There was no way I'd have found a new dancing job the way things are the moment in the business, especially without my dance partner. And even though I don't desperately need the money, it somehow feels right to stay close to Lola. As well as that, I feel I need to stay close to keep on top of what they find out. So I am not taken by surprise.

But at the same time, being here is hard. The constant gossip and speculation is getting on my nerves. You'd think the crew would have a bit more respect when discussing Lola around me. But all they can talk about is who she may or may not have been sleeping with (I've heard Doctor Stuart, Engineer Rick, Safety Officer Bill, Captain Leo and even Chef Alice mentioned, among others – none of which are true as far as I know), and whether someone killed her because they were jealous. Speculation about where she was when she was meant to be doing the show, whether she killed herself or not, and why. Or whether I killed her.

The investigation is officially ongoing. Myself and a few of the other crew members are being questioned. I am dreading my interview. I'm not sure how I'm going to deal with it. I'm not a very good liar.

I am fully expecting neither Heracles or the police ever to get to the bottom of what really happened. With so many of us on board that night, it's not like they can interview two thousand crew and six thousand or so passengers. And the day after Lola went missing, we docked, and most of the people on board went their separate ways. It would have been impossible to keep everyone in place long enough to question everyone. And they'd have needed interpreters, because a lot of them didn't even speak English. Plus, as we were out at sea when it happened, in international waters and with no body, it's possible there won't even be an inquest. Like the crew and the passengers, the police will move on quickly and Lola will soon be forgotten, probably by everyone except me.

It doesn't happen often, people going missing from the ships. And the cruise companies don't shout about it when it does. On the rare occasions it hits the papers, it's usually because whoever went over has a family who is desperate to know what happened to their loved one and has made a big fuss. They write to MPs and embassies, they set up Facebook groups and GoFundMe campaigns, some of them even employ private detectives. But even when all that goes on, there are rarely any definite answers found. That's what I'm hoping for. Lola is gone. The full truth coming out won't help anyone. Not her, and definitely not me.

At the end of the day, I go back to my suite and run myself a bath. It's a two-storey suite with one of those free-standing baths for two people with jacuzzi jets on the upper floor. It takes ages to fill but it's worth it. When I'm not working, there's very little else to do as I'm hardly in the mood for drinking in the bar with the others, so I like to spin out these mundane activities for as long as possible. I tend to lie in the bath and look at the stars through the glass wall, then I get out and wrap myself in a huge fluffy robe and maybe watch a film on the enormous TV in the living room. Or I wallow in the water even longer and watch something on the smaller TV in the bathroom, though sometimes the steam makes it tricky. I've nicked some of the 'suite-level' toiletries from the supply cupboard; they're nicer than the bog-standard ones they shove into cattle class – not that we're supposed to be using those either, but whatever. It's the little things that help me get through the days. As I ease myself into the hot, scented water tonight, I think of Lola's lifeless body in the cold and churning ocean and can't help but let out a sob.

I close my eyes and slide down under the water, holding my breath, trying to shut out my thoughts, the awfulness of everything that's happening. As I resurface, I think I hear the room door on the lower floor of the suite slam shut.

'Who's there?' I shout, leaping out of the bath and grabbing the plush robe I've left next to it. I rush down the stairs but there's no one.

Perhaps I imagined it. It's all been so stressful lately – it's making me jittery. I turn to go into the bedroom and my heart leaps into my mouth. There's something on the bed.

I KNOW WHAT YOU DID. IF YOU DON'T WANT ME TO TELL, MEET ME AT MUSTER POINT M FOR INSTRUCTIONS AT MIDNIGHT.

The note is written in spidery capitals and must have been put there while I was in the bath.

Someone came into my room? Who would do that?

I throw the note down as if it's on fire and put my hand to my mouth. My legs feel quivery and I sit down on the huge bed. One of the advantages of being staff during this lay-up

44

over when we have clients on board is we get to sleep in the passenger staterooms rather than our usual stinking below-decks cupboards. But that's very little comfort right now.

The note has to be someone winding me up, surely? No one saw what I did, I'm sure of it.

And yet . . . what if they did? What do they want? I peer at the writing – scrawling, childish capitals. No clue there at all. I need to find out who sent it and what they know. And if they do know anything, I will need to deal with it.

8

Stuart

14 January 2022, 22:00
The Caribbean

Being a ship's doctor is a pretty cushy number at the best of times, but being a ship's doctor while we're on lay-up could hardly be easier.

While cruising may have changed in the last decade or so and is no longer solely the preserve of the well-heeled retiree, the over-seventies still make up quite a large proportion of the clients, in my experience. And while the larger boats like this one now come with water parks, nightclubs and kids' zones, cruising still remains an easy way to get from place to place while everything is done for you, which is always going to appeal to the older demographic. You get on the ship, you're fed, watered and entertained, you wake up in a different place where you are taken somewhere nice with everything arranged for you, then you're brought back again. In the meantime your room has been cleaned and your nightclothes laid out for you. If you're lucky, someone will even have arranged your towels into an animal or a rocket shape and the end of your loo roll into a fan or a pretty point. You don't have to think about anything. It's almost like being in a care home, except with better scenery and nicer food. So it's hardly surprising that the third-agers love it.

And it's the older population on a cruise ship that tends to keep me most busy. Some of them are simply hypochondriacs used to seeing their doctors on a weekly basis who will come and see me about any minor issue, 'Just in case, Doctor', though the fact that they have to pay quite handsomely for the privilege usually keeps the real time-wasters at bay. That is, except for the really rich ones who will insist on a cabin visit at almost twice the cost, simply because they can.

But even without taking them into account, on a typical cruise there will be falls, diabetic incidents, perhaps a heart attack or a stroke. It's not that uncommon that I have to arrange an airlift. And sometimes people die. There is a reason that cruise ships come with on-board mortuaries, though you won't find them in the brochures. They get used more than you'd imagine. If there's nothing that can be done to save someone, there will be no air ambulance – it's a waste of time and money for all concerned. The body will travel with us to the next major port in what amounts to a giant fridge in a discreet room in my health centre, not that far from where people are still eating, drinking and taking their salsa classes. I doubt many of the passengers know that.

Of course, I do see the younger passengers in my surgery too on occasion, usually because of drunken injuries of one sort or another. There aren't too many of them, because a cruise ship is almost like a giant soft play centre – it's pretty difficult to hurt yourself unless you're doing something really stupid. And one of my deputies usually deals with the crew, their kitchen injuries, their broken fingers when they get into fights and, now and again, their STIs. That guy Rick, for example, has got through pretty much every venereal disease I learned about at medical school, and quite possibly some that I didn't.

On a lay-up like this, I don't anticipate having anything much to do at all. My presence is a legal requirement, but the crew members are all young and healthy – mainly under thirty, bar Captain Leo, who is a robust old sea dog and has never visited my surgery. And there's only a comparatively small number on board, the troublemakers having already been weeded out and not selected to stay on for the lay-up, so I'm not expecting many fights or alcohol-related injuries. Plus everyone has more space and less work to do than usual, both of which help keep the stress levels, illnesses and accidents down. Instead, I'm spending my time sunbathing, enjoying a bit of afternoon delight with Alice the chef, and the odd sweetie from my medicine cabinet when I find myself dwelling on what happened back in the UK too much. Everyone is pretty bored already, so you have to take your pleasures where you can.

Antonio came to see me yesterday. He said he's feeling 'anxious' after Lola's disappearance and wondered if I had anything herbal he could take. I wrote him a script and told him I could give him a few benzos to keep him going, but he shook his head and said he didn't want to be dependent on anything like that.

So instead I did my sympathetic doctor's spiel of asking him if he had any friends on board he could talk to, suggesting some breathing exercises or some CBT when he was back on land. There's nothing too wrong with him, in my opinion, he's just grieving. I think he'll be OK.

Lola, on the other hand, was a totally different matter. She went through those drugs as if they were Smarties. Pretty girl. After that one night we spent together, shortly after I joined the ship, I had a look at her medical form before deciding to steer well clear in future. And, indeed, to behave in a manner more befitting my profession.

At least, I did until this lay-up when I started hooking up with Alice, but I don't think normal rules count out here. I guess she's officially my patient, but she also kind of isn't in that I've never treated her for anything and it's fairly unlikely I will, given we'll be here for such a short time. Plus there really is nothing else to do. I'm pretty confident Alice isn't going to tell anyone, anyway, and Lola certainly isn't now.

Lola had a history of depression, anxiety, self-harm and at least one suicide attempt. I saw her regularly to keep an eye on how she was doing and tweak her various prescriptions. Anecdotally, as far as I understand, she shagged pretty much anything that moved. Male or female. Alice has been disconcertingly vague about whether there was anything more to them than platonic friendship, though I think she does that partly because she knows it puts hot girl-on-girl images in my head.

But back to Lola. I certainly wouldn't want anyone to find out what happened between me and her – even if it was only one night.

9

Antonio

14 January 2022, 23:50
The Caribbean

Before I found the note I was exhausted, pleasantly woozy after a few vodka shots in the bath and looking forward to going to bed. With no clients on board, our working hours aren't quite as hectic as usual, but we're expected to put in a full day to earn our meagre money, which is even more meagre when there are no tips. Compared to being a dancer, cleaning all day is much more boring even if not quite as physically tiring. It's not helped by the fact that the WiFi is dodgy at best, so I often end up listening to the same old music and podcasts time and time again. I'd almost forgotten what it's like to put in eight hours of such bone-crushingly tedious work, and how privileged I was to make my money from dancing, even if work often went on well into the night. How lucky I was. Am. This is temporary, I remind myself. I won't be a cleaner forever. Although, God. Dancing without Lola. It's hard to imagine. Who will be my partner now?

But the note sent a shot of adrenaline through me more powerful than any line of coke I've ever taken (only ever with Lola, when she was teasing me for being straight and boring – drugs aren't really my thing at all) and now I'm wide awake and buzzing. It has to be a bluff, surely. I'm almost sure that no one saw what happened that night.

And yet . . . there's still a chance that someone saw or heard something. Was there something I missed? Does someone know what I did?

My whole future rests on this. I can't take the risk of someone telling. I can't go to prison. I would die. Literally die. If someone thinks they know something, I need to know who. And what they plan to do.

Muster point M is a grim spot, just below the waterline, in what would normally be just above the crew area. With no passengers here while we're on lay-up, we've spread out to use all the nicest places around the ship and there is no one down here. Normally we're tucked away in dingy cabins off the I-95 without any natural light or air, squashed in like sardines. The muster point is next to some steps which take you up to a deck on the waterline where you can get into a lifeboat in an emergency. I feel a bolt of panic as I wonder if that's why whoever it is has asked to meet me here – are they planning to throw me overboard if I don't agree to their terms? I'm fit and reasonably strong, but there are plenty of men on board much bigger than me, so it's entirely possible that whoever is trying to blackmail me could beat me in a fight. Fuck. Fuck. I should have thought this through and brought a weapon – a knife or something. I glance at my watch, ten past midnight. Where are they? Are they trying to wind me up? Is it a double-bluff even – someone who is trying to work out for themselves if I'm behind Lola's disappearance?

I look along I-95, which seems to go on forever on a boat of this size, broken only by huge doors which will close automatically in case of fire or flooding. You wouldn't want to be down here when anything like that happens. Doesn't bear thinking about.

I've turned the lights on in my section of corridor but looking further along, it quickly fades away into darkness. With the boat stationary and all the people on board hanging out in the luxe guest areas, it's uncharacteristically silent down here and I'm not sure I've ever felt quite so alone. I picture again Lola falling into those vast, black waters and a wave of nausea crashes over me. Along the corridor, something clatters.

My breathing quickens and I start to hyperventilate. *Slow down!* I tell myself. Inhale, one two three. Exhale, one two three. Inhale, one two three. Exhale, one two three.

But it's not working. My chest constricts and my hands start to tingle. I feel like I'm going to faint. I'm going to die, down here, alone, and no one knows where I am. Is that what they planned? Did they get me here so that . . .

Calm down. Calm down. I sit on the ground, put my head between my legs and eventually manage to slow my breathing, the way I was taught in therapy to stop myself catastrophizing. When I check my watch again it's 12:30. No one is here. They're not coming.

I stand up, dust myself down and look around myself again in case there's something I've missed – another note maybe, telling me what I need to do. Where to go. What do they want from me? I run my hands along the flaking beige paint on the exposed pipes, see if there's something tucked behind them.

There's nothing. I need to get back to my room.

Most of the lifts on board have been taken out of service as they're not needed with so few of us here. I don't want to draw attention to where I've been by going further out of my way than I need to, because I don't want anyone asking me why I'm prowling around the ship in the middle of the night. So by the time I'm back up at my room at Deck 14, I'm pretty out of breath. The natural adrenaline boost has gone and I feel shaky and even a bit tearful. I just want to go to sleep, forget it all and wake up tomorrow with things back to normal. With Lola still here, though obviously that's not going to happen. The note is pretty sick as a prank, but probably nothing more than that. People get so bored holed up together like this. I'm probably overreacting.

I head back in to my suite. And I can't quite believe what I see when I open my door.

10

Alice

14 January 2022, 23:50
The Caribbean

There are loads of great suites on the ship, but I've accidentally managed to bag one of the most impressive. None of
us is allowed in the very best suite, the Owner's Suite, with
its private spa and glass grand piano, as the threat of a visit
from CEO Nico hangs over us at all times, even on lay-up.
This is probably to make sure we are behaving ourselves
and getting on with our work (though his visits are always
sold to us as morale boosters, like anyone cares), so that
suite, the best on the ship, has to be reserved for him.

This one, the Stargazer Suite, as well as having one fully
transparent wall, which is common to many of the best
suites, also has a glass ceiling so you can lie in bed and

look at the stars on clear nights. The ceiling and wall turn opaque at the touch of a button or, somewhat alarmingly, into mirrors at a second touch. Stuart loves that feature, loves to be able to watch himself in bed, whereas I prefer to leave the glass clear. No one can see in, but it feels like they might be able to, and I like that.

Afterwards, I am lying on my back looking at the stars when I become aware that Stuart has propped himself up on his elbow and is looking at me.

'What?' I ask, suddenly self-conscious, pulling up the sheet so it covers me.

'I was just thinking that apart from what you look like naked, I don't know much about you,' he says.

Stuart and I get together like this fairly often. Neither of us has much to do on board, we're a little bit older than most of the rest of the crew, and it just kind of worked out like that. He's pretty fit and very eager to please in bed. But that's all there is to our relationship, such that it is – we don't chat much, and that suits me fine right now.

I sit up, turn away from him, and start putting on my clothes. 'Not much to tell,' I say airily. 'Part of the reason I took this job was to escape all the kitchen gossip and be somewhere different. It's kind of nice to start with a clean slate.'

He trails his fingers along my back. 'Sounds to me like you're running from something.'

'No I'm not,' I say, more tetchily than I mean to, standing up to get away from his touch. Why can't he leave it? Soul sharing wasn't part of the deal here as far as I'm concerned. 'I could say the same about you. Why are you here?'

His face falls. 'There was . . . something at home I wanted to distance myself from.' Hmm. You and me both, I think, but I don't say anything.

He swings himself up out of bed, pads over to the kitchen area and opens the American-style fridge which guests rarely use to keep anything more than their champagne cold – or fresh milk for their tea if they're Brits. 'I think you're right – let's not talk about our pasts. Better to live for the present, isn't that what they say? Carpe diem and all that. Want a beer before you go?'

11

Antonio

15 January 2022, 01:00
The Caribbean

Just inside the door of my suite, there is a neat pile of clothes on the floor. At first I think they are mine, though I didn't leave them there and certainly not so neatly. Why would someone come into my room and do something like that? But when I look closer, I realize they're not mine at all.

The colours are wrong. There are pinks, yellows and pale blues, the kind of colours favoured by Lola. My hand flies to my mouth and heart rate quickens as I move closer and realize what they are.

They're hers. Lola's. I pick up the hoodie on top of the pile and press it to my face. It still smells of her, her perfume which she always wears and never deviates from.

I put it to one side and sort through the others, which are all neatly folded as if taken directly from a cupboard. These clothes would have been over-sized and roomy on her, though they'd come up small on almost anyone else as she is so tiny. Not is. Was, I think, tears springing to my eyes. What state would her body be in now? Would there be anything left of her?

I push the thought away. I need to stay focused, not descend into wallowing in self-pity. She is gone, and there is nothing I can do about it now.

At the bottom of the pile are a couple of scarves, the winter kind which she would have had no call to wear out here in the Caribbean, but she must have brought with her for some reason. I don't recognize them, but the perfume is the same. They must have been hers.

I pull on one of the jumpers – it's too tight for me but it's comforting to wear something of Lola's – and wrap one of the scarves around my neck. I lie down on the bed, for a moment, calmer now as it almost feels like she is there.

But why would someone leave these in my room? Our tiny workers' cabin was cleared of her belongings when we came into port, when it became apparent that she had gone missing. I was too distraught to think about it at the time – I'm not even sure who did it or where her things ended up. I wasn't paying attention. By the time we were back on board, everything had gone and it didn't occur to me to ask where. Lola was no longer here – that was all I cared about.

And even though wearing something of Lola's feels almost like coming home, the fact that someone left these things here for me to find is a worry. Who would do that, and why? Is it some kind of prank? A sick joke? A warning?

Is it a message? What does it mean? Why would anyone do this?

Is it someone who knows what I did? It must be the same person that left the note. That said they knew what I'd done.

But what am I supposed to do now? And what will happen next?

I wish Lola was here. She would know what to do.

12

Antonio

15 January 2022, 10:00
The Caribbean

'Thank you for coming to see me today, Antonio,' the super-intendent says. 'First, may I say how sorry I am for your loss.'

I nod, a lump already in my throat. I'm so nervous. 'Thank you,' I say hoarsely.

'I understand that you and the, erm, missing woman, shared a cabin. Is that correct?'

'Yes. That's right.' I feel sweat beading on my forehead. Calm down, I tell myself. Just answer the questions and don't offer any extra information. He doesn't know anything. There's no way he could, I tell myself.

'And when was the last time you saw her on the night of her disappearance? Can you remember?'

'It would have been about nine o'clock, I think.'

'Nine o'clock in the evening?'

'Yes.' I notice that I am jiggling my knee up and down and will myself to stop. I'm making myself look guilty, I know I am. He makes a note. I take a deep breath. Calm down, calm down.

'And how did she seem then?'

'She was . . . upset.' I'll need to tell him that. Other people will have seen her. I think. Won't they?

He makes another note. Fuck. 'I see,' he says. 'Did she tell you why she was upset?'

I shake my head. 'No.' I feel myself go red. Shit. Can he tell I'm lying? 'She wouldn't tell me. But then she didn't turn up for the show, which is when I knew that something was seriously wrong.'

'That's not typical behaviour for her? Not the kind of thing she'd done before?'

'No. Lola, she liked to mess around and all that but . . . she'd always turn up for the show. She loves performing.' I pause. 'Loved.'

Tears come to my eyes and I wipe them away. 'I think she must—'

'We don't deal in speculation here, just facts, please,' he interrupts me.

'She had tried to hurt herself before, so it's possible that . . .' I say. Oh God. This is so awful. My poor Lola. What did I do to you?

He nods. 'So I understand. Is there anything else you want to tell me which you feel may be pertinent to the investigation?'

62

'She . . . no.' Should I tell him about the clothes? Would that help Lola?

No. She is gone. It would only complicate things. If I told him about the clothes, I'd have to tell him about the note, that someone knows what I did, and surely that would only lead on to . . .

'There's nothing,' I say. 'I don't know why she was upset. I don't know what happened to her. I only wish . . .' I break down into tears, and thankfully he calls an end to the interview.

13

Antonio

16 January 2022, 13:00
The Caribbean

I barely slept last night, both traumatized by the police interview and unable to stop turning over and over in my head what the note and the clothes might mean. I don't get anywhere with it, but I'm pretty sure that one way or another, they're not a good thing.

I almost told the policeman about the note and the clothes when he interviewed me, because I'm so tired I can't think straight, but I'm relieved now that I didn't. Whatever their significance, I'll need to deal with it myself. In my own way.

I get through my morning duties on autopilot, which isn't exactly difficult as it's cleaning after all – I don't need to concentrate. But today that isn't a good thing as my mind races, going to dark places where I don't want it to go.

Lola is dead and I am going to prison. I'm sure of it.

I've been withdrawing more and more from the rest of the crew during the lay-up; I can't bear the looks of pity from some or wariness from others. Most of them give me a wide berth anyway – I get that I'm not exactly fun to be around these days.

At lunchtime I am sitting at a table, alone as usual, staring glumly at my phone, trying to get the WiFi to work so I can find out what kind of sentence I can expect if anyone finds out what I did.

It's not working, as per, but I can see my reflection in the screen. I look terrible – bags under my eyes, and a stain on the ratty T-shirt I've been wearing for days as it's easier to pick it up from the floor and put it back on again each day rather than find something new to wear. It's starting to smell, but I don't care.

I'm still listlessly trying to make the Internet work when someone puts their tray down in front of me. I put my phone face down on the table – I don't want anyone to see what I was searching for, and look up. It's Leo. 'OK if I join you?' he asks.

I shrug. 'Help yourself. I'm off in a minute anyway,' I say, waving vaguely at my tray, which is still covered in food. 'I'm not very hungry.' I have almost no appetite these days. Eating seems pointless. I can barely taste anything and my stomach is always in knots.

'How are things?' he asks, in an unusually gentle tone of voice. 'You must miss Lola terribly. You know, if you've changed your mind and you'd rather take some time off, that can be arranged. I can make sure there's a dancing job for you once we're on the move again. I'll talk to HR. I don't want you to worry about that.'

I shake my head and bite my lip. I feel tears welling. Oh God. I don't want to cry in front of Leo. I take a deep breath. 'It's just so hard,' I say, my voice hoarse, 'thinking of her in the sea, all alone.'

Leo shifts awkwardly. I stare at the table. I wish he'd go away. I don't want to talk about this with anyone, but especially not with Leo. 'I understand,' he says, though he looks embarrassed and I'm quite sure he doesn't understand. How could he? 'We all miss Lola, but of course it will be more difficult for you, being so close,' he adds. 'Hopefully, in time, there will be some more . . . answers . . . maybe they'll be able to tell us . . .'

He tails off, not finishing his sentence, but I know what he's obliquely referring to. In time they might find Lola's body.

She may wash up somewhere, or she may well not. Where she went overboard, we were miles from land and the ocean was several hundred metres deep. There would have been sharks and other carnivorous fish. As she hasn't yet been found, the likelihood is, she never will be. I know that but I try not to think about it. A wave of nausea washes over me and I take another deep breath.

'Have a think about it,' Leo adds. 'If you want to take some time off, it isn't a problem.'

I shake my head. 'No. Apart from anything else, I want to stay here. Close to the sea. Close to Lola.'

And close to the investigation.

14

Alice

17 January 2022, 02:00
The Caribbean

It's pitch black when I wake up and at first I think the unbearable sound is my alarm clock going for the breakfast shift but then I realize it's still the middle of the night and it's the muster alarm.

Fuck's sake. I bet someone's got drunk and set it off for a dare – everyone is already bored out of their minds – or it's gone off by accident.

But it's about the worst sound in the world – no doubt designed that way so you can't simply stay in bed and ignore it as I would otherwise be hugely tempted to do – plus there are massive bollockings and even punishments for anyone who doesn't take them seriously, even when we all know they're going to be a waste of time. It's almost certainly not a real emergency, but there is an outside chance that it may be an official drill; according to legend, it wouldn't be the first time Captain Leo's decided to do one in the middle of the night when there are no passengers on board.

I grab my life jacket and shuffle along the corridor in my slippers to our muster point – with the reduced numbers on board, we have just one. I'm hoping that they're not going to carry it through and make us put on immersion suits and board a lifeboat (again, not unheard of for Captain Leo's drills, apparently) because I'm not exactly dressed for it, still in my PJs.

It's clear that everyone else is of the same opinion. No one is exactly rushing, and it takes a while for everyone to arrive and touch in with our key cards. On the way I notice a few people slipping out of rooms they shouldn't be. Safety Officer Bill is the only one fully dressed and looking properly awake – he's smartly dressed, brandishing an iPad officiously and wearing a fluorescent tabard. Everyone else is bleary-eyed and wearing something hastily chucked on or in their pyjamas. At least I don't feel out of place.

A few minutes later, as it seems like the trickle of people turning up has petered out into nothing, the muster siren is finally turned off and there is a collective sigh of relief. Bill peers at his iPad.

'Right. Two missing. Rick from engineering and Antonio from housekeeping.'

My kitchen staff all seem to be here, thank God. I don't want to have to be disciplining someone for not turning up

68

for this or, even worse, be a man or woman down if they decide to sack someone.

Both Bill and Leo take the drills very seriously. They won't let Rick and Antonio off lightly for not bothering to get out of bed. I'm not that surprised at Rick not being here – he's a lazy bugger and likes to think of himself as a bit of a rebel – but I'm surprised not to see Antonio. He usually toes the line.

'OK. It took fifteen minutes for everyone to get here and we're still two short,' Bill continues. 'It's not a brilliant performance, which means we'll have to do it again at some point, I'm afraid.' Everyone groans. 'I'm not doing it for my own benefit,' he snaps. Bill is officious and a bit of a knob at the best of times, but to be fair, no one is really their best self at two fifteen in the morning. 'But for now I'll let you get back to bed. Mara, Danny, if you can kick the absentees from your departments out of bed and send them up to my office ASAP, please. As in now. Not in the morning. This can't wait. Drills need to be taken seriously. Thank you.'

15

Stuart

17 January 2022, 02:30
The Caribbean

I haven't even made it back into bed when someone is hammering on my door.

'Stuart! Stuart! You need to come and help! Now!' someone is shouting.

I open the door. It's Bill. He seemed fine about five seconds ago at the drill, so what can suddenly be so urgent?

He's deathly pale and shaking. 'I think he's dead!' he says. 'You need to come. I don't know what happened. I don't know what to do.'

What is he talking about? 'Who?' I ask, grabbing my bag. 'Who's dead? Are you sure?'

'Please, you need to come. See if you can do anything,'

he pleads. 'Something's happened. He's, he's, oh God, I don't know . . . I've just left him there but, Danny's there, he's trying to . . . you need to come. Maybe you can . . . I don't know. Oh God. I've never seen a dead body before.' He turns away and strides off down the corridor. I grab my bag and follow, my heart pounding.

PART THREE

16

Eight years earlier

July 2013
Inverness

Noise. So noisy. All around me, noise.

'Can you hear me?' someone shouts in my ear.

'Uhhhhhhhh,' I groan. I can't speak. Everything hurts. I'm moving. I'm on a trolley, I think. There is a bang, and clattering. Something tightens around my arm.

'Her blood pressure's dropping!' someone else shouts. I feel a hand tapping my face. 'You still awake, love? Stay with us now. Squeeze my hand.'

'Wh . . . wh . . .' I breathe and try to squeeze but I can't feel anything. 'I . . .'

'You're doing great,' someone else says. I am barely conscious but I register that he sounds kind. 'I'm going to

put a mask over your face now, help with your breathing.
Nothing to worry about. Try to stay awake.'

I feel something on my face. It smells of plastic. I don't
like it. I try to turn my head but I can't.

'Lie still now, we're going to take very good care of you,'
the voice says. 'Can you tell me your name?'

'I don't . . . I don't . . .'

And then there is nothing.

I open my eyes. My head is thudding like I've been bludg-
eoned. There's a beeping sound. I look around the room. It's
white and smells of disinfectant.

The sound is coming from a machine by the bed; it's got
a screen with little wavy lines on. *Beep beep beep.* The
machine has wires attached to it, which in turn, are attached
to my arm. I'm in hospital, I suddenly realize with a wave
of panic. I try to sit up but my head swims and for a second
I think I am going to throw up so I lie back down again.

Why is nobody here?

Where is Dad?

'Hello?' I call out lamely. My throat is dry and my voice
little more than a whisper. 'Is there anyone there?'

Nothing. No one. I can hear people clattering past outside
in the corridor, but no one comes in.

I move my head gingerly again and see a button with a
picture of a person on it. My right arm, the arm closest to a
big red button with 'call' written on, is wrapped in a huge
bandage and throbbing. Ow. I twist myself round to reach
across to it with the other arm and a sharp pain shoots across
my ribs which makes me cry out and fall back onto the bed.

I take a deep breath, steel myself and roll over again. This time I manage to reach the button and press it. A red light comes on and there is a dull buuuuuuuuuurrrr sound.

I press another button next to it and the head of my bed moves upwards.

Better. I can see more now. The room is very bare. No furniture in the room bar a very plain-looking chair and a nightstand by the bed.

There is nothing on either the nightstand or the chair. Nothing at all. Where are my clothes?

Suddenly terrified, I try to sit up but the shooting pain makes me yelp and fall back onto the mattress. Tears spring to my eyes.

Why am I here?

I turn my head to look out the window but I can't see anything except a grey sky.

There is a sudden noise and the door bursts open.

'Good God, you're awake!' says a bosomy, friendly-looking nurse. She bustles over to my bed and presses another button, making the red light go out. 'How're you feeling?'

'My head hurts,' I rasp. 'And I'm so thirsty. Can I have some water?'

She frowns. 'I'm not sure. I'd better get someone in to have a look at you first. Let me call the doctor.'

She bustles off again, leaving the door open. I lie back on my pillows, exhausted.

'Hello? Can you hear me?'

I open my eyes. A woman in a white coat is standing by my bed. 'I'm Doctor Lyons.' She lifts my left eyelid and shines a little torch into it, and then does the same with the other. 'Good, good,' she says. 'Can you tell me your name?'

'My name?'

She nods. 'Yes.'

I stare at her blankly.

Only then does it occur to me that I don't know my own name. 'I, um, I'm not . . .'

She nods again. 'OK. Try not to worry. Amnesia in these kinds of cases is almost always temporary.'

'Amnesia?'

'When you can't remember things.'

'I know what it means.' My throat hurts. 'Can I have some water, please?'

'Yes, I think so.' The doctor nods at the nurse, who scuttles off and returns almost instantly with a jug of water with a jaunty red lid and a plastic beaker. She pours water into the glass, puts a straw in and hands it to me. 'Small sips at first,' she warns. 'You haven't had anything by mouth for five days.'

The water is deliciously cool as it slips down my throat. I rub some on my lips, which feel dry and cracked.

'Five days?' I croak. 'I've been here five days?'

'Yes, that's right,' the doctor agrees.

'What happened to me?'

She sits on the edge of my bed. 'We think you were in an accident. Hit by a car. You were found lying in the road, having suffered some injuries.' She inclines her head towards the bandage on my arm. 'A badly scraped arm, cracked ribs, some cuts and bruises, and it's quite possible you've suffered a concussion which can also cause memory loss.' She pats my leg. 'But memory almost always comes back with time. We've examined you thoroughly and there is no sign of serious head injury.'

'And Dad? Does he know I'm here?'

The doctor frowns. 'I'm afraid we haven't yet worked out who you are. You had no ID on you when you were brought in, no phone, no belongings, nothing. We were hoping you might be able to tell us who you belong to, if and when you woke up. If you can let me know who your dad is, I can make sure he's contacted as a matter of urgency.'

I close my eyes and try to picture something. But nothing comes to me, apart from Dad. 'I can remember what he looks like. But, uh, I can't remember my name. Or his. I don't know how you would contact him.' I feel scared and embarrassed and tears come to my eyes. What kind of person can't remember their own name?

Doctor Lyons pats my hand and smiles awkwardly. 'That's OK. Plenty of time. Now that you're awake I think it will only be a matter of time. We'll arrange for a psychiatrist to come and see you tomorrow if you feel up to it to help you piece together the bits you *do* remember and make sense of them. For example, until now we didn't even know if you spoke English. We thought maybe you'd come from abroad. And that that's why no one had reported you . . .' She trails off.

'No one has reported me . . .' I prompt.

'From the enquiries we've made so far, no one seems to have reported anyone fitting your description as missing locally. But I'm sure there'll turn out to be a logical explanation for that,' she adds briskly.

'You must have got it wrong,' I insist, tears now brimming and rolling down my cheeks. 'Dad must have reported me missing. I never go anywhere without him. He'll be beside himself. Someone needs to find him and tell him I'm OK. He'll come and get me.'

My eyelids grow heavy and I fall back on the pillows.

17

I sleep a lot. Though I've only been awake for a day I've had loads of visitors. Not proper visitors; Dad still hasn't come, just various medical people. They come in, take blood and other samples no one would want to hear about, ask questions, check my pulse, shine lights in my eyes. At one point they put me in a wheelchair and push me through the corridors to go for some scan or other. I say I can walk but as soon as I try to stand my head goes all swimmy and I realize I can't.

'It's OK, you're just weak from being in bed,' the nurse tells me. 'You'll be fine in no time.'

As the doctor said she would, a psychiatrist comes to see me too. She asks me lots of questions about what I remember, but I can't come up with anything, other than that I can picture Dad very clearly and that he will be looking for me.

I'm really worried about him – he will be frantic. I can't remember any other family, friends, or where I live, however many times and however many different ways she asks me, or how many sketch pads she puts in front of me. I'm not even sure how old I am, though the doctors think probably between fourteen and seventeen.

The most interesting visitor is the policewoman, PC Oaks. She is very young and pretty. She sits in the chair, close to my bed, fiddling with the edge of my hospital-issue blanket. A social worker Ellie sits next to her, watching me carefully.

'We've been going through the missing persons register to see if there is anyone who might possibly be you,' PC Oaks tells me. 'We've checked all the girls who have gone missing recently, and they've all been ruled out for one reason or another. So now we're having to consider historic cases, which takes more time. Obviously we will keep you updated as soon as we find anything of relevance. Which I'm sure will happen – I don't want you to worry.'

But how can I not worry? I don't know who I am and no one seems to be looking for me.

The nurse bustles in as PC Oaks and the social worker leave. 'You OK, dear? Anything I can get you? You must be bored, all on your own here with nothing to read. Do you want me to bring you some magazines from one of the wards? There are always some lying around.'

'Yes please, that would be nice,' I say. I'm not entirely sure what she means by magazines, but something to read would be good.

'Or do you want to watch TV for now? You're probably still tired, so that might be easier.'

'TV?'

'Yes, here you go . . .' She picks up a remote control and points it at the screen on the wall, which fizzes into life.

'Oh TV!' I say. 'Yes. Yes, please.'

I watch TV for the rest of the day. It helps take my mind off my dire situation.

TV seems both familiar and unfamiliar. I've a feeling I've seen something like it, but not quite the same. And after a few hours, I feel totally drained. I've watched everything from smiling people winning money by answering questions correctly, to a programme showing children with distended stomachs who are dying because they haven't got enough to eat, which makes me cry. There are programmes where people cook amazing-looking dishes and a team of judges choose which is the best, and ones where two people just sit in chairs and talk to each other.

I don't recognize anyone, but the day passes quickly between that and thumbing through the magazines which the nurse brings in for me. It's fun to look at some of the pictures but all the stories seem to be about allegedly famous people I've never heard of. I guess that's what amnesia does to you.

The next day, I am staring mindlessly at the TV when PC Oaks and Ellie appear again about an hour after breakfast. I'm watching a programme where they seem to change topic every few minutes with seemingly no links between the sections at all, people come and go into the studio to be interviewed and now and again there are what I eventually work out must be adverts. It doesn't seem familiar in any way and I'm starting to find that quite disconcerting.

'Good morning,' PC Oaks says. 'How did you sleep?'

'Fine thanks,' I reply, warily, not looking away from the screen. I instinctively know that I'm not going to want to hear whatever it is they have to say and so I try to put it off as long as possible.

They both pull up chairs and sit next to my bed. 'Would you mind turning off the TV?' Ellie, the social worker, says quietly. 'I'm afraid we have some bad news.'

I point the remote control at the TV and switch it off, a feeling of dread rising within me.

Ellie reaches out and takes my hand. 'I'm sorry to have to tell you this, and there's no easy way to say it, but the man who we believe you called your father is dead.'

What? 'Dead? No, he can't be,' I say. I feel myself start to shake. Not Dad. No.

'The police were called out to a farmhouse after some ramblers reported . . . well, you don't need to hear what they reported right now, but they found your . . . a man's body there.'

My breath catches in my throat. 'A body?'

'Yes. I'm sorry to have to tell you this, it very much looks like he killed himself.'

Tears rise in my eyes and start to fall down my cheeks. I don't wipe them away.

'But how do you know it's Dad?' I ask. 'He could be anyone.' They've got it wrong. They must have.

'Samples taken from you while you were still asleep match those found around the house – on tissues, a hairbrush and your toothbrush,' PC Oaks says gently. 'It seems that we have almost certainly found where you were living. So by extension, the man . . . found there is believed to be the man you were living with.'

'But you said he's dead? He can't be!'

The officer pauses before saying, 'That's the other thing. This will come as a shock, but I'm afraid that while you appeared to have been living at the house, the man whose body we found could not be your biological father. But we think we know—'

What? What are they saying? 'Know what!' I cry. 'You said my dad was dead and now you're saying he's not my dad! Which is it?'

PC Oaks takes a deep breath. 'As I was saying, we think we now know who you are. The man who you appeared to be living with is dead, I'm afraid, but he was not your natural father. We know this from the same samples taken from you. We have also checked your samples against our databases—'

I shake my head. 'I don't understand. You say he's not my father, but you don't know who I am either.'

PC Oaks sighs.

'We do know who you are. We found a match on our database of historic cases.' She pauses. 'You're Anna Roberts. You were abducted as a four-year-old. I'm so sorry.'

My heart starts beating faster. '*Abducted?* When I was four?' I shake my head. 'No, I don't think so. You must've got it wrong. I remember my dad perfectly. I can picture him. From recently, I mean. Not from when I was four.'

Ellie tries to take my hand. I snatch it away. 'I understand this is difficult to hear, but samples were taken from Anna's home when she went missing, more than a decade ago. Yours match hers.'

85

'But my dad . . .' I trail off.

'We have been in touch with your mother, your birth mother, Karen, who can't wait to be reunited with you,' Ellie continues. 'As for the man who you called your dad, the man found where you were living . . . we don't know exactly who he was yet. We are trying to work that out, but . . .'

I shake my head. What are they talking about? This is all too much to take in and simply doesn't make any sense. 'I'm sorry, I still don't understand.'

'The man who you lived with wasn't your real father,' Ellie reiterates.

My breath catches in my throat. 'That's not possible,' I insist.

She pauses. 'There were numerous DNA samples taken from your personal items when you were abducted as a four-year-old and – well, there's really no doubt that you are Anna Roberts. And as I said, the blood taken from the body we found in the house where you seemed to be living indicates that he couldn't be a close biological relative of yours. It's not possible because of your respective blood groups.'

I shake my head. 'There must be a mistake. You need to check again.'

This time she ignores my objection. 'The doctors say you appear to be well nourished and your injuries are new and likely to have been caused by being hit by a car so . . .' Ellie trails off. 'At the moment we have no way of knowing if you were abducted by the man you were living with, or came to him at a later date, or indeed why you were with him at all. Unless there's anything you . . .'

'He was never anything but a great dad to me.' Or at least, as far as I remember. Was he a good dad? I'm pretty sure he was. When I think of him, all I can remember is feeling loved.

Tears prick at my eyes, and Ellie puts her hand gently on my wrist. This time I don't snatch it away. 'We very much hope that's the case, um . . .' I can tell she wants to use my name here and fresh tears come at the thought that I can't remember it – though somehow I'm almost certain it wasn't Anna. 'You'll continue to talk to the psychiatrist and your memory will hopefully come back, and then you'll be able to . . .'

I sit upright. 'There's nothing to tell! That much I remember. He was a good and kind man who looked after me.' I swipe angrily at the tears, which are now coming thick and fast.

'OK,' Ellie says, in the tone of voice you might use to talk to someone very stupid, or maybe a wild animal. 'The other issue, of course, is reuniting you with your family . . .'

'I don't want to be reunited with anyone!' I yell. 'I want my dad! Now please, leave me alone.' I throw myself down on the bed and childishly turn my back on the two women. I hear them tiptoe out of the room and gently close the door behind them.

18

I cry and cry and cry until eventually I fall asleep. I dream of a house with a large living room, a big roaring fire, a kitchen table covered in books. It's my house, I realize. Where I live. Lived. With Dad. My room is upstairs, where there are even more books. Dad's room is along the landing. There is a bathroom, but the water is often cold and the bath which stands in the middle of the room is cracked and mottled. It's nothing like the clean, white bath here with as much hot water as I want, or the tiny, neat white bathrooms I've seen on TV since I've been here.

I wake up covered in sweat, realizing that it wasn't a dream, it was a memory. Wasn't it? I remember the smell of Dad, woodsmoke and something else, mysterious and manly. In the evenings sometimes when it was cold we would huddle under a scratchy blanket on the sofa and watch films. We didn't watch TV programmes, not like I've been watching here in hospital, but we watched films. Dad always chose them. Sometimes they were in colour but often they were black and white.

That's why the TV seemed different. Films. Longer. Less shouting. More story. No adverts.

It is still dark, but it feels important that I have remembered something, and I wonder if I should tell someone. I switch on my bedside light and buzz for the night nurse. A few minutes later she comes in.

'Everything OK?' she asks in a soft voice.

'Fine,' I say. 'I just thought I should let you know I'm remembering some stuff.'

The nurse smiles and pats my arm. 'That's great. I'll leave a note that the psychiatrist should come and see you tomorrow. Did you remember your name?'

'Laura,' I say, the name springing into my head seemingly out of nowhere. 'My name's Laura.'

'I had a dream last night and it was all familiar. I think it was a memory. Where I lived was a farmhouse, right?' I describe the house from my dream last night, and Ellie nods as PC Oaks takes notes.

'Yes, that's right,' she says. 'So can we assume your memory is starting to come back?'

I shrug. 'A little.'

'But you still don't remember much of your life there? Or where you were going when you were hit by the car?'

'I remember watching films with Dad. And lots of books at the kitchen table. Oh – and my name – Laura.'

Ellie smiles and writes something in her notebook. 'Laura. Hello, Laura. It's lovely to meet you properly. Don't suppose you remember your surname?'

'No. Sorry. No idea. Dad called me Laura. Or Lala.'

She nods briskly and jots down something else. 'You mentioned books. So you can read?' she asks hesitantly.

I laugh, but it comes out more like a bark. Embarrassing. 'Of course I can read! I love reading. I read at least one book every week. Dad insists.' I pause. 'Insisted.' Tears well again and I fight them back.

Ellie nods. 'Good, good. But you still don't remember if the man . . .'

'Dad?'

'The man you call your dad, if he . . . hurt you?'

I slam my hands down onto the bed. 'No! He never hurt me. It's the last thing he would do. I don't remember much but I do remember he loved me. As a father should love his daughter. I'd remember if he'd mistreated me. I'm sure I would.' I pause. 'I still can't believe that he abducted me. He was the best dad. There must be some other kind of explanation. I really think you've got it wrong.'

Ellie clears her throat. 'I understand that this must be upsetting for you, but there is no doubt about this. Since we last spoke, we've been checking with the various local authorities who have no records of anyone of your age living at your address in their schools, or registered with any doctors' surgeries. Do you remember if you went to school? Or ever saw a doctor?'

'I don't remember,' I say. I'd seen schools in the films I'd watched with Dad and read about them in books, but I don't remember going anywhere like that myself. 'I think Dad taught me at home. And I don't think I was ever properly ill, not that I remember, so maybe I didn't need to see a doctor.'

Ellie nods. 'OK. If you were taught at home you should have been registered as being home-schooled, but you're not. At least, no one at your address.'

I nod. 'Right. So maybe Dad didn't fill in the forms. Is that a crime?'

'Well actually . . .' PC Oaks says, but Ellie shoots her a look and she stops talking abruptly.

'We haven't been able to trace any family for the man you call your dad yet as we don't know who he is.'

'No, you wouldn't have done, I remember that much. It was just me and him. He told me we had no other family.'

A wave of grief washes over me as I remember that he's gone and I don't want to talk about this anymore.

'I'm tired now,' I say. 'Can we please leave this till tomorrow?'

They are back again the next day with more questions.

'Did he, um, the man, ever talk about . . . do you remember your mother?' Ellie asks gently.

'No,' I say. 'I never knew her. She died in childbirth.'

PC Oaks nods. 'I see. It's been quite difficult to find out any information about the man you were living with, there was an unusual lack of official documentation in the house. The house we believe you lived in has been rented for around eleven years by a man called Daniel Johnson. Does that name ring any bells? Do you think that might have been the name of your – uh – the man who you called Dad?'

I shake my head. 'I don't know. I always called him Dad.'

'And your friends?'

'Friends?'

'What did your friends call him?'

Friends? I try to picture other people I might have known, but can't picture anyone other than me and Dad. Did I have friends? Did we? Have I just forgotten? Oh God. He can't be dead. He's all I have. I'm sure of it. A sob rises in my throat and then there is a wailing sound, and it takes a few minutes before I realize the sound is coming from me.

I'm all alone.

19

July 2013
Inverness

After a lot of discussion with Ellie, I agree I will meet my 'real family'. While it is constantly reiterated that everything will happen at my pace and in my best interests, it still feels very scary. I am having to come to terms with the fact that Dad isn't coming back, and my original family is desperate to have me home with them. As I am, apparently, not yet sixteen, it's either this or a foster family. So my original family seems like the best option, even if I have no memory of them whatsoever. I get dressed for their arrival and sit on the bed. Ellie is here for the occasion.

'Ready?' she asks.

I nod. 'I'm a bit nervous.'

She gives me a sympathetic smile. 'That's understandable. But there's nothing to be nervous about. The family is delighted you're safe and can't wait to see you again. But everything will go at your pace and nothing will happen or be decided today.' Yawn. How many times has she said this? 'After the meeting, when you're ready, we'll go through the options again and you can decide what you want to do.'

Tears fill my eyes and I brush them away. I want to go home to Dad but that particular option isn't on the table, and never will be. I sniff and Ellie puts her hand on my shoulder. 'I know,' she says. 'It must be a lot to take in.'

'I'm OK,' I lie, straightening my back. I can't stay in hospital forever – I understand that things will need to move forward in one way or another at some point soon.

There is a gentle knock on the door and a woman and a boy – I guess my mum and the brother I've been told I have – come in with PC Oaks. The woman's hand immediately flies to her mouth and tears start running down her cheeks as she murmurs 'My baby!' I shift awkwardly. I don't know what to do. The boy glances at me, gives his mum a look of exasperation and the two of them sit down on two chairs which had already been brought in before their arrival. The woman is wearing a headscarf and I remember being told she has cancer. She is still crying, silently, and the boy pats his mum's shoulder, whispering, 'Mum! Please! We talked about this.'

'Laura – meet Karen and Jesse Roberts,' Ellie says formally. It annoys me when she calls me Laura because she always says it in a weird way as if to make the point that she doesn't consider it my real name, but then again, I don't want her to call me Anna either. I can't think of myself as Anna. It's hard to imagine I ever will be able to.

My legs feel wobbly and I'm glad I'm sitting down. This is the first time I've been out of bed properly since I arrived in hospital, except when I've been wheeled around for tests and scans. My head starts to spin. I try to smile at Mrs Roberts and the boy whose name I've already forgotten but I think it probably looks like some kind of hideous grimace. Mrs Roberts still has her hand over her mouth and tears are streaming down her face. None of us has said a word and even Ellie seems at a bit of a loss as to what we should do now.

Mrs Roberts takes her hand away from her mouth and mumbles something, but it is incomprehensible through her tears. Her silent crying has by now progressed to sobbing, and I'm feeling really awkward. I don't know where to look so I stare at my hands.

'I'm sorry, Mrs Roberts, we didn't quite catch that,' Ellie says in the kind of patronizing tone which I imagine a teacher might use to speak to a mumbling four-year-old. 'Could you repeat what you said?'

She continues sobbing and we all sit in silence for a few seconds. I'm starting to wonder if this was a really bad idea. If I should have refused to meet them. What would have happened then? It is hot and stuffy in the room and I feel sweat prickling on my back underneath my hideous sweatshirt, retrieved especially from the lost property department of the hospital so that I'd have something to wear other than a hospital nightgown.

'I . . . I . . . I . . . I wanted to ask . . . do you . . . remember me?' Mrs Roberts manages to force out between sobs.

I look up and she is staring at me, and then she reaches

over and touches my leg before crumpling against her son, barely able to breathe for crying.

'I don't . . . I mean I can't . . .' I stutter. I tug at the neckline of the sweatshirt and take a deep breath. Why is it so hot in here today?

'As I explained, Laura – as we have been calling her for now – doesn't remember much at all,' Ellie says soothingly. 'The doctors think she may have suffered a mild concussion, most likely as a result of being hit by a car, but they're confident that her memory will come back over time.'

'I've already remembered a few things,' I blurt. 'My name. My house. My dad.'

I look down at the floor, realizing that that was probably the wrong thing to say. Mrs Roberts' sobs escalate and she mumbles something which sounds like it might have been 'That man, why . . .' but it's difficult to tell.

'She's mine!' Mrs Roberts suddenly shouts, pulling herself up straight. 'How dare that man take you away from me all those years! Anna! You're back . . .'

She gets up and lunges towards me, wrapping her arms around my neck and sobbing into my shoulder. I can feel her spit, snot and tears running onto my skin and shift uncomfortably.

I feel nothing except embarrassment and revulsion. I don't know who this woman is and she's scaring me.

There is a tugging at my neck. 'Mrs Roberts,' Ellie says, trying to prise the woman away from me. 'I realize this is a very emotional time for you, but it is also a very difficult time for Anna . . . Laura. She has been . . . away for a long time and will need to get used not just to you but life in general. Please . . .' She gently lifts her off me and guides her back into her chair. 'We all need to take things very slowly. For everyone's sake.'

Mrs Roberts takes out a tissue and she wipes her eyes and nose. She seems a little calmer now. 'Of course. I'm sorry, Anna, it's been so long, I thought I'd never get you back, I thought I'd . . .'

She starts sobbing again.

I look at PC Oaks, who is standing by the door looking totally bewildered.

'Laura? Do you have anything you want to ask or anything you want to say?' Ellie asks. 'Do Mrs Roberts or Jesse look familiar to you?'

Jesse. That was the boy's name. When I was first told it, I thought he must be a girl.

Mrs Roberts looks up at me. The expression on her face sends a bolt through me. It's a desperate mix of hoping and pleading. All she wants is for me to say yes. All she's probably hoped for since her daughter went missing is to have her back. I wonder if I should pretend. After all, if these people aren't my family, with Dad gone, who is? What will happen to me when I leave the hospital? With a stab of loneliness I remember that not only do I have no family, I have no friends either – at least none I remember. Did I have friends? Why has no one come to see me at the hospital? Why has no one come to claim me?

With Dad gone, if I ceased to exist, maybe the only people who would notice are the people in this room and some of the hospital staff.

Mrs Roberts is still staring at me. She reaches out to touch my knee again but gently this time. 'Do you remember me . . . at all?'

I stare back at her. I figure it's best to be honest and slowly shake my head. 'No. I'm so sorry. I don't.'

She leans back in her chair. 'But that doesn't mean anything, does it?' she gabbles. 'After all, you don't remember anything? Isn't that right? Isn't it?'

I nod. 'Not much, nothing specific. And nothing at all from . . . when I was very small.' I mean from before I was with Dad, but I don't want to say that.

'So what happens now?' Mrs Roberts gabbles. 'Can Anna come home with us?' She directs that pleading look she gave me a few minutes ago at Ellie. 'We've been so patient – like you asked us to be. Her room's still the same as it was, ready for her – we don't let anyone else use it – but she can decorate it exactly how she likes, and I can find out about where she could go to school – she could probably go to the same school as Jesse did – what year should she be in? Could she start school in September?' She pauses. 'You can read, can't you, Anna? Did anyone teach you?' Her hand flies to her mouth again. 'Oh God, what has he done to you? Did he . . . hurt you? Oh God, he didn't hurt you, did he? I'd never forgive myself if . . .' She starts bawling again and crumples into her son.

I shift uncomfortably in my chair again. I don't know exactly what I expected from this meeting, but I'm pretty sure it wasn't this. My face feels hot and my mouth is filling with saliva.

'I'm feeling a bit . . .' I mumble, but no one seems to pay any attention. I pull the sweatshirt off over my head, not caring that the manky greying T-shirt underneath is ugly and too small for me. I wipe my hand across my forehead, which is prickling with a cold sweat.

'As I said before, whatever happens now, it all has to happen slowly. Nothing will be decided today,' Ellie says, using that slow, patronizing tone again. 'This meeting has been very emotional for everyone. You and Jesse need to go home and think about how you feel, discuss it between yourselves, and we need to talk to Laura about what her options are.'

'But we can have her back, can't we?' Mrs Roberts shrieks hysterically.

My head is spinning. 'I really need to . . .' I say a little louder.

'Again, we all need to go away and reflect and work out what's best for Laura,' Ellie repeats. 'For the short term—'

'You can't keep my baby away from me now she's back!' Mrs Roberts screams. 'You can't! I need to call a solicitor or—'

'We're not saying we're going to keep her away from you, just that we need to—'

Nausea rises through me and I stand up. 'I think I'm going to be . . .' I mumble, stumbling towards the bathroom, but my legs collapse under me, my stomach spasms and, Mrs Roberts' screams still ringing in my ears, I throw up on the floor.

20

July 2013
Inverness

That night I have another very vivid dream. I am standing at a window in what I think is probably my house, looking down. There is a boy by the front door with sandy hair, with a large cardboard box on a trolley. He is wearing a white short-sleeved T-shirt and I can see the fine golden hairs on his arms glinting in the sun. I am admiring his muscular forearms when he looks up at me and catches my eye.

As I dart backwards into my room I wake with a start, feeling disorientated and strangely on edge, as if there is something I want to do but I don't quite know what.

I sit up in bed and turn the light on. The growing familiarity of the room, even in its starkness, is somehow comforting.

Was that another memory? Or a dream? God knows how I'm supposed to tell the difference.

I turn the light off and lie back down, but I am wide awake for ages.

Tomorrow I'm going to ask if I can see my house. I think it would help.

It feels strange being outside the hospital again. I'm not entirely sure how long I've been there. I watch the buildings whizz past and then thin out as we drive away from the hospital and out of the city. As the buildings get sparser, I find myself relaxing. It occurs to me that I have no memory of being anywhere other than my house and the hospital. But I don't know much about amnesia – maybe that's how it works. Maybe I just don't remember the other places I've been.

'This is it,' Ellie says as we turn right between two old wooden fence posts. A rusty red gate is propped open and there is a large 'No Entry' sign tied roughly to it. I notice a scraggy end of plastic police tape still attached to one of the fence posts.

The car slows as we drive up the long, bumpy track, and I feel a jolt of familiarity as the house comes into view.

It is the farmhouse in my dream. But not the farmhouse of anyone's dreams. It was probably once a pretty, if not exactly impressive or imposing house, but now the paint is peeling and some of the wooden shutters are rotten and hanging off. The area in front of the house was probably once covered in gravel but now most of the stones have become so worn down that it's mainly mud. To either side there are fields which look like they could do with attention, some overgrown vegetable patches, and some pens which look like they were probably once for animals but now stand empty.

The front door is red, or at least it probably used to be, but it's now faded to a kind of dirty rust colour and the paint is peeling.

'Remember it?' Ellie asks as she rummages in her bag and pulls out a key.

'Yes. I do. This is where I lived.' I frown. 'But something is different.'

'There were animals here. Chickens, a couple of cows, some sheep. Maybe that's what you're thinking of?'

I nod. 'Oh yeah. Maybe.' I feel a pang of alarm. 'What happened to them?'

'Don't worry – they were rehomed with the help of an animal charity. As far as I know, they were all fine. I can double-check later if you like.' She tips her head to one side. 'Ready to go in?'

I nod. 'Definitely.'

I follow her into a dark hallway. I push a door open to the right, which reveals a large kitchen with the table I remember as covered in books – as it still is. There's a musty smell but the room looks clean, if a bit dusty, and there is a big black Aga in one corner.

I smile. 'In winter I used to sit over there,' I say, pointing at a threadbare old easy chair next to it. 'It was about the only place in the house which was warm. Apart from by the fire in the living room – I'll show you that next.'

I walk back into the hallway and push open the door on the other side which leads to the living room. 'It's just like it was in my dream,' I tell Ellie, taking in the shabby-looking rug on the bare floorboards, the sagging sofa covered in old blankets and the ancient TV and VHS player and Dad's huge stack of videos.

'It's great news that you're starting to remember stuff, Laura,' she says, 'I'm sure the rest of your memory will come back in no time.'

'Hope so,' I say, feeling strangely cheered by being home, even though it's ultra-weird and sad being there without Dad. It's the first thing that's really felt familiar since I woke up in hospital. 'Can I go upstairs?'

'Of course.'

I bound up the stairs and turn left into my room, which is exactly as I imagined.

'Gosh, it's very bare,' Ellie comments.

'What do you mean? It's got a bed, desk, chair, wardrobe and books – what else would I need?' I ask. There's also my doll's house in the corner which Dad made me when I was tiny. I feel a pang as I have a flash of memory of me moving the tiny figurines around the rooms when I was much, much smaller.

'You don't *need* anything else,' Ellie says, snapping me out of my reverie, 'but most girls of your age have posters on the wall, pictures of their friends, things like that. Other bits and pieces.'

'Like what?' I ask, although I kind of know. I guess real-life rooms are like the ones on TV.

'I dunno. Trinkets. Cheap jewellery. Make-up. Magazines.'

I look around. 'I don't think I had those. I think my room was just like this.'

Ellie nods. 'Fair enough. Maybe you're the minimalist

type.' She pauses. 'And look,' she indicates the corner of the room, 'you had a guitar. Did you play?'

I pick it up and strum a few chords. It feels familiar. 'Yep. I think I probably did,' I say.

'That was something else actually,' Ellie adds. 'You didn't have a phone on you when you were found. Or an iPod or anything like that.' I look at her blankly. 'To listen to music on.'

'Dad and I listened to tapes. There are loads downstairs. You could have a look if you're interested.'

'Tapes?' She sounds surprised.

'Yes.'

'Why didn't you use an iPod or an MP3 player like everyone else? Or even CDs?'

I shrug. I don't know what she means but I don't want to say so. Ellie obviously thinks I'm weird in some way and not being able to remember anything isn't helping. Her phone rings and she wanders over to the window as she talks. She keeps taking the phone away from her ear and frowning at the screen, and I can tell from her end of the conversation that she is struggling to hear. I open the drawer of the bedside table where there are some hair clips (disappointingly plain), hair bands, and a small tape player with a cassette in a plain plastic box on top. An image of myself carefully recording songs from one tape to another flashes into my mind. Casting a glance behind me to check Ellie isn't looking, I thrust the tape into my trouser pocket. For all I know it could be anything – there are loads downstairs like I said to Ellie – but quite apart from anything else, I want something which feels like it is truly mine.

I look out the window down towards the front door. An image of the boy I saw in my dream pops into my head.

Is this where I watched him from? Who was he? Did I know him? Ellie was asking about friends before. Maybe he was my friend? It's so frustrating. I just can't remember.

I open the wardrobe door. 'Can I take some of my clothes with me?' I ask. I rifle through the cupboard and have to admit to being a little disappointed. There are very plain jeans, T-shirts and jumpers. No dresses or skirts, and no bright colours. Not nearly as nice as the things I've seen people wearing on TV or in the hospital.

Ellie frowns. 'I'm not sure. I'll need to check. Better not for now.'

I close the door. 'OK,' I say, vowing to buy myself some new, more interesting clothes as soon as I can, but then a thought strikes me like a mallet.

'How am I ever going to be able to buy myself new stuff like clothes? Or food, for that matter? My dad always did all that.' My throat feels tight, almost as if I can't breathe. 'I don't have any money.'

'Don't worry. Your – erm – your mum, Karen, told me she can't wait to go shopping with you, make up for lost time. I don't think you'll want for anything. Or,' she adds hurriedly, 'if you decide not to go down that route, there are various benefits that you or whoever cares for you will be eligible for.' She squeezes my arm. 'Don't worry.'

I nod, tears rising in my eyes but I force them back. My mum, Ellie said. I've never had a mum. The woman who came to see me in the hospital was a stranger, and it's hard to imagine her being anything else. But I don't want to think about that now. 'Can I go in Dad's room?' I ask.

Ellie nods and I push open the door. My breath catches in my throat. The bed is unmade and some of his clothes are draped over the back of a rickety old chair. It's almost as if he's simply gone out somewhere and will be back any minute. It still smells of him.

I lurch backwards, suddenly feeling sick. 'I'd like to go now,' I say, pushing past her and running down the stairs. Once outside I take a big, deep breath and the nausea starts to subside.

'You OK?' Ellie asks as she catches up with me. 'Did your dad's room make you remember something?'

I shake my head. 'No. Nothing specific. I just miss my dad.'

Dad's funeral is horrific. Attended only by me, Ellie and PC Oaks. A minister mumbles some generic pleasantries about a man he never met and then I watch as a velvet curtain slides slowly around the cheap wooden casket and I hear the conveyor belt take Dad to the incinerator.

For all I know, I'm the only person who will remember him, who will care that he ever lived.

I am numb. I don't even cry.

21

'This is it,' Ellie says, pulling up outside a house on a street in a part of London I'd never heard of: Catford. The houses are all small and squashed together and a helicopter is hovering overhead. 'Your new home.' She pauses and then adds hurriedly, 'As long as it all works out for all of you, of course. I will be keeping in close contact to check that everyone's happy and that there are no problems. Ready?'

In the end, it was agreed that it would be best if I went back to my family. After all, what else was I going to do? I'm fifteen years old, with no formal education and no family or friends. It's basically this or foster care, so this seems like the better option. At least I will be making Karen happy, if nothing else.

'Ready as I'll ever be, I guess,' I say. We both get out of the car and walk up the short path to the ratty-looking green-painted door. I feel a stab of disappointment and then hate myself for it. In my mind, when I'd heard my family lived in London, I'd pictured something grander, like I'd seen in the films. Our farmhouse was shabby, cold and dilapidated, but there was plenty of room, both inside and out. This place looks tiny and there are other houses right next to it. Ellie rings the doorbell and steps back.

The door is opened by Karen, who I am supposed to think of as Mum. We've only met once, in the hospital, and last time I was too upset and overwhelmed to take much in. Today I am feeling calmer, largely thanks to the anti-anxiety medication that was sorted out for me in the hospital to help me cope with everything. I can see that neither of us is very tall, but I can't see any other similarities between us. She is wearing a headscarf again and this time I notice that her eyebrows are clearly pencilled on. Her wrap dress has a bright, lurid print which matches the scarf and I wonder if she planned in advance what she should wear for my home-coming. Did she think about what kind of impression she'd like to make on me, her daughter, as I arrived back within the family fold? I look down at my horrible hospital-issued track-suit bottoms and am embarrassed at my appearance. I wish I'd had something better to wear to be introduced properly to my family. Because I guess that's what they are, like it or not, and I need to try to get used to the idea. It still seems kind of impossible though.

'Laura!' she gushes, leaning forward as if to kiss me on the cheek, and then backing off as if she realizes I might not be ready for that kind of thing yet. I'm relieved that she doesn't try to call me Anna. I'm guessing someone has told her not to. 'We've been so looking forward to you coming.'

She ushers Ellie and me into a small kitchen where a boy who looks a few years older than me is sitting at a table, fiddling with his phone. I recognize him vaguely as the boy who came to the hospital. He looks up when I come in, puts his phone down and smiles at me.

'She's here!' Mrs Roberts trills, 'Laura, you remember your broth—, I mean, my son Jesse? He came to the hospital with me.'

I smile benignly, hoping it covers the unexplainable panic I'm feeling. 'Um, nice to meet you again,' I mumble, feeling my face go scarlet. The boy gets up and comes over to me.

'We're so glad to have you back,' he says, looking straight into my eyes. Is this really my brother? Unexpectedly, he suddenly puts his arms around me and hugs me tight. I feel a bit uncomfortable as I don't know him and I can't think what to do so I kind of pat his back gently and after a few seconds he lets go. He squeezes my arm and says, 'We're all looking forward to getting to know you again,' and goes back to his seat. It sounds like something he had preprepared to say. I wonder if his mother drilled him.

'Would you like a drink, Laura?' Mrs Roberts says. I get the feeling she is deliberately using my name to show that she can cope with not calling me Anna. I can imagine her and Ellie discussing that, how best to handle me. 'Tea? Coffee? Juice?'

'No, I'm fine thanks,' I say, shuffling my feet awkwardly.

'OK. How about we show you your room and let you settle yourself in?'

'Uh, yes, that would be great, thank you.' I suddenly feel like there is nothing I would like more than to be back on my own again.

'Great. I'll take you,' Mrs Roberts says. 'You've had a long journey and I imagine you'll want some time to . . . well.'

I follow her meekly out the kitchen, into the hallway and up a flight of stairs. After the blank sterility of the hospital everything here feels very colourful. There is a small landing at the top with four doors off it. She pushes one open saying, 'This is yours.'

I step inside. Karen wasn't joking when she said they had kept it as it was – it is very clearly a little girl's room. The duvet cover on the bed is plain white but the headboard and curtains are pastel pink and there are stuffed toys everywhere.

'Bathroom's out on the landing,' she says, vaguely indicating the bedroom door. 'I've put a toothbrush and toothpaste, shower gel and shampoo, a hairbrush, towels, sanitary products and everything else I could think of that you might need in here for you,' she adds, opening a wardrobe door and pointing at one of the shelves where all the things she mentions are stacked. 'I hope you don't mind. If you'd rather use your own stuff then that's fine too.'

I shake my head. 'No – I don't really have any of my own things. So far I haven't been allowed to take anything from the house.'

Karen nods curtly and her cheeks redden. 'Well, if there's anything you need, please let me know. She touches my arm

110

gently. 'We're so glad to have you back. I know it will take a while, but I want you to feel at home here.'

I nod, tears filling my eyes as I wish she'd leave me alone now. Thankfully, she does.

I sit down on the bed and press my hands down on the duvet. It feels luxurious after the institutional blankets in the hospital. I brush away my tears. I can't spend my whole life crying. I've got to get on with things. Make a new life. Dad's gone, I can't go back.

I take the tape from my pocket and put it on the bedside table. It's the only thing I have from the past. I wonder if I can ask Karen if she's got something I can play it on? Or would that make me seem grasping? Out for what I can get, now that I've landed on my feet with a new family?

Not new, I remind myself. According to what everyone says, and the science, these people are my family. It's so hard to believe though. I feel a pang. I miss Dad so much.

I sigh. I need to tread carefully. Make an effort to fit in. This family is all I have now. They've managed without me for more than a decade. For all I know, they might decide that having me home isn't all they were expecting it to be. That they'd be better off if I hadn't come back. That me being here is too disruptive, brings back too many bad memories. They might decide to send me away and then . . . and then . . . Tears spring to my eyes and I brush them away.

I open the drawer of the bedside table. Inside there are a couple of plastic ponies with gaudy manes and a colouring book. I look at the pile of teddies in a huge basket. Anna obviously liked her stuffed toys.

I wonder if she had a favourite teddy. If *I* had a favourite. Was this really ever my room? I feel like an intruder. I feel like I shouldn't be here, intruding on a little girl's space.

I get up and open the wardrobe.

It's totally empty, apart from the towels and toiletries Karen mentioned. At least she didn't keep Anna's clothes for all these years, that would be weird. I realize with a stab of panic that all I have to wear is what I am standing in. I don't even have a spare pair of knickers. Why didn't I bring my horrible hospital stuff with me? How stupid was that?

I cross the room and open a drawer to check if there is anything in there I could wear – God knows why; I mean, why would there be? – when there is a knock at the door.

'Laura? Can we come in?'

'Uh, yes, come in.' This is my own room, I realize. I can decide who comes in and who doesn't. Not like the hospital when people knocked but then they always came in whether you liked it or not.

Ellie enters with Karen.

'I was thinking,' I say, 'I should have brought the stuff they lent me at the hospital. I've got nothing to wear.' I blush. I've only just arrived – the last thing I want to do is start demanding things.

A look of impatience flashes across Ellie's face. 'Never mind. I can – post it on to you or something.'

Karen waves her hand. 'It's my fault. I should have got you some basics, but I remember what I was like when I was your age – the absolute last thing I would have wanted would have been my . . . someone as old as me picking out my clothes!'

112

She laughs falsely. She was obviously going to refer to herself as my mum and then decided against it. I bet Ellie warned her about not doing that. I can totally imagine her saying something like 'Let her come to you in her own time.' Thinking she knows what's best for me. Not that I can ever imagine thinking of Karen as Mum. I've never had a mum, nor felt I've needed one. A wave of sadness crashes over me as I think about Dad; it's so intense that for a second I think I'll collapse.

'But if you feel like it and you're not too tired, we could go shopping today?' she is still twittering on. 'I mean, I don't want to rush you if you'd rather take things at your own pace but we totally cleared the day for you so, whatever you want, it can be arranged! And I've been putting some money aside for you over the years – I always believed you'd come back eventually. I prayed for your return every single day. Back when you disappeared our whole church prayed for you. And now our prayers have been answered. Finally.'

I shift uncomfortably. I certainly don't feel like I'm the answer to anyone's prayers. I wonder if she will expect me to go to church with her. Dad and I discussed religion a lot, and I decided I am definitely an atheist. Like Dad was.

I feel tears welling at the thought of him and move the conversation back onto the safer ground of shopping. Even though I'm exhausted after our early flight, thought of having literally nothing to wear is making me anxious. 'If it's really no trouble I guess it would be good to have some clothes of my own,' I say, although this makes me uncomfortable too because I have no money and so am basically assuming she will buy them for me. 'Sorry, I should have brought the hospital stuff with me.'

She waves her hand impatiently. 'No, no, no! It's important that you should choose your own things, reclaim your own . . . identity.'

Whatever that may be, I think.

'If you're sure, then I'd love to,' I say. I don't want to spend the whole afternoon with this woman who is a complete stranger to me, but equally, I am going to need something to wear.

We spend the afternoon shopping – I'm bewildered and a bit embarrassed by how much we buy in somewhere called Primark, but Karen doesn't seem to mind. I realize I have no real concept of what things cost, what is cheap or expensive. I guess Dad must have done all the shopping; I certainly don't remember doing any, at least. And I'm almost certain I've never seen so many clothes in one place. All those colours on all those racks! I'm bewildered by the choice but choose some things which look a bit like things I liked best that I saw in the magazines when I was at the hospital.

Back at home (home?) I go up to my room and put my new stuff away. Even though it's all brand new, having my own things here makes me feel a tiny bit more like I belong. Or at least makes me feel like I might do, in time.

I lie on the bed and pick up the tape, the one and only possession I have from my previous life. I take it out of its scuffed plastic box and put my finger in one of the little holes. I wish I'd brought the player too, but that would have been too big to take without Ellie noticing. I wonder if there is something I can play it on here. I'd love to listen to it, hear what's on it. Maybe it would bring back some memories?

Then again, maybe it wouldn't. There were loads of tapes at home. It's probably just music, like all the others. Something I listened to. I was amazed that Ellie thought having tapes was so weird and old-fashioned. Though thinking about it, there aren't any here, and I haven't seen any when I've been watching TV. I obviously have a lot to learn.

There is a knock on the door. I call, 'Come in.'

It's Jesse. He looks like he has just got out of the shower; his hair is wet and he smells of shower gel.

'Hey,' he says. 'OK if I come in?'

I nod. 'Of course,' I say, sitting down on the bed.

'How was your shopping trip? Get everything you need?' he asks.

I nod. 'It was fine. Good. Thank you.' I feel wary. Jesse seems nice but I don't know him at all and I feel like I need to be careful what I say around him. He says he's pleased I'm back, but is he really? Maybe he might be jealous? After all it's been him and his mum all these years as far as I understand. It must be weird to suddenly have to share her with someone else. Especially someone like me who is being welcomed back like the prodigal son. Or prodigal daughter. He might not want the disruption in his life. I wouldn't blame him.

'What's that?' he asks, inclining his head towards the tape which I had forgotten I was holding.

'Oh.' I blush, putting it back down on the bedside table. 'It's nothing. A tape I picked up when the social worker took me back to my house. I don't think I'm supposed to have it, but I wanted something which was mine from . . . before.' I probably shouldn't tell him, but it slips out. It's exhausting having no one except psychologists and social workers to talk to about anything. Lonely.

He nods. 'I can understand that. What's on it?'

'I don't know. I haven't got anything to play it on. I wasn't supposed to take anything from the house. I only took this.' I feel myself go even redder. 'I'm not even sure why. It was probably a stupid thing to do.'

'Can I have a look?' Jesse holds out his hand and I pass it to him. 'Wow. I didn't realize these things still existed.'

Suddenly an image flashes into my head of lying on a blanket with someone next to me, touching me, and a feeling of . . . of . . . I'm not sure what. And then in another instant, it's gone.

Jesse is frowning at me. 'You OK? You seemed to zone out for a few seconds there.'

'Yeah.' I don't want to tell him about the image I saw. It probably wasn't even a memory. It was probably nothing. My mind isn't exactly reliable these days. 'I was just thinking about what might be on the tape,' I lie.

He puts it back on the bedside table and shrugs. 'Who knows? If I can get hold of a player, we can find out if you like? Though I'm not sure quite where I'd find one. Maybe we can get a cheap one online. No one uses these things anymore. Anyway, Mum sent me up to tell you it's time for dinner.'

22

'What are you planning to do today?' Jesse asks me over breakfast the next day.

'Um – nothing really,' I say. 'I, uh, kind of don't know anyone.' I give him an embarrassed smile. It's getting pretty lame having to say stuff like that over and over again.

'D'you want to do something?' Jesse asks. 'It's a lovely day – I could show you around a bit?'

I smile. 'Thank you, I'd like that.' I'd like to get a sense of where I live now. I haven't been outside yet. In fact, I've barely been outside since I was found. I feel a pang again. I have a strong feeling I spent a lot of time outside in my previous life. In woods. Digging the garden. Tending to animals.

A flash of memory comes back to me – me asking my dad why I didn't have a brother or sister like the children

117

in the books and films, and when could I get one so I could have someone to play with. I'm pretty sure I never had one, and I've a vague idea it upset Dad when I asked.

Jesse grins back at me. He has a dimple in his right cheek which I have never noticed before. I touch my face – I have one in the same place. My brother. So weird. 'Great!' he says. 'Let's sort out some food and make a picnic of it. We can go to the park.'

He takes sliced bread from the bread bin and makes cheese and ham sandwiches, and roots around in the cupboards and fridge to find crisps, chocolate biscuits and cans of Coke. He's stuffing them into a bag when Karen comes in. She smiles indulgently.

'What're you two up to?'

'We're going to go for a picnic in the park,' Jesse says. 'It's a nice day and Laura's barely been out the house – I thought it would be nice to show her around.'

Karen frowns. 'You're going out?'

'Yes. That's OK, isn't it?'

She frowns. 'It's just . . .' she trails off and Jesse sighs impatiently.

'*What?*'

'Laura's social workers, and the police – they think it's best if she keeps a low profile for now.'

Jesse tuts. 'Oh yeah. I remember now. Press interest and all that.'

Karen nods. 'Yes. Especially while we don't . . . while Anna – Laura – doesn't remember much, Ellie thinks it would be very difficult for her to deal with the press. It was such a huge story when Anna went, and while it's been ages since anyone has shown any interest in us—'

'Do you mind not talking about me as if I'm not here?' I snap, and then clamp my hand over my mouth. It's the first time I've been even vaguely rude in this house. 'Sorry,' I mumble. 'I didn't mean it to come out like that.'

Karen smiles and puts her hand on my arm. I manage not to flinch. 'Sorry. It's fine. My fault entirely – that was rude of me. I thought Ellie had talked to you about this. If the press get wind that you might be . . . Anna, back with us, they'll have a field day. If they don't know, you can live a much quieter life, which we think you'll find easier. We're only thinking of you.'

I nod. 'It's OK, I understand. I think Ellie did say something to me about it.'

'So it's up to you, Laura, but I thought it might be best if for now you say you are a cousin who's visiting. And you're already using the name Laura, so you should continue to do that, for now at least. Perhaps we could say your parents have had to go abroad for work? Maybe we could say they're in the army? If anyone asks, which they probably won't.'

This all seems very complicated, but I go along with it, telling her 'Um . . . OK.' I can't imagine why the press would be interested in someone like me, but equally it doesn't sound like something that I'd want. Not that I know anything about the press. Or, indeed, much at all about life outside my farmhouse, it is starting to dawn on me.

'It's just for the short term,' she adds. 'When – I mean *if* you feel ready, we might have to make some kind of official announcement. And even then it will probably be better to withhold your identity from the public. Either way, it will be better – for you – if we decide how and when to do it. Rather than accidentally letting something slip out.'

I nod. 'It's OK. That makes sense.' It kind of does. I think.

'And in case you were wondering, that's also why we haven't thrown a big party to welcome you home or anything. We thought it was better if we kept it all low key. As does Ellie.' She smiles nervously, and I feel terrible for snapping at her. 'Take care.'

'We will,' I say as Jesse grabs my arm and hauls me after him.

'Sorry about that,' he says as he slams the front door behind him.

I shrug. 'It's fine. Your mum's just looking out for me.'

He stops dead. 'She's your mum too.'

'Um . . . yeah.'

He starts walking again and I follow. 'It's OK. It must be weird being dumped into a family like this and having no memory of us, or of who you really are.'

I laugh. 'That's an understatement.'

We walk in silence for a few seconds as Jesse frowns. 'It's a shame you don't remember anything about us. I guess the difference is that I'm a few years older, but I remember you.'

I stop and look at him. 'Do you? What do you remember?' I ask.

He shrugs. 'Fragments. You'd have nightmares sometimes and come into my bed. And there was a time when I pushed you off a swing and you cried. I got sent to my room, but I was livid because I didn't mean to do it.'

I laugh. 'Sorry.'

'But then you brought me a stone from the garden to say sorry. It was round and smooth – a fairly ordinary stone, but you thought it was pretty. I remember your favourite dress was pink with ruffles and a big bow at the back. You wore it all the time. And then one day you were eating chocolate ice cream and you dropped it down the dress. Mum couldn't get the stain out and you cried and cried and cried.'

'I sound pretty annoying.'

Jesse sits down on a bench under a tree and puts the picnic bag on the ground.

'You were. You could be. But you and I . . . we were also great mates. When you were taken, I looked for that stone you brought me from the garden. I couldn't find it and I was inconsolable, apparently.'

I take his hand and squeeze it. 'Awww. Never mind. It was just a stone.'

I let go of his hand, reach down and pick up a random stone from the path we are on. 'Here you go, have this one. All sorted.'

He laughs, and then his expression turns serious.

'Over the years, I've often thought about that stone. I've thought that if I couldn't even look after a stone, there was no way I could have looked after my little sister.'

I feel uneasy at the sudden change in atmosphere. 'Jesse, that's silly. It wasn't your fault I got taken,' I say.

He nods slowly, his gaze not leaving mine. 'I know. Kind of. And . . . I'm not proud of this, but that day . . . I was with you in the garden. We were playing. Then you annoyed me in some way and I stormed back into the house to tell on you.' He pauses. 'By the time I got back out, you'd gone.'

I take his hand. 'You were a child. It wasn't your fault. It probably would have happened anyway, whether you were there or not. You were seven years old! It's not as if you could have done anything.'

He is looking at the ground and there is silence between us. I think I see him surreptitiously wipe away a tear and then look up. 'Mum's sent me to masses of counsellors over the years and they all say the same. That it wasn't my fault. But a part of me still blames myself. A large part.'

'Please don't. You mustn't. You're making me feel bad.'

'I'm sorry. That's the last thing I want to do. This is my issue, not yours. But now you're back, I'm going to make sure I look after you properly.'

He drops my hand and jumps up to standing. I shade my eyes from the sun as I look up at him.

'Anyway. That's all in the past now,' he says, his tone suddenly much more upbeat. 'I've got an idea about something we can do together, to get to know each other again, and it doesn't even involve going out, so it'll keep Mum happy. Over the summer, I'm going to teach you to dance.'

23

I'd assumed there'd just be a manky old cellar at the bottom of the house like there was when I lived with Dad, so I hadn't yet been down the stairs by the kitchen door. I didn't want the family to feel like I was prying into their lives or going anywhere I shouldn't be, so I generally kept to my room, the kitchen and the TV room and didn't go anywhere else unless I was specifically invited to. Not that there *was* anywhere else, as far as I knew. So I'm surprised when I follow Jesse down the stairs to find what looks like a dance studio.

'Wow, I had no idea this was here,' I say. It's a lot smaller than the ones I've seen on TV, with only tiny windows right at the top that you can't even see out of, but there are huge mirrors on the walls on three sides of the room, a barre at waist height along one and a massive speaker in the corner.

'Yep, Mum and Dad were quite the dance floor king and queen a long time ago,' he says. 'They ran a little dance school for kids here for a while. It all stopped when Dad left, just after you were taken. I don't think Mum could manage it on her own. Or maybe she didn't want to, what with everything else. I don't know.'

This is the first time either of them has mentioned my biological dad. There don't appear to be any photos of him anywhere and I wonder when and why he left, but this doesn't feel like the right time to ask. Instead I say:

'She taught you to dance?'

He nods. 'Yep. I used to dance quite a lot as a child, and even as a teenager, because it was a good way to meet girls,' he says. 'And then my mates started taking the piss and I had exams coming up, so I stopped doing anything like competitions. But if we can't go out too much this summer, it might be a fun way to pass the time? It's something to do. You said you play guitar, you're obviously musical. I think you'd enjoy it and I bet you'd pick it up in no time. What do you think?'

'Gosh. That's kind. I don't know about me being musical, but yes please, I'd like that. I watched some kind of dance show which was on when I was in hospital – they were teaching celebrities to dance. I didn't know who anyone was, but I loved the costumes.'

He laughs. 'Oh yes everyone loves that one, whether they dance or not. Which dances did you like best? Ballroom or Latin? Anything you'd like to start with?'

'I can't remember. I'll go with whatever you think.'

'Cha cha cha? That's fairly straightforward. Let's start with that.'

He fiddles with his phone and music comes from the giant speaker in the corner.

'Right, stand next to me,' he says, taking my hand. 'For now, watch my steps in the mirror.' He moves his feet backwards and forwards, saying 'ONE, two, cha cha cha, ONE two, cha cha cha, c'mon, you do the same, ONE two, cha cha cha, ONE two cha cha cha.'

I smile and try to follow and soon we are moving to the same rhythm, laughing as I move my feet and swing my hips like he does. 'Brilliant! You're a natural!' he says. 'Now we'll try it in hold.' He puts his hand on my waist and takes my hand. 'Great. Head up, look at me, that's it, same steps. ONE two, cha cha cha, ONE two cha cha cha. And then we go into the single hand hold and both turn towards the mirror . . . yes that's it! Fantastic.'

We stay in the studio the entire afternoon and by the time we are finished we have a whole routine. I am hot, sweaty and exhausted. But I'm feeling much more at home, and I've barely thought about Dad. I feel a pang of guilt.

PART FOUR

24

Stuart

17 January 2022, 03:00
The Caribbean

It's pretty clear what the situation is as soon as I enter the room.

Rick's boss Danny is valiantly pumping at his colleague's chest, grimacing as he pauses every few pumps to hold Rick's nose and blow into his mouth. 'Come on, come on . . .' he is muttering, and he presses again and again and again.

I grasp his shoulder. 'Danny, I can take over now. Let me see, please. Thank you.'

He lurches away and straight into the bathroom where I hear him vomiting. Poor guy. I'm trained for this kind of thing, but dealing with a dead body is never exactly fun and for someone who's not used to it, it's usually extremely traumatic.

I breathe in sharply as I see Rick's face. I can tell at first glance that he's beyond help – his eyes are open, staring and glassy. His body is in an unnatural position and while I am by no means a religious man, it's usually somehow obvious when someone is dead – there's something different about a dead body to a living one. Like there's an element missing.

Nonetheless I go through my usual checks – feeling for a pulse and shining a light into Rick's unresponsive eyes. His skin is already cooling and there's no resistance in his limbs. As I suspected – knew – there is nothing that can be done. Feeling a little queasy, I gently close his eyes.

Danny comes out of the bathroom, wiping his mouth.

'Is he . . . ?'

''Fraid so.'

Already looking ropey, the colour drains even further from his face.

'There was nothing that you or anyone else could have done,' I add. 'It was too late for that. You did well to have done what you did. To try. You should be proud of yourself. Not everyone would try to perform CPR. It takes bravery and a cool head.'

He nods, but doesn't say anything. 'Think I need some air,' he mumbles, stumbling over to the balcony door and wrenching it open. Through the huge window I see him sink down onto a padded lounger and put his head in his hands.

Leo appears in the doorway looking grumpy and unchar-acteristically dishevelled.

'Bill tells me there's a problem,' he says.

A problem? That's a bit of an understatement.

My mouth is dry and I swallow hard. 'Yes. There's no

easy way to say this, but Rick's dead. I can't give an exact time of death, I'm afraid, but I'd say it was pretty recent.'

'Oh God,' he says, blanching as he hangs back, staring at the body. At Rick.

'I'll get a couple of the porters down here and have him moved to the mortuary,' I continue. 'Then in the morning I'll make a start on the paperwork and get in touch with HR so they can contact his family and—'

'What happened to him?' Leo interrupts. 'He's a young man. Why did he die?'

'Fuck's sake, Captain, this isn't *Silent Witness*,' I snap. Shit, shouldn't have said that. But it's been a long day and however many times I deal with a death, it always sets me on edge. Even more than it used to since what happened before I left for the ships.

Leo gives me a look. Even without the passengers on board, at sea, he is my superior and I shouldn't speak to a captain that way. Especially not Leo, who I've learned in my short time on the ship, is a stickler for convention and hierarchy.

'Sorry,' I say. 'I apologize. It's late, we're all tired, and this was obviously a bit of a shock,' I continue. 'There'll need to be an autopsy when we can get him to land, but there's no immediate sign of physical violence. And from memory, though I will need to check, he had no chronic conditions.' I pause. I shouldn't speculate, but I can't help myself – I know what the most likely result of the autopsy will be and Leo is clearly looking for some kind of answer. 'So my best guess, and I need to reiterate, it *is* simply a guess, is some kind of overdose.'

131

'An overdose? What, as in, drugs?' Leo splutters. 'I have a very strict anti-drugs policy on board, all the crew know that.' A beat passes before he continues. 'Or do you mean he took a deliberate overdose?'

God. I've already said I don't know – why is he keeping on like this? I try to keep my voice steady and even. 'Captain, I'm sorry, I really can't say. There's no way of telling until the toxicology is done, and possibly not even then. And as I must emphasize, an overdose is nothing more than a guess on my part. I'm a GP, not a pathologist. Let's move Rick to the mortuary and organize the paperwork. The sooner we can do that and get his body to land for an autopsy, the more likely we are to get answers.'

He nods. 'OK. I'll contact the port in the morning and see if we can bring forward our next scheduled resupply slot so we can offload him as quickly as possible to . . . wherever he needs to go.'

'Thank you, I think that would be a good idea.'

Quite aside from wanting to get to the bottom of what's happened here, I imagine the crew will be somewhat creeped out by knowing the dead body of one of their crewmates is still on board, cooling in the mortuary.

25

I pushed my book away, stretched and yawned.

'Haven't we done enough for today, Dad?' I grumbled.

He twisted round to look at the clock. Almost four.

He rolled his eyes. 'OK, I guess that's near enough a full day.' He stacked up his books and put them in the cupboard and I did the same. 'What do you want to do now?' he asked.

'Um . . . I think I'll just go to my room and play my guitar for a little while if that's OK?'

Dad nodded. 'Course it is, Sweetpea. I heard you playing last night – you sounded really good.'

I blushed, thinking of the lyrics I was singing last night. Lyrics to the song I'd written myself. I hoped he hadn't heard. Surely he hadn't? 'Thanks, Dad,' I mumbled. 'But it's a bit embarrassing. I'm still working on that song. I'd kind of rather you didn't listen,' I said, dragging my toe backwards and forwards across a crack in the faded terracotta tile.

He smiled and stroked my hair. 'I wasn't listening, my angel. You know how I respect your privacy. I heard you as I was passing your door.' He paused and then added: 'You'll play it to me when it's finished though, won't you?'

'Of course,' I lied, blushing again. I'd have to write a different song for Dad. I didn't want to play him that one. I couldn't.

He moved his hand from my hair to cup my cheek. 'My little girl. So grown up now.'

'Dad!' I grumbled, but at the same time, felt a warm glow in the pit of my stomach. It felt good to be loved. I knew not everyone had that. Dad was always telling me how lucky I was. How most of the world had gone bad, full of danger and hate.

He pinched my cheek lightly and then let his hand fall. 'Sorry. I'm going to go out to the garden to find some veggies for dinner. I'll leave you to play your guitar in peace, 'kay?'

I smiled. 'Thanks, Dad. I'll come and help you in a bit.'

I ran up the stairs to my room and closed the door gently. I pulled a large notebook from my bedside table and propped it up on the music stand at the end of my bed. I tuned my guitar carefully and then started playing, singing very quietly in case Dad was listening.

> You may be the only boy I know
> But I know you're the only one I need
> When I'm feeling lonely and cold
> You light up my fire for me

134

> One day we'll fly away
> Find a place that's just for us
> Far away from anyone else
> Just you and me, you and me.

I smiled to myself. I knew the lyrics weren't brilliant, but I was pleased with the song even so. And I was sure he'd like it too, if I ever got the chance to play it to him.

I hugged myself as I pictured his face, smiling up at me.

'Great curry, Dad,' I said, wolfing it down. He always cooked a mean veggie curry. But I ate as quickly as possible so I could get back to my room and think about the boy who had come by.

People almost never came to the house. Dad said it was because he wanted to keep me safe from everyone, that no one could be trusted. On the rare occasions anyone did come, by tacit agreement I went to my room so I wouldn't be seen. We didn't make a big deal of it, it was the just the way we did things. I'd never really thought much about it. Until recently.

Our drive is very long, so no one ever comes up it on foot. Even if someone turns up unexpectedly, which almost never happens, there's time for me to get out of the way. Dad had already told me he had an appointment that afternoon which was always the signal for me to take my books and go to my room. I was meant to stay away from the window, but over the last few months, whenever someone came, which admittedly wasn't often, I always sneaked a quick peek, just to see who it was. It was such a novelty to see anyone who wasn't Dad or in a film.

135

This time, it was a boy, maybe three or four years older than me. The washing machine was broken, and he had come to fix it. I leaned out of the window as he left, so I could see better. I could see the sun glistening on the blond hairs of his arms as he held a clipboard out for Dad to sign, which gave me a feeling low down in my stomach that I didn't understand.

'Thank you. Bye, Mr Johnson,' he called as Dad closed the door. 'I'll be back in a couple of days once I've got the parts you need. That machine's ancient, so I don't have any suitable parts on the van.' As he turned away he looked up towards me and waved.

I knew I should have ducked back behind the curtain, but I didn't. I smiled and waved back.

26

'Dad?' I asked the next day when we were reading through some boring textbook about the Tudor period, 'will I live here with you forever?'

Dad looked up and frowned. 'What makes you ask that now?'

'Well, it's just that you say the outside world is too dangerous for people like me to go out, but what happens later? Does that mean I can never meet anyone, get married, have children, have a family of my own? Travel? Or live on a Caribbean island and swim in a warm sea? One day that's what I'd really like to do.'

Dad took my hand and squeezed it. 'And I hope you will, my darling Laura. In the future, you will have all those things, if you want to. But for now, you're too young, and you're safer here with me. Where no one can hurt you.' He squeezed my hand again. ''kay?'

I squeezed back. ''kay,' I replied, but I still felt a little weird.

I willed the next few days to pass, wondering when the washing machine boy would be back. I'd thought about him often when I was alone in my room. And when Dad finally told me he had an appointment that afternoon, I knew it was time.

Up in my room I put on my favourite top (red) and brushed my waist-length mousy hair. It was starting to look quite straggly at the ends – it hadn't been cut for years. I'd never been to a hairdresser. When I was little, Dad would cut it now and again. But then one day I told him I wanted to leave it long so he stopped and since then it's been left to grow.

I stood by the window and waited, barely breathing I was so nervous.

About an hour later, by which time my feet had gone numb and I had a crick in my neck, I heard the crunch of a van coming down the drive. My breath caught in my throat and I pushed the curtain further back to improve my view.

This time, he spotted me as soon as he got out of the van and waved. I waved back, beaming at him. I held my breath, wondering if perhaps he would call up to me, both hoping and dreading that he would (what if Dad heard? What would he do if he did?) but he turned away and lifted a box out of the van. I watched his forearms flex as he moved, which gave me the same feeling low down in my stomach as before.

I waited by the window while he did whatever he needed to do to the washing machine and about half an hour later he reappeared on the drive. I held my breath as I saw Dad sign the docket and then pulled the curtain back a little more to be sure the boy would see me as he left.

He looked up and smiled. I felt myself go bright red but even so, smiled and tossed my hair slightly, like I'd seen women do in films sometimes.

'What's your name?' he called out, which made my stomach lurch with both panic and excitement. I put my finger to my lips in the 'be quiet' sign, and shook my head.

He shrugged, turned away and walked back towards his van.

Panic surged through me. He couldn't go! Not like this! Not with him thinking I didn't want to talk to him! Checking that the front door was closed and that Dad was out of sight, I eased the window open and softly called out, 'Hey.'

He didn't hear me, or at least he didn't react, but I hadn't called out very loud as I was terrified that Dad would hear me. 'Hey,' I called, louder. 'I'm sorry. I didn't mean to be rude. I'm Laura. What's your name?'

He wheeled round and looked at me. 'Fred. I'm Fred.' His voice was boyish and reedy.

'Nice to meet you,' I stage-whispered. 'Sorry about just now. My dad doesn't like me talking to strangers.'

Fred laughed. 'Probably good advice.' He tapped his nose. 'Don't worry, I won't tell.'

'Thank you.'

There was a pause. He was still looking at me and I felt myself blush.

'Maybe we can talk next time I come? Quietly, I mean,' he added in a stage whisper.

I grinned. 'Yeah, I'd like that.'

'Perhaps you could come down here then? So that I don't feel like I'm talking to Rapunzel?'

My breath caught in my throat. 'Yeah, OK,' I said, even though I knew that Dad would never let me in a million years.

'Great – I'll be back in a couple of days with a new machine – turns out the old one was beyond repair after all. So I'll see you then.'

'Bye then.'

'Bye.'

I watched as he got back in his van, turned it around and headed off down the drive.

It was all I could do to breathe as I closed the window.

When was the last time I had spoken to someone other than Dad?

Had I *ever* spoken to someone other than Dad? I wasn't sure that I had.

Why had I said I could go down and talk to him? How could I do that without Dad finding out?

Should I even risk it? What if he was one of these dangerous people Dad was so keen to protect me from? What might he do to me? Might he hurt me? Kill me, even?

He didn't look dangerous. But maybe you couldn't tell just by looking?

Should I ask Dad?

I laughed out loud to myself.

No. Of course not. I couldn't do that.

But I wanted to talk to Fred. I did. And not from up here. I wanted to be closer to him.

I didn't really know why. But I knew I needed to find a way.

27

May 2013
Scottish Highlands

For the next few days I could hardly sit still. I did my boring old lessons with Dad at the kitchen table as usual, but it was a struggle to concentrate. Dad would be talking about some ancient king or trying to make me do some algebra and I'd be thinking about how the sun had shone on Fred's sandy hair, the way his forearms rippled as he lifted boxes.

'Laura!' Dad said, bringing me back to the present. 'Come on! You're not concentrating. If x is four, then what is y?'

I sighed. 'Um . . . five?' I offered, saying the first number which came into my head.

Dad pushed his chair back. 'You're guessing. C'mon, Laura, look again.'

I stared at the page but the numbers swam. 'Tell me again why I need to know this? It's just a puzzle. What's the point?'

He sighed. 'It's part of your education, Laura. You need to be educated so you can get on in life.'

'But I never go anywhere. I'm always here. I don't need to know what y is equal to for that.'

As soon as the words were out of my mouth, I regretted them and tried to get them back. 'I'm sorry, Dad, I mean, I know you . . .'

But it was too late. His face had darkened, the way it always did on the rare occasions that I questioned him like this, and I noticed his hands clench into fists.

For many years when I was smaller I'd never wondered about our life here. Dad had always provided everything I need. I'd always felt safe and happy with him. I'd never been hungry, ill or in pain. I'd never wanted for anything. I'd always felt loved.

All those things still stood. But more recently, from the books I'd read and the films we watched, even though Dad chose them all and, I'd begun to suspect, carefully vetted them, it had become clearer and clearer to me that my life wasn't normal. Dad said plenty of young girls lived like me these days. He told me the books we read and the films we watched were very old. He said life wasn't like it was portrayed in those books and films anymore – it had become much more dangerous. He said that parents who really, really loved their daughters did this for them to keep them safe at home with them until they were absolutely sure they were fully prepared and ready to go out into the world. And while I hadn't directly asked him whether this was actually the truth, I had started to think about it more, and to ask more questions. I had started to suspect that he was keeping things from me.

'As I have told you before, I am simply trying to protect you,' he said quietly and evenly, as though trying to rein in his temper. 'When you're . . . older, and ready, you can go out into the outside world. But if I let you go now, anything could . . .'

His voice cracked and he wiped away a tear. 'Oh God, Laura, the thought of anything happening . . .' He rubbed at his eyes with the heels of his hands.

'I'm sorry, Dad, I know,' I said, panicked by the sight of his tears. He always reacted this way when I asked about my future. 'I know you're doing all this for me. But sometimes I feel like it would be nice to have a . . . friend.'

He looked up at me, his eyes glistening. 'A *friend*? Friends aren't always what they seem, Laura. Haven't I taught you that?'

'Uh – yeah. Yeah you have. Sorry, Dad.'

'Aren't I enough for you?' I looked at him, his expression somewhere between pleading and terrified.

A lump rose in my throat and I reached over and squeezed his hand. 'Of course you are, Dad,' I said, because I wanted him to stop crying.

But I was lying.

He wasn't.

I wanted something else.

Something more.

I just didn't know quite what.

Up in my room after lessons, in between perfecting my song, I looked at myself in the mirror.

Almost all of the films Dad and I watched were black

and white, and I didn't look much like the women in any of them.

I leaned in close and examined my face. Unremarkable eyes, pale eyelashes, nose too big for my face, lips too thin, teeth too sticky-out and a bit wonky, and a couple of spots on my chin. I'd once asked Dad if I could get some make-up like I'd seen the women in the films use, but he said no, I was beautiful as I was, and then he started crying, so I didn't ask again.

I took a handful of my mouse-brown hair and looked at the ends, which were scraggy and split. Taking a pair of paper scissors from my desk, I cut off the split bits and watched as they fell to the ground. I shook my hair back and tossed it about a bit.

Better. But not so different that Dad would notice, I hoped.

I unbuttoned the top couple of buttons on my boring navy-blue shirt and leaned into the mirror to peer at myself again. I pushed my elbows together, trying to give myself a cleavage like the women in the films from the 1950s, but it didn't really work.

Was I pretty? Would anyone ever want me?

Would Fred like me?

I hugged myself. He wanted to talk to me. That was a start, wasn't it?

28

May 2013
Scottish Highlands

I spent days planning my outfit even though my choices were pretty limited and eventually settled for my favourite pair of three-quarter length jeans, my one underwired bra, which I think Dad must have bought by accident (my others were plain, greying white and soft) and a V-necked T-shirt which was very slightly fitted.

I twisted my hair up and pinned it, and pinched my cheeks to make them pink like I'd seen a girl do once in some film or other.

Then, I crept down the stairs and out of the back door. Holding my breath, I tiptoed round to the front of the house and hid behind a bush which gave me a perfect view of the driveway. Dad very rarely came to my room – he seemed to make a point of never coming up so I'd 'have my privacy' – so as long as he didn't actually see me leaving,

I felt like I could probably get away with it. Even so, I was so nervous I was almost surprised he couldn't hear my heart beating from the kitchen, it seemed so loud to me.

Fred's van arrived and I watched as he parked, got out and unloaded what must be the new washing machine using a trolley. I held my breath and pushed myself further into the bush as Dad opened the door and ushered him in. I waited, holding my breath – how long did installing a washing machine take? I had no idea.

Almost an hour later he reappeared with the old machine on the same trolley and called a goodbye to Dad, who, to my relief, closed the door immediately.

I stuck my head up above the bush and in a low voice, called 'Fred!'

He looked round, startled, still loading the machine into the van. Then, as he caught my eye, he grinned.

'Laura!' he said, mimicking my muted tone. 'How are you?' he mouthed. 'Why are you hiding in a bush?'

I beckoned him over. 'I'm hiding so he doesn't know I'm talking to you. Once you've got the old machine loaded, you need to move your van if we're going to chat. Otherwise Dad will know you haven't gone.'

He looked around. 'Erm . . . OK. I'll meet you at the bend in your drive. Your dad won't be able to see us there.'

Heart in my mouth, I raced down to the bend in the drive, weaving in and out of the trees and staying well away from the line of sight of the house.

As I heard the van approaching I leaned back against a tree, arranging myself in a pose I hoped look casual and as if I talked to boys all the time, as opposed to never, pushing my too-small boobs out a little bit and running my hands through my hair.

I watched, head tipped to one side, barely able to breathe as the van came close and stopped. Fred got out of the van and slammed the door.

'Hey Laura,' he said softly.

'Hey,' I squeaked, my voice coming out high and strangled.

He moved a step closer and I could smell his aftershave along with a vague hint of something very male – a bit like Dad's bedroom. I breathed in slowly.

'Why all the secrecy?' he whispered.

'Oh, you know . . .' I stuttered. 'My dad's really over-protective.'

He nodded. 'Yeah. Dads can be.' There was a pause, an awkward silence when neither of us spoke. Panicking that he'd go, I blurted out the first thing I could think of: 'Do you like fixing washing machines?'

He laughed. 'Yeah, it's all right as jobs go. I'm looking for something better. Don't want to be stuck here doing this for the whole of my life.'

I nodded frantically as if he'd just said the most profound thing ever, and he looked at me strangely. 'You OK?' he asked.

'Yes,' I squeaked, and then breathed in deeply to try to calm myself down. 'I'm fine,' I said, hoping I sounded more normal, 'I'm a bit out of breath from running down here, that's all,' I lied.

'So how come you're not at school today?' he asked. 'Or the other day? Are you ill?'

I shook my head. 'No. Not ill. I'm home-schooled,' I said. 'By my dad.'

'The protective one.'

'Yeah.'

'And what's that like?'

I shrugged. ''s OK, I guess. Never known anything different.'

'I didn't like school. You're not missing much.'

'That's what Dad says too.'

'And what about your mum?'

'She died when I was a baby.'

He pulled a face. 'That's rough. Shouldn't have asked. Sorry.'

''s OK.'

We both fell silent again, but I carried on looking straight at him. His eyes were bright blue and his unkempt hair was falling in front of them. I wanted to stroke it, to push it away from his face, but I didn't dare.

He touched the end of my hair, making my breath catch in my throat. 'I love your hair. I like long hair on a girl,' he said. 'I like the way you look different to other girls. Most of them all dress the same, skirts too short, tops too tight, covered in make-up. But not you.'

'Thank you,' I croaked.

'They're stupid bitches,' he added, his voice changing, suddenly bitter. 'Slags. They all think they're too good for the likes of me. Not even interested in talking to me. Will barely give me the time of day. But you – you're different.'

He slowly lifted his hand towards my face and touched my cheek. I held my breath.

'You don't have a boyfriend?'

I shook my head slowly, not wanting him to move his hand away.

I stared at him as he leaned in towards me as if in slow

motion, my body crying out for him to kiss me in a way I didn't really understand but a small voice in my head was shouting that maybe it was dangerous, maybe something terrible would happen and . . . His lips eventually touched mine, sending what felt like a bolt of electricity through me.

I froze as his tongue pushed roughly into my mouth and touched mine, both terrified and thrilled. It tasted faintly of smoke and salt and vinegar crisps. I moved my tongue back against his. Was that right? Was that what you were meant to do? It was both the best and worst thing I'd ever experienced at the very same time.

He pulled away and smiled. 'Nice to meet you, Laura. Maybe we can do this again sometime?'

'Yes, um, yes . . . when are you . . .' I panicked. He couldn't go now! What if I never saw him again? What would I do?

'I'll see you next time something breaks down here then,' he said, giving my waist a little squeeze, and then turning towards the van, before turning back towards me and adding as an afterthought, 'Unless you'd like me to come and see you again sooner? How about that?' He paused. 'It could be our secret?'

'Um, I . . .' I said, my mind whirring. I was desperate for him to come back but couldn't say that, could I? In the books I'd read, women didn't do that kind of thing. Did they? I wasn't sure. And the books I was thinking of were fiction. Maybe real life was nothing like that – Dad was always saying that it wasn't any more. That was the reason I had to stay here, out of harm's way. Maybe it was fine to do that kind of thing now. If you weren't the kind of daughter who was kept at home by her dad. If you weren't the type like me that was particularly special, particularly loved. I bet it was OK.

'How about I come back Monday? About 3 p.m.? That suit?' he asked, interrupting my racing thoughts.

'Um . . . no, Dad likes me to study during the day. I think I'd find it hard to get away.'

'About six then?'

I grinned. 'That sounds fine. I'll see you then. Same place?'

'Yeah.' He leaned in and kissed me again, more roughly this time, pulling me towards him so I was pressed against him, putting his hand inside one of my bra cups and squeezing it quite hard, which made me gasp, both scared and thrilled at the same time.

'Brilliant,' he said, touching me under the chin as he broke away from me. 'See you then.'

With my whole body tingling, I put my fingers to my lips as I watched the van drive away, and then ran back to the house.

29

The entire week I was on edge. I could barely sit still. I thought about Fred all the time. Dad sighed and huffed as he tried to get me to concentrate on my books, when all I could do was look at the clock, willing time to pass, for Fred to come again.

When I wasn't with Dad I spent time in my room, playing my song and looking at myself in the mirror. I rearranged my hair time and time again, putting it up in a high ponytail, down low, a French plait, tried tossing it around, messing it up, and brushing it one hundred times like they'd done in some book or other I'd read, but all that did was make it static and frizzy.

Strange feelings ran through me – a yearning for something, without really knowing quite what. I replayed films

I'd watched with Dad in my head, thinking about how the men and women touched each other, how they reacted. What they did together when they were alone.

None of them seemed to feel like I did when Fred touched me – like I didn't want to let him go, like I wanted to press myself against him, until . . . until what?

What happened when it faded to black as they were kissing in the films? What happened then?

There must be something else. When Fred kissed me, it was both weird and scary but also not nearly enough. There was something more, I was sure.

I squirmed in my chair and touched my lips. I looked in the mirror and saw that my cheeks had gone pink.

After spending an hour getting ready – which was quite a feat considering I had next to no clothes and absolutely no make-up – as I reached the tree where I met Fred last time at ten to six exactly, it suddenly occurred to me that he might not come.

Panic surged through me. Maybe he wasn't going to turn up. Maybe after last time he went home and had a good laugh with his mates about the stupid girl he kissed who then believed him when he said he'd come back. Was that the kind of thing boys did? Sometimes people lied, I knew that. Dad was always saying that no one could be trusted, and he'd often point out particularly bad behaviour from men in films and books, reminding me that it was exactly the kind of thing he was protecting me from. Look at how Heathcliff behaved towards Isabella, he'd say. Or what happened to Butterfly in the opera! Or Tess – look at how men treated her and how miserable it made her! And Carmen! What a tragic end she had! You wouldn't want anything like that, would you? he'd warn. Maybe Fred was one of the bad men Dad was so desperate to protect me from. Maybe this was all a big mistake. Maybe I should have never agreed to meet him.

Just as I'd decided that the whole thing was at best a stupid idea and at worst, entirely reckless, and was about to stomp back up to the house, cursing myself, I heard the sound of an engine and Fred's van appeared.

Brushing away the angry tears which had been threatening I tried to arrange myself to look alluring and as if I was never in any doubt that he would turn up, although I imagined by now it was probably obvious that I was hot and flustered. I smiled.

'Hello,' I said, just about managing to keep my voice even.

'Hello, you,' he said as he stepped out of the van. 'Here we are again.'

I blushed. 'Yeah.'

He went round to the back of the van, opened the doors and pulled out a bag.

I pictured Dad, back at the house. Oh God. I wondered what he was doing now? Being down here, alone with Fred, was such a risk. But I had thought about what I would do on the off-chance that he went up to my room; I could tell him I'd gone out for a walk. He wouldn't like it, because I hadn't asked or let him know where I would be, but it was better than . . .

'I brought a few things for us,' Fred said, spreading out a blanket and dropping down to the ground. 'Don't know about you, but I could do with a drink.'

'OK,' I said, suddenly breathless.

He pulled out a bottle of wine and twisted the top off.

'It undoes like that?' I asked.

He looked at me strangely. 'You never seen a screw-top before?'

'Uh – yeah,' I lied. 'Just normally I've seen bottles with corks.'

'Posh round yours then. Red OK?' he asked, pouring it into a plastic cup and handing it to me.

'Lovely,' I said, taking a sip which almost made me gag. I'd never drunk wine before – I'd never seen Dad drink it either. I'd only seen it in films. Dad would occasionally have a bottle of beer or two when he'd been to the supermarket, but that was it, and he never let me have any. The sticky red liquid made me cough, but I managed to force it down. It tasted kind of metallic but not exactly unpleasant. I took another sip.

Fred reached into the box behind him, lifted out a massive packet of crisps, opened it and offered it to me. I smiled and took a handful, instantly regretting it as I didn't know how to eat them without looking like a pig. I tried to balance them on my knee and most of them fell onto the blanket. I pretended to not notice that they had fallen and said: 'Thanks.'

He took a handful of crisps himself and shoved them into his mouth, munching loudly while I nibbled at one of mine. Cheese and onion – not my favourite. But never mind – I wasn't here for the crisps. He eased himself down onto his side and propped his head on his elbow, looking up at me.

'So then, Laura,' he said, once he had swallowed his mouthful, 'why don't you tell me about yourself?'

'Um . . . not much to tell,' I stuttered, taking another sip of wine, for something to do rather than because I wanted to. 'Mainly I'm just here with Dad.'

Mainly. That was a lie. I was *always* just here with Dad.

'How old are you?'

'I'm fifteen.'

'Sweet fifteen and never been kissed,' he said.

'No,' I contradicted. 'You, uh, you kissed me, last time you were here.'

I felt something stir in me at the memory of it.

He gave me a puzzled look. 'It's a turn of phrase. Kind of. Though normally sweet sixteen – it just came to mind. But don't tell me that was the first time you'd been kissed?'

I forced a laugh. 'Of course not!' I lied, because it seemed like the right thing to say.

Fred took a large glug of wine. 'So, when you're not doing your lessons, what do you do, all alone here with your dad?'

I shrugged. 'Watch films. Read. Play my guitar. Usual kind of stuff,' I said, not that I had any idea what the usual kind of stuff was.

'You play guitar? You any good?'

I shrugged again. 'Dunno. I've only played . . . on my own so I don't know if I'm any good. I told Dad I wanted to learn and he bought me a guitar and a book. I taught myself.'

'You taught yourself? Wow, that's impressive.' He touched my knee, which sent a frisson through me. 'I'm about as musical as . . . I dunno, a dead duck. I'd love to hear you play sometime.'

I blushed, thinking about the song I was writing.

'Actually . . .' I said, and then tailed off, feeling myself turn even more crimson.

'Actually what?' he asked.

I shook my head. I couldn't tell him I was writing a song about him. 'Nothing. I could try to bring my guitar down here and play for you sometime, if you like.'

'I would like that,' he replied. He reached upwards and gently took the plastic cup from my hand and put it on the ground at the edge of the blanket. He eased himself down so he was lying on his side and patted the blanket in front of him.

'Come and lie with me here,' he said.

I felt my heartbeat instantly quicken and a lump rose in my throat as I eased myself down onto the blanket, propping my head on my hand, mirroring his position.

He shuffled closer so that his hips were almost touching mine. My breath caught in my throat as he touched his fingers to my lips, and then kissed me.

He reached round the back of my neck and pulled me closer. I moved my hips closer to his and felt something move inside his jeans. He kissed me harder and moved forwards so that I toppled back and suddenly he was lying on top of me and before I knew what I was doing I shouted 'Stop!'

He pushed himself up and looked at me. 'Sorry, I thought you wanted me to . . .'

'I do,' I croaked hoarsely, because even though I didn't really know what he was doing, or what I was agreeing to, I also knew that a big part of me wanted him to do whatever it was. 'I just wasn't expecting that . . . I wasn't ready,' I said.

The feeling of him lying on top of me had both shocked and thrilled me in equal measure and I didn't know what to do with myself.

He looked at me quizzically. 'So I'm guessing . . . you're a virgin?'

'Like Mary?' I asked.

He laughed. 'Yeah, I guess so. Except without the mother of the son of God bit.'

'Um . . . yeah,' I said, although I didn't entirely know what he meant. I wasn't like Mary at all. I wasn't even religious. 'Does that matter?'

He smiled, leaned in and kissed me, more gently this time. 'No. It doesn't matter. We'll take things slowly.' He kissed me a little harder and put his hand down the front of my knickers. Oh God. It felt so amazing. Then he grabbed my hand and put it inside his trousers.

I almost snatched it away I was so shocked by what I felt. But then he put his hand on top of mine and showed me what he wanted me to do, and I tried to relax into it.

30

I am dreaming about an ice cream van and when I open my eyes I realize that the doorbell is ringing.

I get up, put my dressing gown on and brush my teeth. As I come down the stairs I hear Karen saying: 'We have no comment to make. Please leave us alone.'

She slams the door and runs her hands through her thinning hair. As she turns and catches sight of me, she looks shocked. 'Laura! I didn't realize you were up. Come away from the windows into the kitchen, I need to talk to you about something.'

Oh God. My stomach feels like lead. This is it. This is going to be 'the talk' – the one I've been expecting. Where she gently lets me know that she doesn't think I'm fitting into the family and she thinks I'd probably feel more at home elsewhere. I've been away too long. It's too disruptive.

Too upsetting for everyone. I don't exactly feel at home here – far from it – but being turfed out and all on my own would be much worse. I can see that now.

Karen pulls out a chair for me at the kitchen table and, legs wobbling slightly, I sit down. She sits down opposite me.

'Do you want me to leave?' I say, as clearly and as confidently as I can, wanting to get this over and done with as quickly as possible.

She looks up at me and laughs. '*Leave?* Of course not, what on earth gave you that idea?'

Relief floods through me. 'Nothing,' I lie.

She looks straight at me. 'That was a journalist at the door. God knows how he knows you're here but . . .'

I feel like she is expecting me to be upset or worried, but I'm not.

'Can't I just talk to them and say I can't remember anything? If I can't remember, it isn't that interesting, is it? I went, I'm back, my dad – the man who took me – died but nothing bad happened to me and I'm fine.'

She pauses. 'I'm afraid it's not that simple. Social services and the police talked to us about this before you came. We knew there'd be press interest, and that eventually you might have to go public, as it were, but we all agreed it would be better that you had some settling in time first. That's why it hasn't been released to the press yet.'

'What hasn't?'

'The fact that you've been found. Because there was no – ah – need for a trial it was fairly easy to keep things quiet. Or so we thought.'

The fact that there was no trial because my dad – my abductor, who they've decided they have no reason to believe was working with anyone else – is now dead hangs unsaid in the air between us.

Karen clears her throat and stands up. 'I think the best thing would be to call Ellie and maybe the police, and see what they think we should do. Meantime, don't answer the phone and stay away from the windows at the front, OK? They can't print photographs of you as you're underage, but for now . . . it's just better if you stay out of sight to be on the safe side, I think.'

I nod solemnly. ''kay.'

I go up to my room and gingerly pull the curtain back. Outside there's a man in his mid-twenties talking on his mobile and an older, fatter man with two cameras slung around his neck.

There's a knock on my bedroom door and Jesse comes in.

'Hey,' he says.

I smile. 'Hey.'

'How's it going? Mum says the press have turned up.'

I sit down on the bed. 'Apparently. It's hard to see why they'd be interested in me. I was taken ages ago. I'm back, I'm fine. Nothing to see here. Nothing to say.'

Jesse sits down next to me.

'They were around a lot too when you went. When you were taken.'

'Really?'

'Yeah. There were always police here then, helping us go out the back and stuff when I wanted to go to school, telling them to leave us alone if they came too close. There's nothing

161

the police can do about the press standing on the pavement if they're not causing a disturbance, because that's public property, but they can't come into the garden.'

'You remember that from when you were seven?'

'Nah. Just looked it up online. So that I'll know if any of them are overstepping the mark.'

I still haven't quite got used to the notion of 'online' because I'm almost 100 per cent sure we didn't have anything like that at home, but I nod sagely as if I know exactly what he means.

He puts his arm around me and I rest my head on his shoulder. 'It's OK,' he says. 'I'll make sure they don't bother you. I said I was going to take care of you, remember? I meant it.'

The next morning when I get up there are four people on the pavement outside the window – two men with cameras around their necks and two bored-looking young women holding takeaway coffees and fiddling with their phones.

One of the men looks up and catches my eye, making me dart back behind the curtain and giving me a strange sense of déjà-vu.

I have a shower and look at myself in the mirror, leaning in closely to examine my skin.

Am I still the same person as the four-year-old girl in the pictures on the walls downstairs? And even if I am, why should the press care?

'Morning, Laura,' Karen says as I get down to the kitchen. 'Sleep well?'

I nod, rubbing my eyes. 'Yes thanks. Did you?'

She pulls a face. 'Not really, if I'm honest. I don't like the press being outside. It takes me back to when . . . when you . . .' she tails off, waving her hand and then touching her face in a way which may or may not have been wiping away a tear.

'Anyway, I need to speak to you about something. I've just got off the phone with the police. There have been some, um, developments in your case and they want to talk to you about it so that you're fully apprised of . . . what happened.'

'What kind of developments?' I don't know what she means.

She puts her hand on my arm gently, and I struggle not to pull it away. 'I don't know all the ins and outs, as they are going to talk to us together, but as I understand it, they've built up a bit more of a profile of who your, um, the man you called your dad was. They think something has possibly been leaked from the investigation, which is why the press has started turning up. So PC Oaks and Ellie are on their way now to fill us in.'

31

Later that day, PC Oaks and Ellie arrive, along with another policewoman and another social worker who are to be my new points of contact now that I'm in London. Karen ushers them into the living room with me and then goes out to the kitchen.

'How are things going, Laura?' Ellie asks. 'You settling in OK?'

I nod. 'Yes. Fine thanks. Karen and Jesse are both being very kind to me,' I say vaguely. I'm not interested in talking about that now. 'Karen said you had some information about my dad – can you tell me about that?'

'I will. We'll wait for Karen to come back and then PC Oaks will tell you all about what they've discovered.'

We make pointless small talk about how I'm getting on until Karen comes back in with a tray of tea.

PC Oaks clears her throat and takes out a file.

'Laura. As we already discussed in the hospital, it seems that the man you considered your father called himself Daniel Johnson in recent years, though it seems he kept himself to himself as much as humanly possible. As we suspected from papers found at the house once it was thoroughly examined, and we and have now confirmed from dental records, this was a fake ID and his real name was Andrew Mugton.'

There is a sharp intake of breath from Karen but she doesn't say anything. I feel numb, as if all this is happening to somebody else.

PC Oaks continues. 'While it is a little difficult to build up a full picture as all this happened some time ago, we have ascertained from various sources that Mr Mugton's partner and daughter sadly died in a car crash. This happened around six months before you were abducted.'

My hand flies to my mouth. Dad had a girlfriend and child who died? Tears spring to my eyes. Poor Dad. All those years, he kept that to himself. I glance at Karen, who is drinking her tea, stony-faced. Ellie reaches over and takes my hand. 'Do you want PC Oaks to continue?' she asks gently.

I nod.

'It is believed from talking to people who knew him at the time, though we have no concrete proof, Mr Mugton may have suffered a breakdown following the death of his own daughter in the crash, and snatched you as a consequence. At the time you were taken, you would have been around the same age as his little girl who died. Her name was Laura, too.'

PC Oaks looks down at her notes and continues in the same, officious tone. 'By this point, Mr Mugton had entirely disappeared from his previous life. As far as we can ascertain, it was widely assumed that he had been consumed by grief and had killed himself, especially when his car was found abandoned at a known suicide point on the coast.

'There are no medical records for Mr Johnson – it seems likely that he never registered with a doctor using that name – and there are obviously none for Mr Mugton following his presumed death. A birth certificate for Mr Mugton was eventually found at the house he was living in, as well as limited papers pertaining to his new identity. There appears to be no trace of him beyond that after his presumed death, and no documentation relating to you living at the house with him at all.'

PC Oaks glances up at me and then back at her notes. I feel tears come into my eyes and roll down my cheeks. Poor Dad. He must have suffered so much. I had no idea. He literally gave up everything to look after me, to give me the life he thought I should have.

'You appear to have left the house where you were living with Mr Mugton on 20 July 2013 and were hit by a car,' she continues. 'We currently have no idea whether it was your decision to leave, or if there was something else at play, or anyone else involved. However, it seems likely that, knowing your abduction was now likely to be discovered, Mr Mugton took his own life.'

Karen lets out a loud sob, puts down her tea and bolts from the room.

Ellie touches my arm gently. 'Laura? Are you OK? Do you have any questions?'

I shake my head.

'Do you know why I was on the road that night?' I ask hoarsely. 'Why I left?'

She squeezes my arm. 'Not yet. But hopefully you'll remember in time.'

'But Dad killed himself because of me?'

She shakes her head. 'You mustn't think that. He was clearly a very troubled man. You've done nothing wrong.'

I wipe the tears from my cheeks. 'I think I'd like to just go to my room now, please.'

Ellie nods. 'Of course. It's a lot to process. If you have any questions, give me a shout. And I've booked you in to see a counsellor next week – I think it would be useful for you to have someone outside of the family to talk to. I hope that's OK.'

'Fine,' I say. Whatever. I don't care.

I just want my dad.

32

Jesse

August 2002
Catford

It is hot and sunny and I am playing on the path in the front garden. I've got all my cars out and I have made a road for them with some stones. It took ages and my fingers are all dirty but I don't care because now it looks really good, like a proper road and I am driving my cars up and down. 'Brum, brum, brum.'

'Can I play?'

I don't like my sister playing with my cars because she is not very careful and sometimes she drops them on the ground and once she broke a wheel and then it wouldn't go round anymore and it was my best car.

'No. I want to play on my own today. Brum, brum, brum.'

I don't look at her. She will probably go away if I ignore her long enough.

'But I want to.' She stamps her foot. She is wearing her sparkly shoes.

'But I don't want you to. Brum, brum, brum.'

I don't look up but I can tell she hasn't gone back to the dolls she was playing with on the grass and is waiting for me to say she can play because her shadow is still on me. She is annoying. I wish she'd go away.

'Let me!' she wails. 'I want to!'

I shake my head. 'Brum, brum, brum.'

Suddenly, her sparkly shoes are kicking the stones away, the ones I spent all morning arranging. She is spoiling my road!

'You're mean!' she shouts.

'I'm telling Mummy what you did!' I shout back. I pick up as many cars as I can because I don't want her to touch them, and run into the house. Mummy is in the kitchen.

'She spoiled my road!' I yell, trying not to drop my cars. 'I made it all nice and she spoiled it because I wouldn't let her play! You need to tell her!'

Mummy makes a sighing sound and turns to look at me. 'Why wouldn't you let her play?'

I stick my bottom lip out. Mummy always takes her side. It's not fair. 'Didn't want to. They're my cars. Not hers.'

Mummy puts her hand on my shoulder. 'Come on, poppet. You're so good at playing nicely with your sister usually. Let's go back out and see if we can come up with a game you can both enjoy.'

I shake my head. 'Only if she says sorry for spoiling my road first. And she can only have one car.' Mummy tips her head to one side and makes that face she does when she doesn't like what I'm saying. 'Or maybe two, if she promises to play properly,' I add.

Mummy smiles and nods. 'OK. Good boy. We'll talk to her about that too.'

Mummy lightly touches the back of my head as my arms are still full of cars and guides me back outside. My road is even more scuffed up and the dollies are on the grass, but there's no one there.

Mummy runs to the gate, knocking my shoulder and my cars all fall down. The gate is wide open and one of the sparkly shoes is on the ground. 'Anna!' Mummy calls, running one way along the pavement and then the other way. 'Anna!' Where are you? Anna!' she screams.

Mummy starts to cry and so do I. She runs back into the house, grabbing my arm as she passes, pulling me along with her. She lurches towards the phone.

'Why weren't you watching her?' she screams as she picks up the receiver and jabs at the 9 on the phone three times just like we were taught to at school. 'You should have been watching her!'

33

Jesse has been giving me more dance lessons, and he says I'm a natural. And while I don't know about that, I love it when we dance. It's such fun.

Today, he is teaching me to rumba. I've put on an old pair of Karen's dance shoes and I love how simply putting on the heels changes the way I move. Jesse puts his hands on my waist as he stands behind me, and we look at ourselves in the mirror as he shows me, how to move my hips in what's apparently called a pendular movement. He counts as he reminds me of the moves over and over, ONE two three four, ONE two three four, ONE two three four. He opens a cupboard full of colourful material and chucks a circle of shiny red fabric towards me – something called a practice skirt – which I put on over my leggings. I twirl and shimmy and it flares around me as the music plays; he takes my hands and we move in time together. It's such fun. Jesse is so patient and I love being down here. When the music is on and I'm dancing, I don't need to think about all the other stuff. Whether I'm Anna or Laura, or someone else entirely. Whether there are journalists outside. Whether I will ever feel like Karen is my mum. Or whether it was me running off which made Dad die. I can forget about it all while I'm dancing.

Later we are sitting together on the ratty old sofa which is in the dance studio, drinking Coke and eating cake which Karen made yesterday. It must be late – I can see from the chink of window near the ceiling at pavement level that it is getting dark. I'm both exhausted and exhilarated by the dancing and Jesse and I are sitting in companionable silence.

'Can I ask you something?' Jesse asks suddenly.

I nod and swallow my mouthful of cake. 'Of course.'

'Do you really not remember anything?' he asks.

'About . . .' I prompt, feeling a sudden stab of unease. Does he think I am making my amnesia up? Why would I want to do that?

'About before you were taken,' he says. I sit back in my chair. 'It's just, it seems so weird that you were here with us for four years and you don't remember me, or Mum or Dad, or our house . . .'

'Well yeah, I guess it might seem strange, but then again, I don't remember much at all, even about stuff that happened later,' I say. 'I remember my house – I mean where I lived after I was taken – and my . . . the man who I thought was my dad, but not much else.'

I have a sudden flash of what might be a memory of lying with someone on a blanket and feeling weirdly excited. But it's so vague and might not even be a memory for all I know, though it's happened a few times now.

'I don't remember anything else about my life there or how I came to be found in the road the way I was,' I say again. Which is the truth. 'And so it doesn't seem that surprising to me that I don't remember about a time even earlier than that.'

Jesse nods. 'I guess. And I suppose if I think about it, I probably don't remember much from when I was four. Or even from when I was a bit older. Although . . .'

He pauses.

'What?' I prompt.

'One thing I do remember vividly is my dad leaving. How he slammed the door and left Mum crying. And how he didn't even say goodbye to me. Just went. And that was that.'

I squeeze his hand. 'I'm sorry. That must have been tough.'

'Yeah.' A few beats pass. 'Mum won't ever talk about it. It wasn't that long after you were taken.'

As well as there being photos of Jesse's dad in the house, I think this is only the second time Jesse has mentioned him and Karen, not at all. I haven't asked why, but it seems pretty clear he's been cast out from both of their lives.

'So . . . you're not in touch with him?' I ask tentatively.

He shakes his head. 'No. He left without looking back. He's not interested in me, so I'm not interested in him.' His voice is tense and bitter – I haven't heard him sound like that before. 'We're better off without him. Mum agrees.'

We continue with our cake in silence for a few more minutes until Jesse says:

'I don't know about you, but I could do with some fresh air. How about if we go out for a bit? I feel like I haven't been out of the house for days.'

I put my plate down. 'But Karen said . . .'

He waves his hand. 'Never mind what she says. It's late, most of the reporters will have gone by now. And it was all right when we went for a picnic the other day, wasn't it? Nothing happened. We'll go out the back, like Mum and I used to last time they were here. Mum's been going to and from church the whole time without them noticing. It'll be fine.'

It seems like Jesse is right – nothing untoward happens as we slip out. The moon is bright as we walk and chat. It feels normal and natural. Comforting.

We stroll round almost the entirety of the park, enjoying the cool air. I ask Jesse to tell me about his school. It sounds totally different from the ones I'd seen in films which were usually boarding schools where it was just girls or just boys and everyone wore uniforms.

When I'd imagined what it would be like to have a brother, I'd pictured someone almost exactly like Jesse. He would make me feel protected and safe, as well as being someone to talk to and tell my secrets to. I feel a pang of resentment at Dad for taking all that away from me and then I feel guilty and sad.

'Better get back before Mum notices we've gone,' Jesse says suddenly, breaking my train of thought and tugging at my hand. 'We'll go back in the way we came out.'

34

August 2013
Catford

'That's her!' someone calls as we approach the passage at the back of the house; a man next to them lifts his camera and a flash goes off in my face.

'Anna! How does it feel to be home? Where have you been?' the man shouts.

'Oh shit,' Jesse says, grabbing my hand and pulling me after him as he tries to open the gate. 'Fuck – it's locked. Come on, run!' The reporters chase after us as we run back around to the front of the house where there's a whole load more who start baying 'Anna! Anna! Over here!' as they thrust tape recorders, microphones and cameras in my face. So much for them having gone home, or not being allowed to use pictures of me – there seem to be more of them than ever. 'Where have you been, Anna! Who took you?'

'Get out of our way!' Jesse bellows, pushing through the gate, dragging me after him. 'And don't even think about coming beyond this gate or we'll call the police!'

'How does it feel to have your sister back, Jesse?' one of them calls as he shoves his key in the lock, pushes open the door and drags me through it, slamming it behind us.

'Where have you been?!' Karen shrieks the instant the door bangs, running out of the kitchen. 'Why didn't you answer your phone? I've been worried sick!'

Her face is tear-stained and there's a wild look in her eyes.

'Sorry,' Jesse mutters, running his hands through his hair, 'battery's dead. Why did you lock the back gate?' he snaps.

'I didn't want the reporters to use it! How many times have I told you . . .' Karen yells, but Jesse interrupts, shouting back: 'Mum, leave it, please! We're back, it's fine. No harm done. Forget it. Get off my case!' He turns and punches the wall, so hard I think I hear a crack.

'Fuck!' he shouts, following up with a kick to the wall which makes me flinch. He stomps up the stairs, shaking his hand at his side as he goes and then slamming his bedroom door behind him. I am shocked. I've never seen him like that before. Karen pats my shoulder nervously.

'Are you all right, Laura? The press going after you like that outside – that's a horrible thing to have to deal with. I will make a complaint as you're underage and they shouldn't be harassing you. They know that. It's me they're waiting for really. Or Jesse.' I'm surprised she doesn't say anything about Jesse's outburst. I guess if she's ignoring his behaviour, I probably should too.

'Don't worry, I'm fine,' I say. I pause. 'Should I go and see if Jesse's OK?'

'I'd leave it an hour or so. Give him time to calm down. It's usually better that way.' Ah. So she has seen that kind of temper from him before.

A little later I knock on Jesse's door. 'Who is it?' he calls grumpily.

'Laura,' I say. 'But I can come back later if it's, um, not a good time.'

The door opens. His eyes look red as if he's been crying. 'Don't be silly,' he says. 'I'm glad you're here. Come in.'

It's the first time I've been in Jesse's room. I think it's the nicest one in the house. It has polished floorboards covered with a huge cowskin rug. There is a desk covered in paper and an iPad on the double bed playing a film, which he picks up and switches off before launching himself onto the bed and arranging a big pile of pillows against the wall.

He turns to face me, his back against the wall, and stretches out his hand towards me. 'Come and sit with me,' he says.

I sit next to him on the bed.

'Are you OK?' I ask. 'I've never seen you snap at your mum like that before. And . . .' I touch his hand. His knuckles are grazed. 'Is your hand all right?' I ask.

He squeezes my shoulder. 'Yeah. I'm fine. I shouldn't have snapped at her. And hitting the wall – that was stupid. I'm sorry I behaved like that. But there have been times when . . . God she gets on my nerves. Makes me see red. It's hard to describe.' He pauses. 'It's not something I'm proud of, but sometimes I've come frighteningly close to hitting her. When I feel like that, I just need to get out of her way.'

I nod as if I understand, but I don't. I didn't like seeing him angry, and I feel as if it's my fault.

'I'll apologize to her later, it'll be fine,' he adds. 'No harm done. She's forgiven me before, she'll forgive me again.'

'If it wasn't for me, none of this would be happening,' I say, tears rising. 'I wouldn't be surprised if . . .'

I tail off. Jesse shifts so that he is facing me.

'If what?'

'Nothing,' I say, blushing.

'Were you going to say you wouldn't be surprised if we wished you'd never come back?'

I bite my lip. 'Well, yeah.'

He removes his arm from around my shoulder and frowns.

'Is that really what you think?'

I look at him. 'I don't know,' I say softly. 'I can see that it's a big deal for Karen me being here, and I believe you when you say that you're glad I'm back, but it's all causing so much disruption. And now the journalists are outside and sometimes I wonder even if Dad did take me, which it looks like he must have done, we'd all have been better off if I'd stayed there with him and everything could have stayed the same. I don't feel that me coming back has made anyone happier. It's just made everything harder for everyone, plus now my dad is dead, and there's nothing I can ever do to change that.'

I feel tears running down my face before I'd even properly realized they were coming.

'Don't cry,' he whispers, leaning towards me and wiping away a tear as it falls. 'I know you miss . . . your dad. It's a lot to deal with. But you being here . . . it's brought us all back together. You've nothing to worry about. It will get better, I promise. I'm going to look after you now.'

PART FIVE

35

'Suffocated?' Leo says. 'They're sure?'

Every few weeks the ship is allowed to return to shore for us to stock up – it's called 'bunkering' and is one of the many new words I've learned since I've been on board. Our slot was brought forward, given the circumstances, and Rick's body was offloaded for an autopsy with his family's permission. Though it turns out he didn't have much family, poor bloke, having been brought up by a grandmother who has since died. A few days later, we had the results.

'I've got the report here,' I say, gesturing with the paper. 'In layman's terms, it very much looks like Rick was suffocated with a pillow from his bed, judging by the fragments of fabric they found in his mouth.'

'Right. So . . . it was definitely deliberate?' Leo asks.

I sigh. It seems like a bit of a stupid question at first, but in actual fact, to be fair, there is a chance that he wasn't deliberately killed.

'Well, there is something else. There is the possibility that it could have been some kind of sex game gone wrong,' I add. 'There were minor injuries on his wrists, which were consistent with him being, um, restrained. They were found to be fairly recent, but it's impossible to tell exactly when they occurred, so it may not have had anything to do with the suffocation. They may have been inflicted at a different time, especially given that Rick wasn't restrained when we found him.'

Leo rubs his forehead and I see his cheeks colour. For all his worldly seadog saltiness, it's clear he finds this kind of subject embarrassing.

'Right. This S&M stuff is a bit beyond me, to be honest,' he says.

'Well, me too,' I say, 'but each to their own and all that. Over the years in my capacity as a GP I've seen the most unlikely sex injuries on the most unlikely of people.' I clear my throat. 'But either way, whether it was deliberate or accidental, given that he was suffocated, there would certainly have been someone else involved, who failed to report it or, as far as we can tell, take any steps to try to help him.' I pause. 'He was found fully clothed, but that doesn't entirely rule a sex game out. People get their kicks in all kinds of different ways.'

'Indeed,' Leo agrees, looking like he would choose to be anywhere else rather than here having this conversation with me.

184

'Also, Rick had quite a lot of diazepam in his system,' I continue. 'It's a prescription tranquillizer but not one that he is personally prescribed to my knowledge – at least not by me. It's not exactly uncommon or tricky to get hold of, either from a doctor or on the black market. He had taken more than a therapeutic dose, but not enough to be fatal in most cases. Whether he or whoever administered the drug knew that is impossible to say.'

'I see,' Leo says. 'Given this new information, I imagine the police will be called in again.' He rubs his forehead. 'But since they've already checked the room for forensics and all that, perhaps it won't be necessary.'

I get the sense Leo doesn't like the police being on board. Maybe it's because he feels they undermine his authority, or perhaps he feels he has something to hide. Either way, he makes no secret of the fact that he likes to be in control. In charge.

'I don't know,' I say. 'All I've had is this report – no other communication with them as yet.'

'People are in and out of these rooms all the time: cleaners, maintenance people . . . everyone,' Leo continues. 'I can't imagine the police will find anything definitive. We're offshore, the crew are from all corners of the globe, we're not really a priority for a small island police force.'

It's not clear to me whether he thinks this is a good or a bad thing, and it doesn't seem my place to ask.

'And as far as anyone thought until the autopsy, Rick's death could well have been an accidental overdose, like you said initially,' he adds. 'I can't imagine any investigation being very thorough, to be entirely honest. By the time they get anywhere significant with it, we might well be back cruising again. We'll be pretty low priority, given that we're only passing through.'

Is he trying to convince himself? Or hoping no one looks too closely? I guess anyone would be unsettled by a death on their watch. He is, after all, in charge here. The buck stops with him.

'I thought I'd seen it all in my many years at sea, but this is new to me,' he says. He draws his hand across his face. 'I guess we'll have to tell the crew that there could be a killer on board.'

36

Alice

21 January 2022, 13:00
The Caribbean

Rumours have been flying around the ship since poor Rick was found dead.

I've been trying not to pay too much attention, as I liked Rick and the things they are saying are pretty derogatory. So far we seem to have everything on the table from him owing money he couldn't pay to dealing drugs which he had stolen from someone else.

For me, he was simply someone fun and easy to hang out with, who knew just about everyone on board and all the gossip, but according to what everyone else is saying, it seems like he had hidden, murkier depths.

Since his death, I've learned that he was widely considered

as 'up for anything' with just about anyone, male or female. One of the other theories circulating is that he was killed by a jealous lover, angry that Rick had been doing things with someone's girlfriend (or boyfriend) that he shouldn't have been.

I guess it's possible, though I find it hard to believe anyone would want to kill Rick. He was a bit rough round the edges, sure, but I never saw any malice in him.

Leo stands up at the beginning of lunch and makes an announcement:

'The autopsy results following the death of your friend and colleague Rick have now been returned.' He clears his throat and shifts awkwardly. 'There's no easy way to say this, but it seems that he was suffocated with a pillow while there was a large, but not fatal amount of drugs in his system.'

There is a collective gasp. 'You mean he was murdered?' someone calls.

'No. That's not what I'm saying. Rick sadly died. It may have been accidental. There is no need for panic, I assure you. If anyone has any concerns, I would ask that you please come and see me directly. The last thing we want here is unsubstantiated speculation and rumour. And it goes without saying that if I get wind of anyone contacting the press about this, it will result in instant dismissal. I hope you'll show some respect for the deceased young man and his family, quite apart from anything else.'

I notice that Leo steers clear of mentioning the circumstances in which someone might accidentally be suffocated, and I suspect that's as much to spare his own blushes as to protect Rick's dignity. From what Stuart told me earlier, the captain had been almost as appalled at the thought of bondage below decks as the possibility that one of his crew members had been murdered.

37

Stuart

22 January 2022, 19:00
The Caribbean

Having been informed of the autopsy results, Nico is back, which is absolutely the last thing any of us wants. As the doctor who signed the death certificate, I'm summoned to Leo's office where Nico is, for want of a better word, laying into Leo almost as if he thinks he killed Rick himself.

'This is a big blow for Heracles, Leo, as I'm sure you're aware,' Nico says. 'After that dancer going overboard like that, this is the last thing we need. And don't think I've forgotten about that incident with the passenger electrocuted in his hot tub a couple of years back. It was only down to luck rather than judgement that we managed to keep that out of the papers.'

'That was hardly my fault or, indeed, anything at all to do with this,' Leo interrupts.

Nico holds up his hand. 'Whatever. My point is, it's yet another thing which paints Heracles in a bad light, and which, once again, is happening on *your* ship.'

'That's hardly fair,' Leo protests, 'I've offered nothing but exemplary service since—'

'I don't want to hear it,' Nico snaps. 'Let's just get on with the business in hand. As far as the investigation goes, what's happening there?'

'We're waiting to hear,' Leo says, his voice sounding strained. 'The local police had already been in and done whatever they do in Rick's room, and they came back today following the autopsy results. I believe they have now found some traces of what could be hair from another person. But with so many people in and out of everywhere and everyone living at close quarters like this it's very difficult to . . .'

'We should get everyone DNA tested,' Nico snaps, clicking his fingers. 'Everyone. Whoever killed Rick has to have been someone on board. All the crew should be tested. Then if the police find anything, we'll be ready. Prepared. Heracles will pay for the tests – I will authorize it personally. We need to be seen to be doing something. Then if the press do find out, we can argue that we're already doing everything possible to help find out who did this.'

'I'd rather play down the whole "murderer on board" thing,' Leo says. 'At the moment none of the crew seems unduly worried by it, which is good news for both of us from an operational point of view. It would be a nightmare if they started to feel unsafe and wanting to leave part-way through the lay-up.'

'Forcing them to have tests isn't going to play out well,' I interject. 'I'm sure a lot of them won't want to be tested, and I'm not sure about the ethics of—'

'I don't give a fuck about the ethics of testing!' Nico rages, slamming his hand down on the table, making the glasses and bottle rattle. Leo and I both visibly jump. 'A man has been killed here on one of my ships. I need to know who did it and ideally, why. What if the same person who did this killed that young dancer?'

'It's extremely unlikely that Lola was killed by someone else,' Leo says, 'there's no evidence whatsoever to suggest that. It will have been a suicide. I would bet my last dollar on it.'

'Given her medical history, it does seem the most likely scenario,' I agree.

Nico ignores us both.

'What if they go on to murder someone else because we are sitting on our arses doing nothing about it?' he rages. 'Anyone who doesn't want to be tested is welcome to resign, though I will ensure that the police will be informed, both here and in their home country. And you can make sure they know that, please. I'm not having two unexplained deaths on my ship, and potentially risking more, not on my watch. We could have a serial killer on our hands for all we know. Bookings are already down – I can't have any more bad press.'

'I'm sure your doctor here . . .' Nico continues, looking at me for the first time.

'Stuart,' I prompt.

'Yes, Stuart, you can get things in motion. OK?'

'Yep. I'll get right on it,' I say. 'Though there will be the logistical issue of getting the tests to us, and then back to a lab – it's not something that can be done on board, obviously, and—'

'We'll throw money at it,' Nico snaps. 'Get the tests helicoptered in and out if necessary. Or send them on a tender, I don't know. You and Leo can work together on it to sort the details, but I don't want us being out at sea to stand in the way of us finding out what happened. How long do these kinds of tests take usually?'

'In all honesty, it's not something I have any experience of, and given where we are and the amount of people, it will be more than a few days, I think. But I'll look at the options and come back to you tomorrow,' I say. The truth is I've never been involved in anything like that before and have absolutely no idea. But I don't think that's the answer Nico's looking for.

He nods. 'Thank you. No expense spared. We need to get to the bottom of this.'

38

June 2013
Scottish Highlands

'You're keen,' Fred said, because I was already waiting by 'our' tree when his van pulled up the next time. The track from the road to our house must have been about two miles long – I was at least a mile from the house and this tree was easy to spot because it was one of the biggest. We couldn't be seen either from the house or the road here and I didn't imagine Dad would bother to come all the way down here without good reason. It was almost perfect.

I grinned. 'I was looking forward to seeing you,' I said.

He laughed. 'You know what I like about you, Laura?'

I felt myself blush. 'Um . . . no?'

'You don't play games. You say what you mean. There's none of the usual "let's pretend I don't like him to make him like me more" or not calling to make a point.'

'But I don't call you. I don't have a phone.'

He smiled. 'Believe me, you're probably better off without one. Everyone on your back twenty-four hours a day . . . it gets stressy sometimes.'

I nodded. I wondered if that was one of the things Dad was trying to protect me from. Stress. Admittedly I did have very little stress in my life.

He spread out the blanket on the ground as usual and we lay down. He kissed me and touched me, doing everything I have dreamed of him doing since he was last here. Things I couldn't even have imagined, that seemed weird and strange but at the same time, somehow right. And I knew that, when he was gone, it would be all I thought about until next time.

Afterwards we lay back on the blanket while Fred smoked a cigarette.

'Why is your dad so protective, do you reckon?' he asked, propping himself up on one elbow and looking down at me.

'Dunno. Maybe because my mum died when I was born and we don't have any other family? Because I'm all he has now?'

'Maybe. Doesn't it . . . get on your nerves though?'

I sat up and crossed my legs so that I was looking down at him. 'Kind of,' I lie. I'd never thought much about it until now. I thought it was normal. 'But I'm used to it. I added. 'And I know he only does it because he cares about me – doesn't want me to get hurt. He says the world's a dangerous place.'

'And you put up with that?'

I shrugged. 'Yeah. He's just keeping me safe.' I paused. 'But . . . since I've met you, I do kind of wish we could go out somewhere together. Like a real couple might.' Like I'd seen in the films. That must be real, surely? 'That would be fun.'

He rolled over onto his back. 'We could do that.'

My stomach lurched with excitement. 'But Dad would never agree to it.'

He put his hand on my knee and trailed it gently up towards my thigh and then into my jeans again. 'But he wouldn't have to know, would he?'

Fred and I agreed a date for a few days later. I literally counted the hours until it was time.

After dinner I yawned extravagantly and stretched. 'I'm so tired, Dad. I think I'm going to head upstairs to read and have an early night.'

He frowned. 'It's very early. I hope you're not coming down with something.'

'No!' I said, perhaps a little too firmly – the last thing I wanted was Dad barging in to check I hadn't died in my sleep or if I needed some paracetamol. 'No – I'm sure it's nothing a good sleep won't sort out. I feel fine, just tired. I just feel like a bit of time to myself,' I added, hoping I wasn't pushing my luck. 'About to get my period,' I lied, to make sure he wouldn't ask any more questions. 'That's probably all it is.'

Dad smiled indulgently. 'OK, Sweetpea. You sleep well and I'll see you in the morning.'

'Thanks, Dad. You too. Night.'

'Night, darling.'

Up in my room I quietly changed into my favourite jeans, which were slightly more fitted than the others and, I noticed, tighter on me today than usual. Was I putting on weight? I made a mental note to stop baking so many cakes. I picked out a T-shirt with plastic jewels studded into it which Dad had bought me for my last birthday, brushed my hair and twisted it up the back of my head, securing it with a clip.

I looked in the mirror and pinched my cheeks again. My eyes were dark with excitement. In the absence of any proper make-up I smeared on some lip balm which Dad bought me because I told him my lips were getting dry. It wasn't lipstick by any stretch, but it gave them a little sheen.

'Not too bad,' I whispered at my reflection, before piling my pillows under my duvet in case Dad decided to put his head round the door, closing the curtains and opening the window.

I sat on the windowsill and leaned out towards the tree branch which used to scare me when it waved around in the wind when I was small. It was by now bigger and stronger, and I hoped it would support my weight. I'd examined it from underneath as well as from my room over the previous few days and figured that, even if it broke, I'd probably be OK as it wasn't all that high. Not really.

I swung out and the branch bent, dipping down so low that I almost touched the ground. I let go and dropped the last couple of feet. Brilliant. That was easier than having to swing myself along the branch to the trunk to climb down like a monkey as I had imagined I would need to do.

I crept round to the front of the house and ran all the way down to the end of the drive. I was totally out of breath by the time I got there. I didn't want to risk Fred driving up even part of the way in case Dad saw or heard him.

Nothing must go wrong this evening – I was determined to make our night out happen.

I jiggled up and down on my feet as I waited. It wasn't cold but I was so excited I couldn't stand still. Eventually I heard the faint sound of an engine and a few seconds later, Fred's van came into view. He leaned out the window and said 'Ready? In you get.'

I got in and Fred leaned over and put his hand on the inside of my thigh, kissing me roughly. He looked and smelled different. He had a T-shirt on rather than his usual work overalls and smelled of shampoo.

'You look nice,' I said.

He took his hand away from my leg and put it back on the steering wheel. 'And you look as good as always,' he said. I blushed, wondering if he meant that I always wore pretty much the same old boring clothes and I wished, not for the first time, that I owned something more glamorous to wear for him. 'This is something a bit different, isn't it?' he added. 'Being away from your garden. What do you want to do?'

'Oh, um, uh, I don't mind,' I babbled, partly because I didn't mind as long as I got to spend the evening with Fred and also because I had no idea what kind of things might be an option. What did people my age do when they went out? Dad had never told me, other than that it was all too dangerous for me to take part in. The books I'd read and films I'd seen didn't give me any true idea – they were so old. I didn't think people went to balls in country houses in long dresses anymore, and Fred had a van rather than a car with a roof that came down that we could drive about in with me wearing cat-eye sunglasses and a headscarf like in some films I'd seen. A thrill of excitement and nerves ran through me. We could go anywhere. Anything could happen.

Was this a bad idea?

No. I was with Fred. He would look after me. He liked me; he had said so. I would be safe with him. I was sure of it.

'Have you eaten?' he asked, jolting me out of my thoughts.

'Yeah.'

'OK . . . so we could go for a drink, cinema if you fancy it, or something wacky and wholesome like ice-skating or bowling. Or, I got paid yesterday, we could get a cheap hotel room and, y'know . . .' He reached over and slid his hand between my legs – pressing hard.

'Um . . . bowling sounds good?' I interrupted, some-what hesitantly because I wasn't entirely sure what bowling was. I pictured something like throwing little balls at each other like I'd seen in the French films Dad made us watch sometimes in a futile attempt to try to improve my language skills. It seemed a bit dark to be doing something like that now, but then again, what did I know?

'Bowling it is then,' he said, taking his hand away from me and putting it back on the steering wheel. He sounded terse, like I'd made the wrong choice. He had obviously wanted me to opt for the hotel room, and while I loved how it felt when I did that stuff with him, as I never went anywhere, I wanted to experience some-thing different.

But I knew how to sort it out. 'Tell you what though,

how about first . . .' I said, reaching over and unzipping his fly as I knew that doing that to him would put him in a better mood.

39

June 2013
Scottish Highlands

Bowling turned out to be nothing like the gentle game I'd seen in the films. As we went into an enormous building, we were hit by a wall of noise – music, shouting, laughing and crashing sounds. It was overwhelming – I'd never seen or even imagined anything like it – and I guess it must have shown on my face as Fred frowned and asked, 'You OK? You want to go somewhere else? We could go to that hotel after all? Nice and quiet there . . .'

I shook my head and forced a smile. 'No. No, this is great. Thank you.'

He sighed and shrugged.

'OK, you're the boss tonight,' he said and then, 'Two, please' to the boy behind the counter as he handed over some money. I blushed, wanting to offer to pay my share but not having any money.

'I'm sorry I don't have any . . .' I began but he waved his hand at me.

'It's fine. My treat. Just got paid, like I said. What size are you?'

'Pardon?' I looked down at my clothes and blushed again. 'Umm, I think about a 14?' Dad always bought my clothes for me but that was what the labels said on them. Usually they came in plastic bags when he'd been to the supermarket.

He laughed. '*Shoe* size.'

'Oh!' I exclaimed, wondering why he wanted to know. 'Four, then.'

The man behind the counter handed over a pair of blue and red shoes which Fred handed to me. 'Here you go.'

'Oh, OK thanks.' I tried but clearly failed to look like I wasn't a little taken aback by this; and Fred looked at me quizzically.

'You *have* been bowling before, haven't you?'

I blushed again. 'Um . . . no, not really,' I said. 'It's not Dad's kind of . . . well.' I trailed off. It was too embarrassing to say that I *literally* never went anywhere. I'd never explicitly stated that to Fred – I'd simply said that Dad was very protective and wouldn't let me out on my own with a boy.

I was more and more beginning to doubt what Dad had told me about lots of girls my age living the way I do. Unless Fred just didn't know about any of them, which then again, I guess he wouldn't if they were at home all the time like me.

It was so confusing.

I looked around at the clothes the other girls were wearing – some of them were in skirts shorter than I'd ever seen in the films we watched and tops that almost showed their boobs. Both girls and boys had rips in their trousers and they wore all the colours of the rainbow. There were people with pierced noses and strangely coloured hair. Rows of earrings. Blue nail varnish. So many things I hadn't seen before, obviously not in real life, as I never saw anyone except Dad, who always wore pretty much the same thing every day, but I hadn't seen anything like it in the films either.

The music and shouts were incredibly loud and the lights were so bright and there were loads of unfamiliar smells too. It was getting hard to think straight. I wasn't sure what to believe any more.

'Your dad really does keep you on a tight leash, doesn't he?' Fred observed, frowning.

'He worries about me,' I snapped, an unexpected flash of anger rising in me at him criticizing Dad like that. 'He cares about me. A lot.'

Fred put his hand on my waist and kissed me hard, shoving his tongue roughly into my mouth.

'Yep – he certainly does,' he said as he pulled away from me. 'But anyway, it's good news for me if you've never been bowling – means I might even have a small chance of winning, for a change.'

I laughed, and leaned in and kissed him, gently, the way I preferred it, not that he'd ever asked me. I thought people might look at us, doing something like that in public, but no one seemed to care.

'Come on,' he said, indicating a bench to the left with a jerk of his head, 'let's get our shoes on and you can lose your bowling virginity.'

The bowling balls were surprisingly large and heavy, and it took me a few goes, but eventually I managed to throw one in a straight line and even hit a few pins down. Between each turn the screen, which as if by magic had our names on, changed and there'd be a little cartoon either celebrating your go (Fred) or lamenting how many pins you missed (me). It was amazing – I'd never seen anything like it.

And the clothes people wore! I still couldn't get over them. So many different styles. It was noisy, yes, but people seemed happy. Even the ones who were shouting didn't seem angry.

It didn't look dangerous to me. But maybe not everywhere was like this. Maybe the dangers lay elsewhere.

Most of the girls here were about my age, some were even younger. Some were in big groups – just girls, or a mix of girls and boys – and others were in couples, like me and Fred. Sometimes they kissed or held hands.

Why wouldn't Dad let me do things like this? Was it really so dangerous? What did he think was going to happen? No one looked frightened or frightening. They all looked like they were having fun.

Why did I always have to stay at home?

After Fred had trounced me at two games, we went to the bar and ordered drinks – beer for him, Coke for me. He led me to a booth in the corner where we sat next to each other. He reached under the table and put his hand between my legs.

'Fred!' I exclaimed, looking around wildly. What if someone saw? He nuzzled my neck wetly.

'Don't worry, no one's looking,' he mumbled thickly, before adding, 'You're not like other girls, Laura.'

I felt like my stomach was falling away. I had been doing my best to be normal, to act like other girls my age, but I was quite clearly doing something wrong. It was hardly surprising though – I had no one to compare myself to. And I could see now that my clothes were all wrong. Boring. Too plain. The wrong colours. Everyone else looked better than me.

I squirmed away from him. 'What do you mean?' I asked. I could feel tears threatening.

He looked at the expression on my face and laughed, which made me feel even worse. He rolled his eyes.

'Don't look like that. It was meant to be a compliment. There's no bullshit with you. You say what you mean, there's no game-playing, you even,' he leaned in closer, 'let yourself do the things we both want to do without angsting about it all the way other girls tend to do.' He leaned in even closer and kissed me, pushing his tongue into my mouth again. 'Do you want to play another game or shall we . . .'

I really did want to play another game, it was so exciting to be out, but I didn't say so. I could tell what Fred wanted now. And I wanted him to carry on wanting me. So I said what I thought he wanted to hear.

'No. Bowling was fun, and it's been amazing to come out, but let's not play another game. Let's go back now.'

We headed back to the house and settled down in our usual place at the bend of our drive on a blanket. I lay back and let him undress me.

'Laura. Wake up.'

I opened my eyes. Fred's face was above me as he shook my shoulder. 'We must have fallen asleep. C'mon, you'd better get back, as had I.'

I sat bolt upright. 'Oh God! What's the time?' I babbled as I leapt up, jamming my boots onto my feet and hoicking my jacket back on.

'It's about three,' Fred said, looking at his watch.

I relaxed a little. The moon was so bright it seemed really light; I had assumed it was almost morning and was worried Dad might already be up – sometimes he was a very early riser.

I put my arms around Fred and kissed him. 'Thanks for an amazing night,' I said.

He shrugged. 'It was just bowling.'

I didn't want him to go. 'Can we do it again?'

'Yeah. If you like. Why not? As long as we still get to do this . . .' he indicated the blanket, 'too. Same time next week?'

I grinned. 'Yeah. Can't wait.'

I watched as he drove away and then crept back up to the house. I didn't want to risk Dad hearing the front door open, so I went in the back door and tiptoed up the stairs.

I didn't turn the light on but started stripping off my clothes as quickly as possible so that if Dad did hear something, I could say I'd been in bed for ages and had got up to go to the loo.

As I pulled the covers back to push the pillows I'd so carefully arranged earlier I nearly jumped out of my skin as the light flicked on.

Wearing just my pants and bra, I turned round to see Dad, fully clothed, standing in the doorway of my room holding a shotgun which was pointed directly at me.

Slowly, he lowered the gun.

'Where the FUCK have you been?'

40

Stuart

22 January 2022, 23:00
The Caribbean

'So have you ever slept with Rick?' I ask Alice, after one of our usual sessions that evening. Unsurprisingly, there's an odd atmosphere on board. Rick's death has caused a lot of speculation, and not only about how he died. I'm surprised he put it around *quite* as much as it's rumoured he did, as he wasn't exactly a looker, but I suppose some people have hidden depths.

Alice swings herself up out of bed and puts on my discarded shirt.

'We were good mates, and to be honest, all this speculation about his sex life is beginning to piss me off,' she says. 'I wish people would have some respect,' she adds, not answering the question.

Hmm. Interesting. 'I'll take that as a yes then,' I say.

'It's not a *yes*, it's a none of your business,' she replies, uncharacteristically snappy. 'Did *you*? It sounds like he wasn't that fussy,' she adds, somewhat snidely. 'Why are you asking anyway? I didn't have you down as the jealous type.'

'No reason. Just curious. Making conversation. From what I understand, he was quite a shagger. But to answer your question, even though you haven't answered mine, I'm only into women – and one at a time at that. Unless it's my birthday or a special occasion,' I joke.

The image of my one night with Lola flashes into my mind and I push it away. 'So who do you reckon killed him then?' I continue, wanting to move the subject away from who has had sex with whom. That night with Lola was certainly a night to remember, but it was hardly my finest hour.

Alice sighs. 'I don't know, Stuart. I doubt anyone does. Except the killer.' She pauses. 'Is that what you're actually asking? Whether I killed Rick in a fit of jealous rage because he was my secret boyfriend rather than simply my good friend, or . . .' – she picks up a pillow and presses it over my face – 'as part of some kind of kinky game?'

I laugh and try to push the pillow off, but she doesn't let it budge. As she holds the pillow over my face and I feel her straddle me again, I have to admit, it *is* kind of hot. She grinds against me and presses the pillow against me a little harder, and for a second it flits through my mind that maybe she did this to Rick too but then I am inside her again and I'm not thinking about anything at all.

41

June 2013
Scottish Highlands

'I just went for a walk, Dad,' I said as calmly as I could manage. 'I couldn't sleep.'

Dad's face was puce and he was kind of opening and closing his hands at his sides. For a second I wondered if he was going to hit me. But he'd never done anything like that. Why would he do it this time?

Because I'd never done anything as bad as this.

'I was FRANTIC!' he yelled. 'You've been gone at least two hours. Maybe even longer for all I know. WHERE WERE YOU?!?!'

'I went for a walk!' I shouted back, picking up the duvet and wrapping it round me, suddenly aware that I was almost naked and not wanting to be in front of my dad. Stick to your story, I told myself. He doesn't know. He can't prove otherwise. 'I can't be stuck in my room all the time! I felt like some fresh air! It's not a crime, is it?'

'DO YOU THINK I WAS BORN YESTERDAY?!?' His right hand flew up and I flinched, but he didn't touch me, instead he ran it through his hair and started pacing the room. 'Why on earth would you go for a walk in the middle of the night? In the dark? It doesn't make any sense.'

'Like I said, I couldn't sleep,' I repeated, trying to keep my voice low and steady even though my knees were trembling so much I could hardly stand and for a second or two I thought I might even wet myself. 'It's no big deal. I'm fine. No one died. I don't understand why you're so upset. I'm tired now, so I'd appreciate it if you'd leave me alone to get back to bed.'

Dad stepped closer to me, so close that I could feel his breath on my face and little flecks of spit as he spoke. 'Have you done this kind of thing before?' he asked.

'Uh – yes,' I said, because it seemed like the best answer at the time. 'Loads of times. And nothing bad has ever happened. It's nice being outside at that time. Peaceful,' I improvise. 'Almost magical.'

'Why didn't you tell me?' he wailed, somewhere between a shout and a whine. 'God, Laura, I do all I can to keep you safe and you're out in the middle of the night wandering around on your own!'

'Nothing's going to happen!' I yelled. 'There's no one here, is there? Just me and you.'

'You could fall. Twist your ankle. Not be able to get up. Freeze to death. Have you thought of that?'

'It's summer,' I muttered.

'Or there could be poachers. With shotguns. Or kids out doing . . . I don't know what. It's not safe, Laura!' His voice was becoming high-pitched, almost hysterical. 'Nothing is safe out there! You're only safe in here with me!'

'Fine,' I muttered. 'I won't do it again. OK?'

Dad nodded curtly. 'Good. Thank you. From now on, you don't step foot outside this house without my say-so, OK? Day or night. If you're going for a walk, you tell me.' He pauses. 'Ask me, I mean,' he corrects himself.

I nodded again, panic rising within me. How was I going to see Fred now? ''kay,' I said, hoping Dad couldn't somehow see my inner turmoil.

'And I'm sorry, Laura, but . . . I know I've given you your privacy before up until now, but this changes things. I need to know you're safe. So I'll be coming up to your room now and again to, uh, check you're OK sometimes. I don't want to have to sneak around or be dishonest with you, so that's why I'm telling you this upfront. So we both know where we are.'

Tears welled in my eyes and fell down my cheek. I nodded miserably. ''kay.'

He tried to hug me, but I didn't want him to touch me and held myself rigid. 'I love you so much, Laura,' he mumbled into my hair, 'the thought of anything happening to you is more than I can bear.'

I wriggled and he let me go. 'I'm sorry I scared you, Dad,' I said thickly. 'But I really want to go back to bed now.'

He kissed me on the forehead. 'OK, Sweetpea. I'm sorry I got so cross. You do understand why, don't you?'

I nodded, but only because I wanted him out of there as

212

quickly as possible. I didn't understand. Living like this was no life. I was beginning to see that now.

'Sweet dreams, my angel.'

Once he had gone I threw myself into bed and pulled the covers over me. I cried harder than I could ever remember crying before. How was I going to get out to see Fred with Dad watching my every move? What would happen when he came for our meeting next week if I wasn't there? Would he think I didn't want to see him and never come back again? Or – God – what if he came up to the house to find out what had happened? Would he do that? What would Dad do then? He had his shotgun out when I came in – might he kill him even?

I just don't know. I feel like I don't know anything about anything anymore.

42

June 2013
Scottish Highlands

The next week was awful. Dad walked on eggshells around me, making my favourite foods, letting me finish lessons early, trying to make up for our argument. We almost never argued, but when we did, it always upset him much more than it did me. And we'd never had an argument as big as that one before. But that was because I'd never actually disobeyed him before.

I tried to act normally and pretend that I'd forgotten about our row, but I didn't think I was very convincing. When it came down to it, I didn't particularly care that I had argued with Dad. I was starting to think that was his fault for keeping me on such a tight leash. However, I was extremely worried about what I was going to do about seeing Fred.

Dad was true to his word about checking up on me. He tried to be subtle: during the day he'd come to my room on the pretext of borrowing something or asking me what I wanted for dinner, but each time it was obvious what he was doing. I knew that sometimes he put his head around the door in the night too. Once he even came over and stroked my face, as if he was checking I was still breathing. I pretended to be asleep. I didn't know how else to deal with that. I felt ashamed that it made me cringe, while also feeling furious that he wouldn't leave me alone even at night.

So I couldn't risk sneaking out and getting caught with Dad keeping such a close eye on me, but at the same time I figured he couldn't keep me in the house all the time for ever. Dad wanted to keep me safe, but he wouldn't want me to hate him – I knew that was important to him too. I decided the best thing for now would be to leave Fred a message.

I could have simply written a note, and left it taped to 'our' tree where he'd find it when he came to find me at our usual place, but I wanted to do something better than that. I borrowed the double tape deck and some cassettes from downstairs, telling Dad I wanted to make my own compilation to fall asleep to, found a blank tape and recorded some of my favourite love songs on to it. Then I recorded the song I wrote for Fred, playing my guitar as I sang.

I was a little nervous about it. What if he thought it was too sappy? He already thought I was a bit strange – he'd said as much.

But then again, Fred had also said that he liked that I did and said what I wanted, that I didn't play games. This was what I wanted to do, so I'd go ahead and do it. And he had once said that he'd like to hear me play my guitar too.

Once I had made the tape and was happy with it, I recorded my own copy to keep for myself. Maybe I could play the tape and imagine Fred listening at the same time, I thought. Tears came to my eyes again as I realized that, for the time being, that might be as close as I was able to get to him.

While I was helping Dad clear away the dishes after lunch the day I was due to see Fred, I slipped into conversation as casually as I could: 'I'm just going to go for a little walk round the garden before we get started on this afternoon's lessons, 'kay? Feel like I've been inside forever.'

I started washing up, deliberately not looking at Dad. I had spent most of the morning rehearsing the words in my head. I figured it was best to present a walk as something I was going to do rather than explicitly asking permission and I added on the bit about feeling like I'd been inside forever to try to make him feel bad about having me on such a close watch. He liked me to get fresh air and exercise anyway, so he couldn't really say no.

'Yes, don't see why not,' he said, equally casually, though I bet it almost killed him to do so. 'Don't be too long.'

Inwardly I grinned, but I kept my face straight. 'I won't.'

Grabbing the tape and my carefully worded note from my room on the pretext of getting my shoes, I hurried down to our usual meeting place. The note said:

Dear Fred,

Dad saw me coming in when we went out. I said I'd been out for some air and he doesn't know about you, but I need to be really careful and can't get out to see you for now – he's watching me too closely. I don't know what to do.

I made you this, think of me when you listen. Don't come to the house, it's too risky, but leave me a note here if you can – I'll check tomorrow. And every day after that until I hear back from you.

I miss you.

Laura xxxxx

I'd never written anything like that before and had no idea if it was OK or if he would think it ridiculous, but I felt somehow lighter as I walked back to the house, knowing that we'd be communicating later, even if it wasn't in our normal way.

When it got to the evening, to the time Fred would be arriving to see me, I listened to the tape I had made in my room and silently cried myself to sleep.

43

The next morning after breakfast I made another excuse to go out and ran down to our meeting place.

My heart leapt as I saw the tape had gone. I wondered if Fred had listened to it, and what he thought of it. In its place was a plastic bag with a note taped to it.

I stroked it with the tips of my fingers. Fred had touched this piece of paper, he had written these words. It said:

Laura – bummer about your dad. Was looking forward to tonight, to seeing you, and, well, the rest 😊 Thanks for the tape – I'm not sure how I'll play it, but I'll try. I brought you this – it's old and basic but my number's in it so you can text me about when you can next get in to the garden at least though the signal seems pretty patchy around here. Hope you can get out soon.

I opened the bag – inside was something small and black with numbers and a little screen, plus a lead with a plug. At first I thought it was a weird calculator, but I read the note again and realized it must be some kind of phone. I'd seen phones in films, but Dad and I didn't have one at the house. And I'd never seen one like this – it was tiny. I pressed the button that looked like it switched it on and the screen came to life. It took me a while to work out how to use it but eventually I tried a button which had a picture of an address book on and there was just one number next to a name – Fred. I pressed another button with a picture of a phone receiver on and held it to my ear.

'Hello?' I said as Fred's voice started to speak but then felt stupid when I realized it was a recorded message. I waited for the beep and then said: 'Fred! Thanks for the phone. Brilliant idea. I'll call you later. I . . . miss you. See you soon.'

I ran back up to the house and up to my room, shoved the phone in its box to the back of a drawer and hurried downstairs to Dad.

As soon as my lessons for the day were over I rushed upstairs, ferreted in my drawer for the phone and switched it on.

The screen lit up and nothing happened for a few seconds, before it went 'BEEP BEEP' incredibly loudly.

'Ssssh!!!' I hissed at it, throwing it under the bed in case Dad had heard and came in to investigate. A couple of minutes later, when he hadn't appeared, I lay down on my stomach to retrieve the phone. Still lying on the floor, I looked at the screen.

'One message' it said. A rush of excitement went through me – it could only be from Fred. I scrabbled out from under the bed and pressed a couple of buttons, my hands shaking with impatience, but nothing happened. It took ages but eventually I found the right button, pressed it and held it to my ear.

'You have . . . one message,' an electronic lady said. 'Message. Received. Today. At. 11.37 a.m.'

Yes, yes, yes, I said impatiently inside my head. Get on with it. Hurry up.

I held my breath as I waited for his voice. 'Laura? Glad you found the phone. Nice one. Um . . . yeah. Let me know when we can meet. Bye for now.'

I listened as the electronic lady came back on and asked me if I'd like to listen to the message again, call back or delete.

I listened again. And again. And again.

Later on, after fiddling around with the phone for ages, I worked out what Fred meant when he said to text – you could use the keypad a bit like a typewriter.

Thanks again for the phone. So pleased we can talk.
Will call you later. Xxx

Two seconds after I pressed send, my phone beeped which took me by surprise.

Careful yr dad doesn't find it ;)

I will be.

I hesitated before adding: I miss you and pressing send.

This time there was a longer pause before he sent:

When cn I cu?

I frowned at the message before texting back:

Sorry don't understand

When can I see you?

Of course. How stupid of me.

Soon I hope. But Dad's really watching me . . . have
to be careful.

OK. Let me know. Already hard thinking about u.

I blushed. I didn't know what to say to that so I settled for:

Will do xxx

I stared at the phone for a few minutes but there were no
more messages. Reluctantly I switched it off and shoved it
to the back of the drawer. I couldn't risk it making a noise
and Dad hearing it.

Over the next weeks Fred and I texted a lot. When I wasn't
with Dad, I was pretty much on the phone while I pretended
to be studying in my room. Late at night when I was sure

Dad was asleep, sometimes I'd even call Fred and we'd whisper to each other. He liked me to talk about what I wanted to do to him when we were together, touch myself down there and tell him what I was doing and what it felt like. It was embarrassing and I didn't really know what to say, but he told me all girls did that and I wanted to be like all girls, not the weird girl who always stays at home with her dad and never goes anywhere. He'd tell me he was picturing me wearing things like little red lacy pants, the kind of thing I could only imagine because I'd never seen anything like that, let alone owned or worn anything but the most bog-standard underwear. The phone only worked when the weather was good and the signal dropped out often, but I tried my best. I liked it better when we talked about normal things like what we'd been doing in the day than all the other pretend stuff.

Meantime, I was on my absolute best behaviour with Dad. I knew that my only chance of getting to see Fred again anytime soon was to make Dad trust me again. I needed him to almost forget that he'd found my room empty and stop checking up on me. It took a while but as the days went by he was more willing to let me go for walks during the day and didn't insist on timing me while I was out. I was often awake late into the night texting or talking dirty (Fred told me what we did was called that) so I was pretty sure that I'd be aware of most times Dad checked on me in the night – it seemed to be pretty much never.

I started to worry that Fred would lose interest. Texting or talking wasn't the same as being together, like that amazing night we went out, or lying together on the blanket, undressing each other, touching each other. So when I could bear being apart from him no longer, when I was once again failing to concentrate on my lessons because I was thinking about him, when I was spending hours torturing myself with images in my head of him with other imaginary girls, I knew I'd have to risk sneaking out again.

Need 2 CU I texted. By now I had learned all the abbreviations. Can't wait anymore

Horny? LOL

I miss u.

2nite?

What time?

Midnight? Usual place?

Y

Cu xxxxxx

44

Stuart

27 January 2022, 12:00
The Caribbean

As I predicted, most of the crew are not at all keen on the idea of a DNA test. There has been a lot of grumbling about their rights and mutterings about coercion but once I reiterate the reasons for it, reassure them that all samples will be destroyed afterwards, only compared against the samples found in the room and not used for anything else, and, most persuasively, that if they don't agree to it they will have to resign and are unlikely to be invited back, everyone consents.

Also, as I predicted, getting the test kits sent out to us was not an easy process – ships moored off the coast of obscure Caribbean islands don't exactly have a letter box, and we only go back to shore about once a month for bunkering. A helicopter was duly chartered, which is costing an absolute fortune, but thankfully that's not my problem.

Now I've got the test kits, it'll take a couple of days to get everyone through the surgery, swabbed, and the samples labelled, and then they'll need to go back and off to the lab, again probably in a helicopter. I guess Nico feels he needs to be seen to be doing everything he can.

Even without the extortionate transport costs, this little operation is costing a bomb and may yet be a total waste of time. We don't even know if the small forensic team found anything useful in their search other than some hairs. Things in the Caribbean happen slowly and it's not easy to stay in the loop when you're literally out at sea.

But if Nico and Heracles want to spend their money this way, then who I am to question it?

I get back to my paperwork.

45

July 2013
Scottish Highlands

I knew it was a huge risk, but I needed to see Fred. It had been too long. Much too long. It had helped a bit, being able to text and have whispered conversations under the covers late at night. But it was never going to be as good as seeing him in real life.

So even though I was barely able to sit still all day, I tried to at least give the impression of concentrating hard on my lessons. I washed up after lunch and dinner and generally behaved like the dutiful daughter that I am the vast majority of the time. I didn't want to give Dad any reason to think he needed to check on me once I'd gone to bed – as far as I knew, he hadn't done so for ages.

We watched a film together, one we'd already seen countless times, and then I went up to my room. I played my guitar for a while so that Dad could hear I was there. I practised the song I wrote for Fred over and over, and then got into bed fully clothed and switched off the light so that if Dad looked in he would think I was asleep.

Can't wait 4 later xx I texted

My phone beeped Me 2

I started to wish I'd arranged our meeting for earlier – waiting, especially in the dark, staring at the ceiling, was torture. An hour after I'd turned out my light I heard Dad go to bed and at 11.50 p.m., after a quick check in the mirror, I climbed out of the window and ran silently down to our usual place. To my delight, Fred was already there. My stomach flipped over as his face broke into a grin and I ran towards him, into his arms and we kissed hungrily.

'How much time have we got?' he asked, already pulling my T-shirt up over my head.

I shrugged. 'Don't know. Probably best not to be too long. Dad's started to relax a bit about me but he's still kind of keeping an eye. But I couldn't wait any longer to see you . . .'

To my surprise my voice caught in my throat and tears sprang up in my eyes. Fred pulled me towards him. 'Hey. Don't cry. Come on, no time to waste.'

Much later, I tiptoed up the stairs carefully avoiding the squeaky board, glancing at the door to Dad's room which was closed as usual. I gingerly opened my door without putting on the light as usual and:

'There you are,' came Dad's voice out of the darkness. I yelped and flicked on the light.

'What are you *doing*?' I shrieked, my heart racing. 'You made me jump out of my skin!'

There was a weird expression on his face – not quite anger. Disappointment, maybe? I'd never seen him look like that before. He was holding something in his hands but I couldn't see quite what. 'Been out for another *walk*?' he sneered.

Oh God. 'Yes,' I whispered hoarsely. 'I couldn't sleep.'

He raised his arm and I flinched as he hurled something across the room. It smashed against the wall and broke into several pieces – my phone. It ricocheted back towards him and he stamped on it, again, again and again, then picked up the pieces and stormed out of the room. I heard a splash and then the sound of the toilet flushing.

Bile rose in my throat. 'I'm sorry, Dad . . .'

He barrelled back into the room and grabbed me by the shoulders. '*Sorry?!*' he spat. 'You're *sorry* are you? I've spent all these years trying to keep you safe, protect you and then you do this, literally the first boy you see, *literally* the first boy, and you're doing God knows what, given the state of those messages and . . .'

His face crumpled as he let go of my shoulders and sank down on my bed. He started sobbing, loud, hiccupping sobs as he buried his face in his hands. I touched his shoulder gently. 'Dad, please don't cry . . .'

Tears were running down my face. He looked up at me. 'I'm sorry, Laura. I failed you.'

I start to cry too. 'No. You didn't,' I say. 'You were trying to protect me, I understand that.' I thought he meant that he realized he'd sheltered me too much and had realized he

228

had to let me live a little. He hadn't failed. I knew he loved me. I should have—

'I FAILED!!!' he burst out. 'This boy – he got to you! You could be pregnant! He could have killed you, or hurt you. I can't let you carry on seeing him, he would hurt you eventually, they all do . . .' he babbled.

'He hasn't hurt me! I love—' I broke off.

'Oh Laura,' he said, his voice low. 'You don't love him.'

'How do you know?' I cried.

Dad took me in his arms, but I stiffened. I didn't want him to touch me. 'I love you. No one can love you like I do,' he said. He moved away and held me at arm's length, looking into my eyes.

'You understand that, don't you?'

I dipped my head and wiped my nose. I didn't doubt that Dad loved me. I needed him. But I needed Fred too. Perhaps if I talked to him, we could . . .

'But it's OK. I've nipped it in the bud,' Dad added, interrupting my rambling thoughts.

What did he mean? What had he done? Had he . . .

'You'll be fine now. Just me and you,' he said hoarsely. I could tell he was on the verge of tears. 'You don't need anyone else. You'll be safe here with me.'

I didn't look at him.

'Things are going to have to change,' he continued, his voice firmer now. 'I'm going to have to keep a closer eye on you. I should have realized.' He touched my cheek and I flinched. 'I know you're cross with me right now. But it's only because I love you. You'll see that when you've calmed down. Goodnight, Sweetpea. I'll see you in the morning. Sleep tight.'

He kissed me on the forehead before leaving the room. I heard him lock my bedroom door behind him.

He'd never done that before.

I loved Dad. And I knew he loved me. But I couldn't live like this. Like a prisoner. Without seeing Fred. And I needed to know if he was OK. What did Dad mean when he said he'd nipped it in the bud? Had he done something to him?

I took my coat and opened the window. I had no idea where Fred lived and now no phone to call him, but I had to find him. I had memorized his number. It was the only phone number I'd ever known – it was burned into my memory. I would find a way to get to him. I grabbed a branch of the nearby tree and swung myself out. I ran down the drive and towards the road. By the time I got to the end of the drive, my chest was hurting so much from the exertion I couldn't run any further, desperate as I was to get away. I started walking in the direction of the town, the way I'd driven with Fred. I heard a car coming towards me and stood in the middle of the road, waving frantically. Could it even be Fred coming back for me? To rescue me? Could he have somehow known what was happening? Maybe Dad called him before he smashed the phone? Oh God, unless Dad somehow made him come back so he could . . .

'Help me!' I cried. There was a thud. Pain. And then, nothing.

46

May 2016

'I was never a prisoner' – Anna Roberts speaks out on her 18th birthday

By Arianna George, *Daily News*

The nation breathed a collective sigh of both relief and shock when Anna Roberts – who had been abducted as a four-year-old – was found in 2013, more than a decade after her disappearance, suffering from amnesia after having been hit by a car, but otherwise in good health. She had run off from a farmhouse in rural Scotland where she had been held for several years – the place she had come to see as her home.

'I didn't "escape",' Anna, now eighteen and living under a carefully guarded assumed name, corrects me when I ask about her memories of this night. 'It wasn't like that. It took a while for my memory to come back, and it did so only in dribs and drabs, but that house was my home, where I lived with my dad. It wasn't a prison. Not at all.'

Wearing a short skirt and over-sized jumper and fiddling with her long, peroxide-white hair, she sighs. 'Dad and I had had a row that night. It took a while after I was . . . found, but eventually, with the help of hypnosis, I started to gradually remember what had happened that night. But all teenagers argue with their parents at some point, don't they? I wasn't trying to escape – I was just angry. I'd have gone back. Probably that same night, as I had nowhere else to go. If he hadn't . . . if I hadn't . . .' She pauses and bites her lip, exposing almost-invisible braces. 'Well. Everyone knows what happened then.'

I ask if she remembers what the row was about. She pauses and looks thoughtful before replying. 'Yeah. I do. Just normal teenage stuff, the kind of thing everyone argues with their parents about. It's not important what it was, and I don't want to talk about that now.'

Following the death of her abductor and the discovery of who she really was, Anna was returned to her family in Catford. That can't have been easy after an eleven-year absence, I suggest.

'It was far from easy,' she tells me. 'I was just . . . thrown back into this family and, yeah, they were kind and pleased to have me back, especially, uh, Karen, my mother, I suppose she is, but at the same time, they were strangers, you know?'

232

She picks at a thread on her skirt. 'It was . . . hard. It still is hard. I get that Dad abducting me was a bad thing to do, and the therapists they make me visit can barely shut up about it, but . . . as far as I'm concerned, he was my dad, the man who brought me up. He was the only family I'd ever known. He took good care of me. He did everything for me. He was nothing but kind to me and when he died, and when I left, I missed him terribly.' She pauses. 'I still do. Every single day.'

But aren't you angry that he snatched you from your family? I ask.

'Part of me knows I should be,' she concedes. 'But no. I'm only sad that things ended the way they did. That Dad died. He shouldn't have done. That shouldn't have happened. He didn't deserve that.

'I often ask myself how things might have turned out if I hadn't left. It might have been better if I hadn't. I was happy, and well-cared for, and my dad would probably still be alive. Everything was fine for us, there's no reason to believe that things would have changed that much.'

I ask if she's heard of Stockholm Syndrome, and she rolls her eyes. 'Yes. The therapists are always banging on about that too. They're wrong. It's patronizing. They didn't know Dad and me. How we were. I don't have Stockholm Syndrome and I never did.

'As a child, I didn't know any other parent. Dad took good care of me. Of course I was going to love him like a father. Anyone would, however they came to be there. It's not rocket science.'

But does she not feel she missed out on her childhood? School? Friends?

'I might have been sheltered,' she says, becoming more defensive, 'but I had a very happy childhood, with everything I needed. Dad saw to it that I was well educated. He had me read at least a book a week. I'm good at maths. I learned where all the countries are. History. All the prime ministers. Kings and queens. Practical things too. How to care for animals. Grow vegetables. Wire a plug. He absolutely wanted the best for me. And if things hadn't . . . turned out the way they had, I'd have gone on to live a normal life like anyone else. I'm sure of it.'

While Anna's new name and image remain officially protected, this hasn't stopped certain websites reporting on her antics. I ask about the reports that she is, these days, something of a wild child.

She flicks her hair. 'I go to a lot of parties,' she says. 'And it's no secret among my friends that I like a drink. It's one of the many causes of friction between me and, uh, Karen. Then there was that time when I had to go to hospital to have my stomach pumped. She got really upset about that. But if she was less restrictive about what I can and can't do then . . .' she trails off.

How about her other family members? How does she get on with her brother? She visibly brightens. 'He's great. I adore him. We spend a lot of time together. He can be a bit overprotective sometimes, but apart from that, we get on really, really well. He respects me and he always has my back.'

234

With her new identity, she says she is trying to put the past behind her. Anna insisted before agreeing to this interview that her anonymity must continue to be protected. 'I've changed a lot,' she said. 'I don't want to be recognized as who I once was. I'm not Anna Roberts anymore. And I'm not the child who always stayed at home in Scotland, though I'm still using the same name I used there, that Dad gave me. For now.' She pauses. 'I've never, ever felt like Anna. I don't tell people what happened to me when I was a child – it's none of their business. If they know, they know, but mostly they don't, and I prefer it that way.'

And what does she plan to do with the rest of her life? 'I just want to get on with things,' she says. 'I don't want to be "that girl who was abducted" the whole of my life. I want to travel – be in places where people don't know about my past. Reinvent myself again. I love to dance – I'm hoping to pursue that.' She pauses. 'I want to live the kind of life my dad wanted for me.'

47

Jesse

June 2016
Manchester

'Hey,' I say, opening the door of my somewhat scuzzy student
house to her.

She smiles. 'Hey,' she says back.

As usual, she looks very different to the last time I saw
her, even though it wasn't that long ago. Her invisible braces
are straightening her teeth and even altering the shape of
her jaw. She's changed her hair, yet again. It's short and jet
black and suits her now pixie-like face with its sharpened
features. She's lost even more weight, and I can see from the
well-defined muscles of her arms she must have been training
hard too. She never seems happy with how she looks, and
is forever trying to change her appearance.

She gives me a hug. 'You going to invite me in then?'

I open the door wider and step back against the wall so she can pass. 'Of course. In you come.'

We walk through to the kitchen and I switch the kettle on, moving aside a pile of dirty plates and dumping them in the sink as I do so.

'Exams OK?' I ask.

She wrinkles her nose. 'Yeah. I guess. Mainly. The ones I turned up for, at least.'

Oh for fuck's sake. Why didn't she go to them? But I know better than to tell her off. There's no point. She'll do what she wants to do. She always does.

'How are things going at home?' I ask.

She sighs. 'Pretty much as you'd imagine. Your mum and I aren't getting on, as per, but you already know that. I think we'll both be glad when I move on. Which now my exams are out the way and I'm eighteen, I can do. All I need to do is get a job, and then I can be independent. Like you.'

I want to say, 'You could come and live with me and we would never need anyone else, I will look after you and provide everything that you need,' but I don't. It'll just make her want to run, again. Panic. Say she needs to be left alone. It's always such a fine line with Laura.

'And the dancing? All good with that?'

She grins. 'Yes. Really good. We did well at Blackpool and my teacher's suggested I audition to be a pro on *Strictly* next year. If I made it, I'd be the youngest pro ever. Imagine that! Little me on the TV. You'd be proud.'

'And you're still dancing with the same guy?' I ask, lightly, casually, as if I'm not livid with jealousy about every moment she spends with him. *I* taught her to dance, and I loved every second of it. She's now a better dancer than me, I haven't danced properly for years now, but I still wish she was still *my* partner instead of his. 'What's his name again?' I add, as if I don't spend several hours a week looking at his perfect fucking face on Insta, wondering if he's using her like so many men do, and wanting to seek him out and punch him in case he is. 'Toby, is it?'

'It's Tony, as you well know.'

I snort. 'What kind of name's that for a twenty-year-old?'

'A perfectly good name that his parents saw fit to give him as a baby. He would probably ask why you've got a girl's name,' she teases.

'So he's all right, is he?' I ask, ignoring the jibe. 'You get on OK?'

She smiles. 'Yeah. He's a nice guy, a great dancer and fit as. We look good together. The judges love us as a pair,' she says, seemingly deliberately giving nothing away.

If Laura thinks he's fit then there's no way they're not shagging. She has sex with anyone and everyone she feels like without thinking twice. I worry about her. Not only for her health, but also that eventually she's going to end up with the wrong guy. Someone who'll beat her or rape her or even worse. One issue I don't have to fret about is her potentially getting her heart broken – she seems much more up for the party and the sex than any relationship, but I do wish she'd be a bit more careful. A lot more careful. These things can end very badly.

Even though I've been at uni and she's been at home, we've stayed close. She comes to see me often, partly to get away

238

from Mum, I think, but also because she trusts me and confides in me. She doesn't have any close friends that I know of, just people she gets pissed and goes out on the pull with. She doesn't want people to know that she was Anna Roberts. I'm not sure if it's that that prevents her making proper friendships, or if it's simply her fucked-up childhood.

We chat on WhatsApp most days too and speak on the phone often. I know all the ins and outs of her life and I love that. I'm her big brother, and it's my job to protect her.

She knows she can rely on me, that I'm always looking out for her. And that's what she needs in her life – stability. Whatever she throws at me, tantrums, mental health episodes and more I am always there for her to pick up the pieces. No one else is.

Mum tries hard, but in spite of it all, they've never got close. I think Mum wanted it so much it made Laura shut down and push her away. And then came the fights, blame, breakdowns, and more blame. I feel sad for Mum that after getting what she had always wanted, Laura coming back, it hasn't made her happy in the way I'm certain she thought it would. She'd use words like 'miracle' in the early days of her return, but I don't think she feels that way about it now. The whole thing has clearly taken a huge toll on Laura, mental-health-wise. Me too, I think, though to a lesser degree. Thanks to many years of tedious therapy, I've now pretty much got the panic attacks under control, as well as the anger issues, at least most of the time.

Laura is still opening and closing random cupboard doors. 'I'm starving,' she grumbles. 'Any danger of anything to eat around here?'

'I haven't got much in,' I say. 'Tell you what – I'll take you out for dinner. Celebrate the end of exams for both of us.'

We go to a restaurant that's a little out of my normal budget, but where I can be fairly confident we won't bump into anyone I know. It's not that I'm embarrassed by Laura – certainly not – but when she's around, I like to keep her to myself. Catch up on where she's at and also avoid her flirting with or getting off with my mates. That's happened in the past, and it's awkward all round. I hate it when she does that. Plus, I have something specific I want to talk to her about this evening.

'What are you planning now you've finished school?' I ask, trying to sound as if this isn't a leading question and something I've been thinking about for weeks. I'm worried that with no direction, she'll go even further off the rails, and I don't want that to happen. I need to make sure she's OK. Look after her.

She shrugs, taking a bite of her monkfish. 'Not sure. Whatever gets me out of the house quickest. I might go travelling. Though I need to earn some more money first. I've just done a press interview which they paid me a stupid amount of money for, but I want to spend that on getting these' – She indicates her boobs – 'done. Your mum won't let me have Dad's money for that.'

The police eventually found several thousand pounds in cash literally hidden under the floorboards in the house Laura had been living in. I can never bring myself to call that man her dad. He had no family left, so after a lot of legal toing and froing, it was decided the cash would be held in trust for Laura – by Mum – until her twenty-first birthday, much to Laura's chagrin. And while she's managed to persuade Mum to advance her a small amount for her invisible braces by telling her it would boost her self-esteem, Mum has quite rightly (I think anyway) said no to using money for the bigger boobs or a nose job Laura is so desperate for. She's lovely as she is, she just needs to realize that. But there's no point me telling her; she won't accept it.

'But I did have an idea,' Laura adds. 'I thought instead of working in some dire job in a call centre or whatever for months on end, living in Catford and having to put up with your mum trying to bond with me and going on about how she's praying for my soul every time I stay out too late, I might get a job where I can travel at the same time. Tick all the boxes at once.'

I look up. She's going away? How far? Where to? How will she manage without me there to pick up the pieces? I try not to panic.

'Oh yes? Like what?' I ask, casually, trying to keep my breath steady and even.

'Jesse, you should try this fish, it's amazing,' she says, leaning over the table with a piece on her fork and pushing it into my mouth.

'Mmm. Yes, lovely,' I say, totally distracted and barely tasting it at all. 'You were saying? Where were you thinking of going?'

'This sauce too . . . want to try? It's really good.' She looks up at me and I shake my head. She takes another mouthful.

'I want to work on a cruise ship,' she says finally. 'I've been reading up on it. The ships these days are huge and

241

need masses of people. I'm going to apply for a few jobs – things like bar work and cleaning, there are loads of jobs like that on board, but . . . I had another idea too.'

I am going into full panic mode. She can't leave! I'll never see her. She'll be on the other side of the world – what if she has a crisis and I'm not there to help? I take a deep breath and concentrate on the techniques I've been taught to keep myself calm. I'll allow myself to worry about this later, I decide, but I can't let her know how stressed I'm feeling about this right now. It will only make her more determined.

'What's that?' I ask, my voice unnaturally high and squeaky. My mouth is dry and I take a sip of water.

'I'm going to do an aerial dance course. I think I can persuade Karen – your mum – to give me some of my money to do it as it'll both help me get a job and get me out of her hair, both of which she wants. She'll be impressed by me spending my cash on something constructive and she'll like that it involves dancing – dancing is about the only thing she and I have in common apart from you, brother dear. I can't see her saying no.' She takes another mouthful of the fish. 'You sure you don't want to try some of this sauce?'

'No, thank you,' I say. I feel sick. I don't know what to do. I want her to be happy but I need to keep her close. Otherwise . . . oh God who knows what might happen?

Laura scrapes the remains of her potato puree into the sauce and takes a last mouthful. 'Mmm. That was great. Thanks, Jesse.'

'So why ships? And why aerial?' I ask.

'Well, I thought it would be nice to be able to travel but not have to pay for it, like I said. I thought about trying to get work on a yacht, but it sounds like too much hard work and I don't have the right experience. But cruise ships – they employ loads of dancers. I've been doing some research and apparently aerialists are particularly in demand, because not all dancers have the right skills for that. And it looks fun, doesn't it? Flying through the air? Amazing. I'm trying to persuade Tony to do it with me, but I'm not sure if he's going to go for it.'

'I'll do it with you,' I blurt, before I've had time to think it through. The thought of Laura dangling from the roof of a massive boat with no one to look after her next time she has a meltdown makes me want to cry.

She laughs. 'You'd want to? I didn't think you'd be inter-ested in arsing around travelling the world or anything pointless like that,' she says. 'I thought you were going to be a hot-shot accountant or something, now that you've pretty much finished your degree.'

I was. In fact I'm about to have my second interview for Jay, Jay and Miller, the accountancy firm that pretty much everyone on my course wants to work for.

But Laura is my little sister who I've already severely failed once when she needed me most, and I need to make sure I don't do it again. Plus, what she's suggesting does actually sound pretty fun.

I shrug. 'One day, yeah. Probably. Maybe. But there's no rush, is there? I've been thinking I might like to take a year off first anyway, because Mum talked me out of doing it between school and uni. Only young once and all that.'

This isn't entirely true – I thought about taking some time off after uni to travel very briefly, and then quickly discounted the idea, but suddenly it seems like the best idea in the world.

'Wow, didn't think that was your kind of thing: drifting around the world with no real aim. Or cruising, as it would be in our case.'

'I'm not quite as staid and boring as you think, Laura,' I say, a little more tersely than I mean to.

'Aww Jesse!' she cries. 'I don't think you're boring at all. I just think you're . . . driven. Keen to get out into the world and make your mark and all that. That's what you've always said.'

I nod. 'I am. Kind of. But all the stuff you're saying now makes me realize that I've never travelled much and you're right – why not do it in a way so that someone else is paying? I've got the rest of my life to be an accountant, after all.'

'Exactly!' she agrees, clapping her hands. 'It would be brilliant. Imagine all the places we can go. White sand beaches and warm seas. Turtles even. Fish that look like Nemo and Dory. We could learn to scuba dive and wakeboard. Honestly it would be stupid *not* to go.'

A waiter arrives to clear the plates and offer us dessert menus, which we regard in silence for a minute or two.

'So how about we do this aerial course together?' I say, casually, as if it's no big deal to me either way. 'I bet if we can apply as a ready-made dance couple, any cruise ship would snap us up once we're trained.'

She reaches over and grabs my hand. 'Yes!' she says excitedly. 'And if you do the course too, Karen's even more likely

244

to think it's a sensible use of the inheritance and let me do it without a row.' She pauses. 'She's always liked you more.'

I frown. 'That's not true. You mustn't say that.' I don't think it *is* true – Laura has always been the golden child. Mum would deny it, but she distanced herself emotionally from me from the day Laura was taken, and she's never entirely come back. Laura returning was all she ever wanted.

'It is true,' Laura counters. 'But whatever, I don't care. It doesn't matter.' She reaches into her bag to get her phone and swipes and jabs at it. 'Look – I thought this course,' she says, pointing at a picture of a lithe, tanned, smiling upside-down girl in a hoop hanging from a palm tree underneath the title 'Aerial Dance in Ibiza'.

'I've already been trying out a bit of aerial alongside my normal dance classes,' she continues, 'and you've been dancing pretty much since you could walk, so I figured a few months intensive in Ibiza should be enough to sort us both out.'

'Ibiza?'

'Yep – it's supposed to be the best course – plus it's better than doing it in the rainy old UK, isn't it? And look' – she swipes the screen to show me a picture of something that looks like a shed on a beach – 'this is where you stay, so it keeps the cost down. It's not exactly luxurious obviously, but look where it is! Right by the sea!'

I take the phone and look more closely. The beach looks beautiful.

Her eyes sparkle. 'I'm so excited that you're going to come too!' she says, even though so far, as far as I'm aware, I haven't agreed to anything.

But we both know there's no way I'm going to say no to her. I never do. 'And it will work even better if you come as well so we can work on routines together straight from the start!' she continues. 'We'll be the best in the class and have the pick of the jobs, I'm sure of it.' She claps her hands like an excited five-year-old.

'It'll be so fun! Can you imagine? I think I'm going to have a stage name. Too many people already know about me being Laura, the girl who stayed at home. I need another new start. I'm going to be Lola. Much more exotic than Laura. Who will you be?'

I imagine Jay, Jay and Miller will let me postpone my traineeship, on the off-chance I get selected. But even if they don't, I don't care. Being with Laura is way more important. I'm not having her go off round the world on her own if I can possibly help it.

'I'll be Antonio,' I tell her. It sounds suitably sexy and exotic like Lola, and is a much better name than plain old Tony.

PART SIX

48

Antonio

17 January 2022, 02:30
The Caribbean

Opening the door when I return to my room after the drill, at first I think I must be hallucinating.

She is lying on my bed, her head propped on her elbow, dressed like a boy but looking at me, smirking, as alive as anything. 'Lola!' I breathe.

I slam the door shut behind me, almost as if I think she might float away if I let her. What's going on? How is she here? I was convinced that she'd gone overboard and been swallowed up by the sea! 'But what . . . why . . . how . . .' I stutter.

She gets up onto her knees on the bed, and I rush over to her to hug her. Oh God. She's alive. She's here. I can feel her. She's real. 'Where have you been? What happened? I thought . . . I thought . . .'

I start to cry. Not just tears running down my face but huge, hiccupping sobs that make it difficult to breathe. 'Oh God, Lola, I can't believe you're here . . .' I moan as she pats my back and shushes me like a mother might to a child. I try to rein it in – Lola hates neediness. But I can't. Oh God. This is the best thing ever. I don't think I can cope.

She pulls back from me and wipes the tears from my cheeks with her hand – the same gesture that I've done to her so many times over the years. 'I've been here all the time,' she says. 'On board. Hiding out. Since New Year's Day. Down in the crew area. No one goes down there when there's all the luxury they can enjoy up here. Why would they? It was easy. I had plenty of space. No one came near. I knew they wouldn't.'

'But how did you . . . that woman in the bar saw you fall, didn't she?'

She smiles smugly. 'She thought she did. Maybe that's what she saw. Then again, maybe it wasn't.'

'But if it wasn't you, who was it? Or how did you survive the fall? Or being in the water? Did you have a survival suit? How have you been getting food since . . . ?'

She puts her finger on my lips.

'I will tell you, I promise. All in good time. But you absolutely mustn't tell anyone that you've seen me. And now I need your help, Jesse. You'll help me, won't you?'

49

Lola

Eighteen days earlier
New Year's Eve 2021, 17:00
The Caribbean

I kiss him hard on the lips, roll off him and reach for my cigarettes which are on the floor of the tiny, squalid cabin in the bowels of the ship. Being below the waterline there is no porthole and no natural light or air, and it stinks. He traces his hand down my side as I lean down towards the floor. I know he will be admiring how my toned curves dip in at the waist and then flare out over my hips, and I love the power I have over him. I can get him to do anything I want.

He turns towards me and smiles as I light a cigarette.

'Beats me how someone as fit as you can smoke so much,'

Rick says. 'How can you dance three shows or whatever it is every day when your lungs must be shot to fuck?'

'Almost all female dancers smoke because we're barely allowed to eat,' I say.

He runs his hand up the inside of my thigh, and then traces his finger over my stomach to my boobs. 'You are the fittest woman I have ever shagged,' he says.

I laugh. 'So romantic,' I say, sarcastically, taking another drag on my cigarette before stubbing it out in a near-empty glass on the floor. 'I need to go. I've got the kids' dance workshop to do.'

'But you'll come again tomorrow?' he asks. We've got into a routine lately. Every other day or so I come to his cabin about this time between shows and workshops. When it fits in with both of our shifts. He is pretty good in bed and eager to please, if nothing else.

I root around in the narrow bed, looking for my under-wear. I pull on my knickers and then tracksuit bottoms and a T-shirt, and shove my bra in my pocket.

'I'll try,' I say. 'Though I have my reputation to think about. If you tell anyone, I'll have to kill you,' I add, with a smile and a wink, before leaving.

50

Antonio

New Year's Eve 2021, 21:00
The Caribbean

Lola messaged asking me to meet her as soon as possible in our cabin – she has something she needs to tell me which can't wait. I've no idea what can be so urgent, but she does like to be something of a drama queen sometimes. I've been busy with my dance lessons all day, waltzing lecherous old ladies around the ballroom, I'm tired and can do without a scene. But even so, I'm still anxious to get back in case she's launched herself into some new crisis that I will need to deal with before it gets out of hand.

She's not there when I arrive and at first I wonder if this is some stupid joke that she or even someone else is playing. She knows that if she snaps her fingers I will come running, and sometimes she does it just for fun. I don't think it's the least bit funny, but she finds it hilarious every time. I know I should ignore it, but I can't. It's too risky. Sometimes, she does actually need me, and I can't let her down.

Having the childhood that she had, so closeted, going nowhere and seeing no one, once she was back in 'normal' life she wanted to catch up on all the things she felt she'd missed out on. I can understand that, but she took it to extremes. Parties, drugs, but also boys, and men. Many, many men. She'd have sex with pretty much anyone who showed an interest in her. Still does, if she gets the chance. I'm not sure if it comes from having no real points of reference, no friends, no sense of boundaries, or if she was just totally messed up in the head by what had happened to her.

But it hasn't all been fun and games for Lola over the years, by any means. Alongside all the wild times there's been a lot of anger and doubt. Drugs and alcohol. Addiction and rehab. Sexual diseases. More than one suicide attempt. Lola would tell me off for playing amateur psychologist thinking like this, but I think what it comes down to is she doesn't like herself much. And though sometimes she is more mentally stable than others, she still has serious self-esteem problems.

She wouldn't agree with me, but I'm convinced the boob enlargement, the nose job, the lip fillers, the bulimia (which she denies, but our windowless cabin is small and I hear her), plus the regular Botox and fillers, are all her trying to get away from who she really is. Body dysmorphia. I've sent her links to articles about it, but she laughs it off and says I'm being ridiculous. 'The things I have had done to myself are no different to me dyeing my hair,' she says. She does that too, of course, very regularly, a new colour almost every time. 'I just want to look nice. Nothing wrong with that, is there?' she says. 'No different to you doing all those hundreds of crunches every day to keep your abs in shape.'

She is beautiful, she just can't see it. And over the years, through the ups and downs, I have always been there for her. A shoulder to cry on. Someone to pick up the pieces.

Being on this ship for a few years has been good for her, I think. Doctor Stuart's got her on what seems like a good balance of drugs. She seems more stable lately. And with that, a bit less interested in the shagging around, at least as far as I know. She knows how much I worry about her doing that. It leaves her vulnerable, both physically and mentally. And I think over the years she has come to realize that while other people will come and go, I will always be there for her. So she listens to me. At least some of the time.

The door opens and she comes in. She's wearing the yellow feathery costume she wears for the children's dance workshop she does where she teaches them simple dance steps based around a story about chickens. It's very cute and they all love her.

Her face is serious and I feel a stab of panic. 'Lola, what's wrong? Has something happened? Has someone upset you?' I feel anger rising already. If some bloke has done something to her, I'll . . .

She shakes her head. 'No. Nothing's happened. But I've been thinking. I don't want to do this anymore.'

My heart starts beating faster. 'Do what?' I say, but I think I can guess what she means. She's been weird lately. Distracted. Distant, somehow.

She moves her hand, gesturing around the cabin. 'This. The ships. Almost always on shift, always at someone's beck and call. I need some time away.' She pauses before adding, 'On my own.'

'Lola, let's talk about this—' I go to take her arm but she snatches it away from me.

'Don't touch me. Please. I've been thinking about this for ages and I need to get it out. Let me have my say.'

I hold my hands up and step back from her. 'Sorry. Go ahead.'

She sits down on the bottom bunk and starts pulling her costume off. 'It's not just the ship. I'm sorry to have to say this, Jesse, but it's also you. You always being here, telling me what to do. Being on my back. I get that you're trying to protect me, but it's stifling – I've had enough.' She pulls on a pair of tracksuit bottoms and a vest top.

I swallow hard and nod, fighting back tears. I can't lose her. Not again. I can't.

'Jesse,' she says, using the name that we only ever use in private. She insists on me calling her Lola all the time – something to do with leaving her past self, Laura, behind. It's very important to her that people don't know what happened to her when she was a child. She stands up and looks me in the eye.

'I'm twenty-three years old. I don't need my brother telling me what to do, who I should or shouldn't see, who I should or shouldn't sleep with. I want to have fun, on my own terms. And I don't want to work the ships anymore. I've had enough. I want time to myself. To be in one place. To not live in a horrible cabin with stupid bunk beds and have to work every hour God sends.'

I open my mouth to speak, but she holds up her hand.

'You are overprotective and sometimes, I suspect, even a bit weirdly jealous of the men I see . . .'

See? That's a euphemism, I think to myself, but know better than to say anything.

'. . . to the extent that sometimes it scares me,' she continues. 'I hate how much time you spend fretting about me. It makes me feel responsible for your happiness. And it's hard enough for me being responsible for my *own* happiness. I don't want to be your problem. I've had enough. I want to be by myself. When the ship docks, I'm leaving. Possibly not for good, but at least for a while.' She pauses. 'And you are not coming with me.'

I'm mortified that she will see the tears which are by now coursing down my face. She can't leave without me – she won't cope. I know she won't. Something will go wrong for her and it will be all my fault because I've driven her away. Because I haven't been there when she needed me. Again. Just like when she was snatched. The memory of that moment when I saw the gate open, her sparkly shoe on the ground and Mum screaming has never left me. I've promised her many times since she returned that I'm always going to be here to protect her. She has to let me keep that promise. If I drive her away, I will have failed. Again.

'Fuck's sake, Jesse, get over it,' she mutters. 'Why are you crying? You're being ridiculous. I'm not a child and neither are you. We're adults – independent of each other. Or at least we should be. You need to realize that. Now let me pass, I need to get ready for the show.'

I grab her arms. 'Please, Lola, no! Don't go like this! Let's talk about it!'

She tries to wrench herself away, but I don't let her go. 'I can change!' I yelp. 'I won't be so . . .' Red-hot rage courses through me – after all I've done for her all these years, whatever she's thrown at me, I've forgiven. She can't leave. Not like this. She can't. I can't protect her if she's not with me.

'Let me go, you're hurting me!' she shouts, before twisting herself to lean down and bite my arm. It hurts and I cry out, but I still don't let her go. 'This isn't just about you, it's about what I want!' she screams.

Before I know what I'm doing, I release her arm and slap her across the face. I reel back from her as far as the tiny cabin allows, which isn't much, silent and mortified. I know I have a temper, but I've never done anything like that to her before. Ever. She puts her hand to her face and stares at me. I expect to see tears, or shock on her face, but her expression is one of pure contempt. I try to reach out and touch her, but she flinches and moves away.

I am horrified. 'Oh God, Lola, I'm so sorry,' I moan. I am bawling like a child by now. 'Please forgive me. I will never, ever do that again—'

'I knew it,' she interrupts, her voice cold and low. 'You're exactly like all the others. You were only ever going to let me down. I have my own mind. No one is in charge of me. Least of all you. Now let me pass.'

51

Alice

New Year's Eve 2021, 21:30
The Caribbean

I'm going through the roster with two of the least reliable kitchen hands in my tiny office cum cupboard when the door flies open and Lola barrels in without knocking, sobbing loudly and clutching her arm. The two boys look up in bewilderment and I usher them out – it probably means they won't turn up to their next shift as they'll claim they didn't understand when they were meant to be there, but right now, Lola is more important. She throws herself into my arms and carries on sobbing, so hard I can feel her tiny birdlike body shuddering.

'Lola? What is it?' I ask, stroking her hair.

'It's Antonio,' she wails, pushing away from me and wiping her eyes. 'He hurt me.'

I frown. I don't know Antonio well, but he's never seemed like the type to be *violent*. Then again, I guess you never can tell. 'What?' I ask. 'Hurt you? How do you mean? What did he do?'

'Hit me,' she sobs, barely able to get the words out.

Oh God. Poor Lola. 'Oh sweetie. I had no idea he had it in him. He always seems so gentle, so protective of you. What did he . . . why?'

'He's not as gentle as he looks,' she sobs.

'Oh Lola,' I continue stroking her hair. 'Has he ever done that before?' She moves her head in what I think is a 'no' but it's hard to tell. 'You poor thing. Between us, we'll make sure he doesn't do anything like that to you again, I promise. Was there . . . what happened today?'

I don't disbelieve her, but it does seem a bit strange. What kind of brother hits his sister? It's hard to believe of Antonio. He seems to worship the ground she walks on. Lola's always taking the piss out of him for it – sometimes when we're having a drink she'll send him a text saying she needs to see him and we'll place bets on how long he takes to get there. It's never very long.

But some men have hidden, unattractive depths. Lola is my friend and she deserves to be believed. She moves away from my hug to look at me. 'I told him I was leaving,' she says. She is still crying but seems a little calmer.

I frown. 'Leaving what? The ship?'

'Yes. The ship. Everything. I've had enough. I don't want Antonio telling me what to do any more. And I don't want to be here on board. It's all so suffocating.'

I take her hand. 'Lola, we all feel like that sometimes,

wherever we are, I promise you,' I say. 'It's not just the ships. You should try working in a kitchen! You can't even fart without everyone knowing about it.'

She smiles weakly. I push her hair back from out of her eyes. She's such a pretty little thing, so vulnerable looking.

'And it's bound to get especially claustrophobic on board, with all of us in each other's pockets the whole time,' I continue. 'But it's not all bad, is it? There are lots of good things about being here. I know I haven't been doing this as long as you, but you've said so yourself before. Don't rush into anything you'll regret, please. Don't throw everything away just because Antonio's being an arse. We can report him, get him removed from the ship. It shouldn't have to be you that leaves. It should be him.'

She shakes her head. 'But it's not just him. I don't want to do any of this anymore. I need some space – I don't want to be stuck in here with everyone all the time, with Jamie shouting at me. So many shows and lessons to do. All the time. There's no let up. It's not what I want.'

For a second or two I wonder if she is drunk, or on something. She seems muddled and unclear about what the problem actually is. What it is that's really upsetting her.

'And I'm too old to be bossed around by my brother,' she wails. 'Look,' she indicates her arm where a bruise that looks like a handprint is already growing, 'look what he did to me. That, and slapped me.' She pauses.

I'm confused. 'So it *is* Antonio you want to get away from? Not just the ships?'

She starts sobbing again. 'No. No. Not only him. He shouldn't have hit me, I know that, but . . . but . . . he's never done it before. He looks after me. He's saved me from myself many times. And maybe he's right, maybe I shouldn't be sleeping around. Everyone thinks I'm a slut. Fuck's sake. I'm such a disaster. I don't deserve him. I don't want him to be sacked on my account. I don't deserve anyone. Everything I touch gets ruined. No one needs me in their lives. Ever since I've been a small child all I've done is messed up people's lives. No good ever comes from me.' By now she is barely coherent she is crying so hard.

I hug her again. Even though she has her ups and downs, I've never seen her as upset as this before. 'Lola, calm down. You're talking nonsense, you idiot,' I say. 'Everyone loves you here, you know that. If you don't want to get Antonio sacked, how about we at least get you moved into a different cabin? Give you some time to think at least. I'm sure that can be arranged. You could talk to Mara about it – I'm sure she'd be happy to help. Maybe you could do that and then see how you feel? Sleep on it. Wait till tomorrow, at least, before you make anything official. New day, new year, and all that. It will probably feel better in the morning.'

There is a pause as she continues to cry. Poor Lola. And what a bastard Antonio has shown himself to be.

As her sobs subside, she pulls away from me again and swipes at her eyes.

'And I know you hate it when I ask this . . .' I say, hesitantly, as given her current state she may not thank me for the question, 'but have you been taking your meds?'

She nods and replies, testily, 'Yep.'

'Maybe it's time to ask Stuart for a review?' I suggest.

Suddenly, she is calmer. 'No. I'm fine now,' she insists. 'I know what I need to do. Thank you for listening. Please don't tell anyone what I've told you. Especially not Antonio. Promise?'

'OK,' I say, 'though if he hit you, I think—'

'Alice! Please! You must promise. No one. No one at all. Whatever happens. It's really important.'

I sigh. I don't think she should keep something like this a secret, but I get the impression that she doesn't have many close friends she feels she can rely on. I want her to be able to trust me. 'OK. I promise,' I say, somewhat reluctantly. 'But if it happens again . . .'

'Thank you,' she says, before turning on her heel and walking out without another word.

52

Lola

New Year's Eve 2021, 21:40
The Caribbean

'All done at your end?' Rick asks. His boss Danny is shouting at him every five minutes through the radio, but I've turned the volume right down. Rick won't care and the constant noise is getting on my nerves. What we're doing is much more important than whatever it is Danny wants done, I'm sure of it.

'Yep,' I say. 'I told Antonio I was leaving. I made sure to shout as much as possible and I picked a time between shifts when there would be other people in their cabins. Someone will have heard me, I'm sure. It worked even better than I could have expected – I even goaded him into hitting me.'

Rick looks shocked. 'He *hit* you?'

I shrug. 'Yeah. I was surprised too, to be honest. I knew he could have a temper but . . . anyway, it reiterates to me that I'm doing the right thing. That we're doing the right thing. I'd never be able to get away from him unless we do this.'

'And you went to see Alice?'

'Mmm-hmm. You'd have been impressed by my acting skills. I was near hysterical, confused, hating Antonio, hating myself. Look' – I indicate the bruises on my arms – 'I even gave my arms a bit of a pounding. Antonio did grab me, but not hard enough to leave a mark. So I helped it along a bit.'

Rick grins. 'Nice one. I'll go and do my bit at ten o'clock like we agreed.'

PART SEVEN

53

Lola

One day earlier
30 December 2021, 18:00

'God that's creepy,' I say. Rick and I have been working on the papier mâché woman for some weeks now, a few minutes here and there whenever one of us can snatch the time. She is hidden in a store cupboard full of old wires and lightbulbs that he has access to and no one else is likely to bother with. We chuck a tarpaulin over it whenever we leave it just in case. We're using an old mannequin nicked from the back room of one the clothes shops as a mould – there are loads of these things about and I can't imagine why anyone would notice that it's gone. The cupboard we are working in is stuffy and windowless but needs must. It's almost impossible to get any privacy on board so this place is as good as any.

'I still don't see why we couldn't simply put one of your dresses on the mannequin and chuck it overboard instead of faffing around with all this,' Rick grumbles.

He's frowning at the model rather than looking at me, so I roll my eyes. Fuck's sake, he is such a thick pain in the arse. All this had better be worth it. It's turning out to be a lot more effort than I'd envisaged and there's only so much of his 'company' I can take.

'Because, sweetie pie, the papier mâché will dissolve quickly, leaving only my clothes. A mannequin is plastic and full of air and would float. It's too risky that it might eventually be found and someone would put two and two together. We'll weigh this model-me down with stuff like sugar or flour which will also dissolve, or random heavy objects which will sink. The water's several hundred metres deep where we are tomorrow evening – I've checked – so it's unlikely anything will ever be found. But belt and braces and all that – better to be safe. And anyway,' I stroke it fondly, 'even if she is a bit scary, I've quite enjoyed making her. Bit like being a child again. I'm going to call her Anna.' I don't tell him the significance of the name. I don't have conversations like that with Rick. Or, indeed, with anyone since I stopped that pointless therapy as soon as I was allowed to make my own decisions.

He pulls me against him and kisses me hard. 'Some kind of wholesome childhood you had, if you spent your time making things out of – what did you call it – paper machine? I've never done anything like this before. My grandma who brought me up never bothered with this kind of thing. Too busy drinking at the local pub. Seems like magic to me, being able to make something stiff and hard out of paper, water and flour. And speaking of stiff and hard,' he leers, pressing himself against me in the darkness.

I wriggle away. 'Not now,' I scold, 'we haven't got time. We need to get on with this. I've brought this white dress I thought Anna could wear – white is most likely to show up best in the darkness and it's got these floaty panels too – give us a better chance of someone seeing it when she falls past the bar.'

He nods. 'Nice one. I'm going to roll up, erm, Anna in a balcony awning to get it up to the top deck. If anyone sees me, I'll say I'm replacing a damaged one. And I've knocked out the security cameras in the relevant places already – the system's so fucked that half of them aren't working anyway so it was easy enough to do.' He pauses. 'You've done all the paperwork, like you said?'

I sigh. 'Yes. You're on the life insurance, like we talked about. Once the insurance people have decided I'm definitely dead, we can get back together somewhere discreet and split the proceeds, me with my new name and papers obviously. Though you mustn't let on that we're an item in the meantime. Maybe we could even get married at sea eventually, by a ship's captain. Though I don't know if that's an urban myth or not. I don't know if they're actually allowed to perform marriages.'

Some of that wouldn't bear close scrutiny but Rick can't believe his luck in being with me, is not very bright and it's all stuff he needs to hear to make sure he gets the job done.

He smiles. 'You want us to get married?'

I look up at him coyly through my eyelashes, the way I know he likes. It makes him feel powerful. 'Maybe. One day. What do you think?'

He laughs. 'Wow, Lola, you're full of surprises. I didn't know you were traditional like that. But yeah, why not? I know we're not exclusive at the moment,' he presses himself against me again, 'but I'd give everyone else up for you. I mean, look at you! You're so fit. I'm totally punching.'

'I said I wanted to be with you, didn't I? So accept it,' I say, somewhat shortly, not wanting to be drawn down this particular avenue of conversation which, along with the lack of air in this cupboard, is making me feel somewhat nauseated. 'Now, do you remember what the plan is? Or do you need me to run through it again? You take Anna up to the top deck, wrapped in the awning like you said, I will hide out in here. Once you are sure that no one and no camera can see you, you throw her off, so she goes past the bar's window – hopefully some of the punters will stop necking their champagne long enough to see her. Then make sure you get back down and continue about your business as usual without anyone seeing you.'

54

New Year's Eve 2021, 22:00
Fizz
The Caribbean

Fizz is the most exclusive bar on the ship. As its name suggests, drinks-wise, it only serves champagne. Everything from the brands you might buy on impulse in the local supermarket to celebrate a special occasion right through to vintage bottles which sell for five figures, or sometimes even more. These bottles are kept in a backlit cabinet behind the bar and when someone buys one, which is more often than you might imagine, there's an elaborate ritual of two bar staff having to use two different keys to open the cabinet. There's a table on a mezzanine with a red rope around it where the purchaser and their guests can go and drink their champagne from Dartington crystal glasses in full view of everyone. Sometimes people choose to purchase a bottle for a marriage proposal or a significant birthday, but quite often it's just because they can.

Tonight it's New Year's Eve and things are a bit different in Fizz. The guests (mainly Heracles suite regulars) have paid a supplement of several hundred pounds to be here. A team of white-gloved waiters are stacking champagne coupes into a pyramid shape. Once the pyramid is built, two take a Nebuchadnezzar – a bottle equivalent to twenty normal champagne bottles – and pour it into the top glass. As it trickles down, the 120 guests take their glasses, and the whole thing starts again.

Fizz has one of the best views on the ship, with one wall entirely made of toughened glass. The pyramids of coupes are being built one after the other by the transparent wall, with a backdrop of a clear sky and many stars. A couple of stacks are always ready at any one time as the clients mustn't be left with an empty glass. There is a delicate gold rope draped in front of them to avoid anyone getting too close and accidentally knocking the pile over, especially as the evening wears on and the guests have enjoyed more and more glasses of bubbles.

Trays of freshly shucked oysters on crushed ice with individual pipettes of shallot vinegar and tiny blinis topped with caviar are brought out as the latest pyramid is completed. A cheer goes up as the two barmen theatrically pop the cork from the enormous bottle, carefully directing it away from the towers of glass.

A woman screams. The two barmen look up, eyes wide, alarmed that the cork may have inadvertently hit someone.

But the screaming woman is pointing at the glass wall as her other hand flies to her throat.

'Someone fell!' she shrieks. 'I saw them!'

'Me too!' someone else shouts.

There is an uncomfortable murmur before a portly man with a vinegar stain on his starched white shirt yells: 'Call the captain! We need to stop the ship!'

55

Lola

New Year's Day 2022, 18:00
The Caribbean

It's stuffy in the bag and my legs are stiff. We considered various ways of getting me off the boat – in a case for a musical instrument, maybe – or whether I should stay on the ship, hiding in a lifeboat with enough supplies to last me until Rick could help me move down to the crew deck once we were sure it was deserted. In the end, being smuggled off in a simple holdall felt like the least risky option. That way Rick could keep me by his side all the time. no one else had to be involved, and I wouldn't die of thirst or starvation if there was a change of schedule.

The only flaw in this plan was the risk of being cooped up in some hotel room with Rick for longer than I would like. Fortunately, the turnaround between the passengers and crew being offloaded and the skeleton crew getting back on board and heading off to the lay-up mooring point would be very short; it was all to happen in a single day. It's expensive to keep a ship in port so they wouldn't want it to be there any longer than necessary. Within twenty-four hours we would be back out at sea with a skeleton crew, only to return once a month or so for bunkering.

Even so, there was no way I was staying in that bag all day, so I got Rick to book a cheap hotel room where we could hide out, telling him I have my period to avoid him trying anything on – he's old-fashioned and squeamish like that.

I simply can't face him pawing at me today. I peer out of the anonymous hotel room at the port below – we're on the fifteenth floor so there's no chance of me being seen from below and obviously we won't call room service.

As crew, we were the last to get off the ship, so it's much less busy down there than it was when we first docked. I don't know if it's my imagination, but I'm sure there are more police around than there would usually be.

I will have officially been reported missing by now. My key card and phone went overboard in an old handbag with the dummy, and I'm hoping the card, phone or even the whole bag might be found to give more weight to the theory I went in the water. It's a long shot, but maybe it will wash up somewhere. Even if not, they will see from my key card records that I didn't open any doors on board after New Year's Eve or officially get off the ship, and obviously the phone will be unreachable. Nobody has seen me since well before Anna went in the water. So there really is only one logical conclusion. Everything is in place.

Jesse will be in pieces. I imagine he will have searched for me frantically, slowly coming to terms with the fact that it was *me* that the woman in the bar thought she saw fall overboard. I think about how he will have felt – from me telling him I was leaving, to discovering I was missing, no doubt panicking as he failed to find me. And now that it will have been confirmed that I didn't get off the ship . . . I dread to think.

He will no doubt be blaming himself, after the argument that I deliberately started. He will probably think, like the rest of those on the ship, that I threw myself off. I hope he doesn't sink too far into despair though, because I still need him.

This is far from the end of the story.

PART EIGHT

56

Lola

Sixteen days later
16 January 2022, 20:00

'Wow. Fabulous. This looks amazing. Thank you,' I say.

Rick's done a great job with the food he's brought down to the deserted crew area for me today – it will last me a good few days, which is exactly what I wanted just in case I need to buy myself a bit of time. I have planned very carefully, so hopefully the extra food won't be necessary. He's brought an entire roast chicken, some potatoes (which are raw but that doesn't matter as there are plenty of kitchens I can use down here stocked with everything I need to cook them). I've also got a few apples, some yoghurts, cans of tuna and, best of all, the bottle of wine I'd asked for.

He shrugs. 'It was pretty easy to get hold of,' he says. 'Alice has been too busy shagging Stuart whenever she gets the chance to pay too much attention to who's helping themselves to a doggy bag.'

Lola smiles coyly. 'Stuart! Ha. Been there, done that, bought the well-hung T-shirt.'

Rick snorts. 'No shit! The dirty dog.' He pulls me against him and gropes my arse. 'Bet he wasn't as good as me,' he growls.

I squirm away. 'Of course not, my studmuffin.' In all honesty, I can't remember – he'd brought along some treats from his medicine cabinet so the whole evening is hazy. 'You'll stay down and eat with me today, will you?' I ask, using the 'little girl' voice that I know Rick, somewhat creepily, likes. 'It gets lonely down here on my own.'

'Yeah. It'll all be worth it in the end, won't it? Not that much longer now.'

'Can't wait,' I say. This is true. But not for the reasons he thinks.

I put the potatoes on to boil and carve the chicken onto plates. I open the wine and pour us a glass each.

'Tell you what,' I say, 'I'd really like some salad to go with this. I've hardly eaten anything green lately. Any chance you could nip up and get me some? The crew'll be eating about now, won't they? Can you just put some on a plate with some other stuff maybe and say you're going to eat it in your room?'

He rolls his eyes but then says: 'Anything for you, my sweet,' giving my bum a squeeze as he leaves the room.

Once the potatoes are boiled, I drain and mash them with

some butter, cream, and pepper, divide them in two and then crumble a few of my best sleeping pills into his half. I put the potato on the plates with the chicken, pour two more very large glasses of wine, and wait for Rick to come back.

After we've eaten I yawn theatrically and tell Rick I'd like to get an early night.

He yawns too. 'How about you let me stay the night? Just this once?' he pleads. 'I'm pretty tired too. No funny business, I promise. Please?'

Before we were on the lay-up, we were both in separate shared cabins and anyway, I always had to get back because otherwise Jesse would give me the third degree about where I'd been. I don't have that excuse now, but I don't want Rick staying the night, and not tonight of all nights. It simply can't happen.

I shake my head. 'We talked about this. I do want to be with you,' I say as I trail my hand across his chest, 'but it needs to be casual for the moment. I need my space. And I think you staying down here with me makes it more risky. You might be missed, and I mustn't be found. That would ruin everything. If anyone twigs that I'm not dead, there'll be no life insurance. Plus I'd probably be in prison for perverting the course of justice or something, and you possibly would too so . . .'

He nods. 'Understood.' He yawns, stretches and then squeezes my bum again. 'I'll see you in a couple of days. You've got loads of food now and, like you say, probably better I don't come down too much. Though it's hard to stay away,' he leers, pulling me against him.

I push him away, pretending I'm being playful but actually, I want him out of here ASAP. He needs to get back to his room before the drugs take their full effect – I don't want him passing out in a corridor somewhere. 'Maybe I've got something particularly special in mind for next time,' I tease, knowing full well that there won't be a next time. As long as everything goes to plan.

He groans. 'I can't wait. Let's not make it too long, hey? I'm going to go now before . . . well. I'll see you very soon.'

'Yep. Later,' I say.

I spend the evening in the crew gym and then reading just about anything I can find left behind in the crew rooms which I haven't already read. The Internet and TVs aren't working down here so I've had to make my own entertainment. I'm an avid reader – have been since I was a child. Not for the first time, it occurs to me that being hidden down here is not that dissimilar to my childhood – cut off from everything with no information coming in from the outside world. Unable to go anywhere and with only one person for company.

Tears come to my eyes. Even now, more than a decade on, I still miss my dad. Not my biological dad, obviously, but my dad who brought me up. Years of therapy might have *objectively* made me see that what he did was wrong, snatching me from the family I've still never quite been able to consider my 'real' family. That my unusual upbringing has, probably to an extremely large degree, contributed to my messed-up state of mind, my *promiscuity* as the therapists call it (from my point of view, I simply enjoy sex and don't see the need to equate it with love or a relationship), and the need to take a cocktail of prescription drugs to keep me stable.

But, as far as I'm concerned, my dad quite literally gave up his life for me. He wanted me so much that he turned his back on society and did everything he could to bring me up so that I would be safe. What kind of love could be greater than that?

Admittedly, his idea of keeping me safe was warped, of course I can see that now, but I strongly believe that he wasn't a bad man. He was doing what he felt was best for me.

When I was a child, I felt nothing but loved. It was only when I left him that things started going wrong. And I would never have left if it hadn't been for a certain someone coming into my life. Even though I was angry when I left that night, I know I would have calmed down. Dad and I could have carried on as we were and everything would have been OK. If it hadn't been for him.

It's payback time.

57

Lola

17 January 2022, 02:00
The Caribbean

I don't want to set off a fire alarm from the crew area as I'm pretty sure they'll eventually be able to tell from where the alarm was set off and I don't want anyone coming down here to check what's going on in the bowels of the ship where I am hiding.

Since we arrived on board for the lay-up I've subtly been asking Rick about who is sleeping where, pretending that I'm interested in hearing about the lap of luxury that everyone is living in, but actually I've been working out who is likely to be where so I can plan a route where I'm least likely to be seen. Every time Rick leaves, I've been marking where everyone is sleeping on the deck plans I got

Rick to bring me, and I've picked the most direct route which takes me past the fewest people. I've already had Rick make sure there are no cameras in service around his room or on the route he takes down to me (the most direct possible), as obviously we don't want nosy old Bill spotting anything unusual in his movements. As it turns out, hardly any cameras are in use at the moment anyway.

I put on non-descript jogging pants, a dark-coloured hoodie and a baseball cap so that, from the back at least, I could be just about anyone. It's 2 a.m., so everyone should hopefully be in bed – it's not like when we have passengers on board and things are open twenty-four hours.

I smash a fire alarm trigger on Deck 10 and duck into Rick's room with the access-all-areas key card I stole from his pocket a few days ago. He's always losing things, probably assumed he dropped it and would have no reason to have suspected me of stealing it anyway. I want to make sure no one is nearby when I do what I need to do, and to make doubly sure I have a clear run back.

As I hoped he would be, Rick is in bed, lying on his back and snoring. He's not used to taking the pills like I am so even the muster alarm is unlikely to wake him. I look around. It's a beautiful room, much better than he deserves. On the mezzanine I can see the free-standing bath with its own huge window so that passengers can watch the sea go by as they sit in the oiled and scented hot water. There's a private bar area which would usually be full of high-end spirits, but for the lay-up it's been stripped so there's only a solitary bottle of cheap vodka and a half-empty bottle of tonic. The living room area features two enormous leather sofas with thick, creamy cashmere throws and a coffee table between them with a gorgeous marble chess set. I pick up the white king – it is cold and heavy in my hand and satisfying to hold. I feel a stab of loneliness – Dad and I often used to play chess. I usually beat him. But I haven't played for years now.

The loneliness and self-pity I'm feeling quickly gives way to anger. I cross the room, take a pillow from the bed and squeeze it between my hands. It is huge, square, duck down and encased in Egyptian cotton. For the really important passengers, the case would be personally monogrammed. It's a totally different world up here to ours below deck. Rick is probably enjoying more luxury and privilege during this lay-up than he's ever had in the rest of his life, not that he deserves it in the slightest.

He gives a kind of snorting snore and stirs. I brace myself, ready, holding the pillow in front of me, but he settles back down to sleep.

In a gruesome echo of one of his favourite positions, I climb onto the bed and straddle him, fixing his wrists to the headboard using some cable ties I found in a maintenance cupboard of the crew area. I laugh quietly to myself. If he was awake – he'd be loving this. So far.

He doesn't stir. I'm about to press the pillow into his face, but I feel another flash of anger. Why should he have a peaceful death, not knowing what hit him or why? Dad didn't have that privilege when he died. He was probably full of angst – must have been, given that he was driven to take his life. I want Rick to feel fear. To regret what he did, even if only fleetingly. I want his last emotions to be panic and remorse, though perhaps the latter is too much to hope for. I'm not sure if someone like him is capable of remorse.

'Rick,' I say, still sitting astride him. No movement. Another snore. 'Rick!' I call louder. I'm not too worried about anyone hearing me – these top-end suites are sound-proofed to within an inch of their life and everyone will be at the muster station by now, probably being bollocked by Bill for being too slow to get there.

He still doesn't wake up, so I slap him across the face, hard. My palm stings, but it's immensely satisfying.

This time he makes an unintelligible noise and opens his eyes. He tries to move his hands but from the puzzled look in his eyes it seems like he can't work out why he can't. His eyes are unfocused.

'Lola?' he whispers thickly. I slap him again. 'What . . . why,' he mumbles.

I lean down, putting my face close to his. 'This is for what you did,' I hiss, 'all those years ago.'

For a second I think I see a flicker of something – reali-zation? recognition? – in his eyes, but then they defocus again. 'I never, I didn't . . .' he is mumbling, but it's difficult to make out.

But I don't know if he is listening. His eyes close and he falls back to sleep. His breathing is shallow. I'm not surprised. I gave him a lot of pills; I may not even have needed to take this final step, but I wanted to be sure.

I press the pillow into his face. There is a small movement of his hips and his head as he tries to buck me off and his wrists strain briefly against the ties. I stare out of the large window, pressing hard, as I wait for his breathing to stop. The moon is full and the stars are beautiful tonight. Dad and I often used to look at constellations together. I miss him so much.

A few minutes later, when I'm sure Rick is totally still, I take the pillow away from his face. His eyes are now open and ghoulish, and I hope that means that he properly woke up, that he had at least some idea of what was going on, even if he didn't have the strength to fight back.

I cut the cable ties with a penknife I brought with me exactly for this purpose, shove them in my pocket, duck out of the room and go to give Jesse the shock of his life.

58

Antonio

17 January 2022, 03:00
The Caribbean

I've only just discovered that Lola's still alive, but that's far from the only surprise she has in store. I can't quite believe what she's telling me.

'You killed him?' I repeat. 'You killed Rick? Just now – when the alarm went off?' I stare at her, so tiny in her baggy clothes, almost childlike. Looking like she couldn't hurt a fly.

'But why? How? What did he ever do to you?' I insist. My incredulity is suddenly replaced with rage. 'Did he hurt you? What happened? I don't understand. Oh God, Lola, I can't believe you killed him! You'll never get away with it! You'll go to prison and then . . . oh God.'

She has come back to me, but I can already see she's going to be taken away. Again. I can't bear it.

Her face darkens. 'You're not going to tell anyone what I did, Jesse, are you? Or that I'm here, on the ship? That I'm alive? You're the only person I trust. The only person in the world.'

I drop to my knees and hug her around her waist, my face wet with tears. 'No, of course I won't tell. But people have ways of finding these things out. They're bound to find something on Rick that links him to you and what you did. Oh God, I can't bear to lose you again! What are we going to do?'

I stand up and start to pace about. Lola reaches out and touches my arm. 'Jesse, don't you see? This is the beauty of it! *This* is why I pretended I'd gone overboard. There's no way someone who's dead can be accused of the murder of someone who was killed *after* they died, is there? It's genius, even if I say so myself.'

I stop pacing and look at her. For all my excellent A-levels and first-class honours degree, she's the one who's clever in the ways that really matter.

'I guess . . . I suppose they can't,' I agree. 'But I still don't understand why you killed him.'

'We can talk about that another time. All you need to know for now is that he deserved it, I promise. When I tell you why, you will agree, I'm sure.' She waves her hand dismissively. 'But Rick isn't important. Our future is what's important now. You don't want to be on the ships for the whole of your life, do you?'

'Well, no, but . . .'

'So listen. I've got rid of Rick, like I needed to. I'm already dead, as far as anyone knows, so there's no way anyone will ever catch up with me. You, dear brother, as my only family, are the beneficiary of my life insurance. Once I am declared dead, you inherit. Then, after a respectable interval, we meet up and split the proceeds. It's win-win for both of us. I trust you 100 per cent, Jesse. You're the only person I could do this with.'

My head is spinning. 'But if this was what you were planning, why couldn't you tell me? The last couple of weeks have been the worst of my life! Not only did I think you were dead, I thought I'd driven you to it! When we rowed! When . . . I hit you! I thought you'd killed yourself. Why would you put me through all that?'

I realize that I'm almost shouting and rein myself in. Tears start to flow again. 'I'm sorry, Lola. I didn't mean to get angry. But I don't understand why you would do this to me.'

'Because you've always looked after me, Jesse. I want to look after you now,' she says. 'I bought myself life insurance a few years back. I've been planning this for some time. Since I joined the ships, in fact. I got Rick to help me fake my own death, telling him he'd benefit. It made it easier for me to kill him too that way, because he trusted me. He thought we were working together. But with him dead, it's you that gets the money. Always has been – I lied to Rick about the insurance. But I needed him to help me first, and I needed to kill him too.'

What is she talking about? 'I still don't understand how . . .'

She rolls her eyes. 'I've got fake ID all ready to go too,' she tells me. 'It's easier to get than you'd imagine. I figured if my dad could get it all those years ago, then so could I. It's way easier now than it would have been in the past. I don't need to stay dead *forever*, as long as I go somewhere no one knows me. And the world is enormous, Jesse! I thought I might buy a beach bar on an obscure little Caribbean island. Then I can live the life Dad always wanted for me: happy, safe and in the sun. When we talked about fantasy futures together, that was always mine. It's like a tribute to him, for all the stuff he did for me.' She pauses. 'I didn't mean those things I said to you the other day, about needing to be away from you. It was only a cover story. I wanted to start a row to add weight to the theory which everyone else has. That I killed myself.'

'But I still don't see—'

'Jesse! Listen to me. You will go and hide out on an island somewhere, sunbathing, surfing, whatever you like. You will apparently be grieving for me – everyone knows we are close and no one is going to be surprised when you decide to leave the ships. You'll be quids in when my life insurance comes through. I've had it way more than two years, so even though my death will, I'm 99 per cent sure, be deemed suicide, the insurance is valid. It will pay out. I checked.'

'But . . .'

She holds up her hand. 'Please, Jesse, listen. I then turn up with my new ID, new name, a new hairstyle and maybe the bigger boobs I've fancied for a while. I'm trusting you here, like I said, that we'll split the proceeds of my life insurance. I'll spend my days and nights hanging out in my beach bar in the sun serving cocktails. You can come too if you like. Wouldn't that be nice?'

Her eyes are sparkling. I can feel myself weakening. 'It sounds amazing. But I still don't understand why you didn't tell me what you were planning.'

She laughs. 'Jesse! Come on! There's no way you'd have agreed to this, is there? No way in a million years. But to be honest, I thought you might have an inkling that I was up to something, even if you didn't know exactly what. When I left you my clothes. Wasn't that a clue for you? I thought maybe that way you'd know I was planning something? That I hadn't died? That I was still there for you?'

What? 'No, Lola, I didn't know anything! Faking your own death and then leaving a pile of clothes is hardly normal behaviour.' Fucking hell. I pause. 'So it was you that wrote me that note? I thought it was from someone who'd seen me hit you!'

'Yes it was me! I needed to get you out of your cabin so I could get myself in. I knew you'd wear some of my stuff if I left it for you, and that way, in case I'd missed anything – though I don't think I have – if any evidence is found of me around the boat where it shouldn't be, it can be put down to you wearing my old hoodies.' She pauses. 'Clever, huh?'

My head is spinning. 'No. Not clever at all. I thought you'd killed yourself. I thought I was going down for manslaughter. And I don't see . . . it all still seems pretty dangerous to me, Lola. It could all backfire on you, you know. On both of us.'

She waves her hand. 'Point proved – I was right not to involve you from the start. You'd have refused to help and tried to talk me out of it. But it's a great plan, and now that

I've done the first bits, there's nothing to be gained by you not getting involved. It's foolproof.'

Can any plan which involves faking your own death really be foolproof? 'But what happens now?' I ask.

'I'll go back to my hiding place in the crew area. No one ever comes down. Why would they when they're all living in the lap of luxury upstairs? All you need to do is bring me some food every other day or so. Rick was doing that but now obviously he can't.' She says this as dismissively as if he's just left to go somewhere else, rather than him being unable to bring her food because she killed him in cold blood. 'Then, when it's time to disembark, you take me off in a suitcase, same way I came in.'

'You came on in a suitcase?'

'Yes! Well, a holdall, it was a better shape to fit into and I've still got it. Why so surprised? Look at me' – she points from her head to her feet – 'I'm a dancer. I'm tiny. And flexible.'

'And then?'

'Like I said! We hide out for a bit. Then we "meet". Go somewhere else. And when the powers that be decide I'm officially dead, which given where I "fell" and the zero chance of survival shouldn't be too long, you get a big payout and we buy a bar. Or I buy a bar, and you go to Monaco or somewhere flash and hook up with supermodels. Whatever we each want. The world is our oyster!'

It seems mad. But the way she's said it, it also makes sense. 'And it's as easy as that?' I ask.

'Yes. It'll be amazing. You'll see. You worry too much, Jesse.'

59

Antonio

21 January 2022, 12:00
The Caribbean

I barely slept the last few nights and don't know what to do with myself now.

After Lola had told me what she'd done, she went back to the crew area. She says I can't come with her, that it's safer if she stays alone. I can go down every few days with food. It's the arrangement she'd had with Rick and apparently it worked out well. There's no point in taking more risks than necessary, it's vital that no one knows she is there. And after all, it's not like she can get up to anything untoward down there, all on her own. At least I know where she is, and that she's safe.

But I am still uneasy. She has killed someone. What if she

is found out? What if she goes to prison? There's no way she would cope, and I will have failed her, again.

I don't know what to do for the best.

I still don't understand why she killed Rick, but I have made a decision about that, at least. I'm going to make her tell me her reasons.

I love Lola with all my heart, but I never would have thought her capable of killing someone. I need to know why she did it.

I'm so confused. But she needs my help and I will do anything, anything, to keep her secret.

Meantime, I have to try to get on as normal. Doing my cleaning. Pretending I'm still grieving for Lola when I know she's alive and well and not even that far away from me. Thinking about her all day, every day. Worrying about whether she will get away with what she's doing. Stealing bits of food for her where I can. Sneaking into the mammoth fridges to fully stock up every three days when I know I'm going to be going down to see her. I live for those days.

'I need to know why you killed Rick,' I say, the next time I take her food down. We are sitting at the table eating rotisserie chicken at Lola's suggestion as it's easy to steal. 'It's keeping me awake at night, wondering, Lola. Please tell me.'

She sighs. 'OK. But you have to promise not to judge me. You haven't been through what I've been through, so you might not see it quite the way I do.'

'I won't judge,' I say, though I can't promise her that because, how can I know? It's hard to imagine a justifiable reason for killing someone, whatever they've done.

She looks down at her hands and states baldly, 'Rick killed my dad. That's why I killed him. He deserved it.'

'Lola, he killed himself,' I say gently. 'You know there was never any doubt about that.'

She lights a cigarette. Rick must have been bringing her those too. I see tears coming to her eyes. 'Yes, technically he did,' she agrees. 'But Rick was the reason he did it.'

I've no idea what she means, but know I have to tread gently. Is this a delusion? It wouldn't be the first time, though to my knowledge, that hasn't happened for a while now.

'What did Rick have to do with any of it?' I ask. The man who abducted Lola, who she calls her dad, has been dead for years – long before she even set foot on the ships. 'They'd never have even met, surely?'

'They never actually met, no. At least, I'm pretty sure they didn't. For a good while, when my memory started coming back, I thought Dad had killed Rick. Or killed Fred, as he called himself back then.'

'Fred?' I ask. I am seriously worried about her now. This makes no sense.

'Yes!' she snaps. 'Even very shortly after my accident I had flashback memories of being with a boy, but I didn't know who he was or where we'd met. Over time, during all that fucking therapy and hypnosis, more and more came back to me until I remembered his name, what he looked like and what he did to me. And as I gradually managed to put together what happened that evening in my mind, I realized that the night I left, Fred would have been far away well before Dad could have got to him. Dad couldn't have killed him, as I had at first assumed. So I started to look for him myself.'

'OK,' I say, trying not to sound patronizing or doubtful. 'But I still don't see what that has to do with Rick.'

'Fred is Rick,' she says. 'Was. Real name Frederick. Fred. Rick. Guess he decided to reinvent himself at some point. Back then he delivered something to our house. We chatted. I wanted a friend. I thought he was my friend. But I realize now that what he was doing was coming to the house and raping me. I didn't put up a fight as I didn't know any different. He was *literally* the only boy I'd ever met, and Dad had seen to it that I had no idea about sex, what was OK, and what wasn't. Dad was very selective about what I read and what films we watched – I knew nothing about sex at all. Had absolutely no idea. He chose to leave anything about that entirely out of my education.'

I don't know what to say. I wonder if she's been taking her medication properly but now clearly isn't the time to ask.

'My teenage hormones though, obviously they developed as normal, as they would in any healthy young girl,' she continues, 'and they really liked the way my body felt when Rick did what he did to me. How it felt when he touched me. But with the benefit of hindsight, everything we ever did was all on his terms. We had sex every which way he wanted and when I couldn't get out to see him, he'd get me to talk dirty to him. He gave me a phone especially for that reason. I was fifteen, a child, and an extremely unworldly child at that, due to being kept at home by Dad. I didn't know any better, didn't know that what he was doing to me was wrong. He wasn't just a rapist but a paedophile too. He deserved everything he got from me, and more.'

What? How can this Fred and Rick both be the same person?

'Lola, I still don't get—' I start, but she interrupts me.

'I talked a lot about what Fred did to me in the therapy that your mum and the social worker made me go to. I didn't want to, but he insisted it would help. Now that I look back on it, I wonder if the therapist was getting off on it too, my descriptions of what Fred liked me to do to him on the three or four times we met. The stuff he used to like me to talk about on the phone while I basically wanked for him. I thought I was doing it for me but I wasn't, it was all for him. I was a child – I didn't know what I was doing.'

She wipes her eyes and starts pacing the room, clearly becoming more agitated. 'I went out into the garden that night to meet him because he wanted me to suck his cock.' she shouts. 'Then Dad found out and I ran away, trying to find Fred. Rick. So I can only assume, as did the police, that Dad knew it would come out that he had abducted me and I would be taken away from him. He would go to prison. Rather than face all that, he killed himself, and thus I am the total fuck up you have before you today. If Rick had never turned up and asked me to do that stuff with him, which he should never have done, none of this would have happened. I wouldn't have run away and Dad wouldn't have died. It's not rocket science.'

'But . . . so how did you . . . how did you end up in the same place as Rick? On this ship?' I ask. 'Isn't that a . . . bit of a coincidence?' I still can't quite believe that they can be the same person. Surely Lola's got this wrong?

'Jesse, for fuck's sake, of course it's not a coincidence!' she screams. Tears are streaming down her face. 'I followed

301

him here. It only took a bit of digging to find him on social media once I'd remembered his name and learned about the Internet, and that was that. All the stuff I told you years back about wanting to go travelling, well, it was true to a degree, but the main reason for joining the ships was that I'd found out where he was working by then and wanted to get my revenge.'

'But why didn't you tell me?' I ask. 'And how did he not recognize you?'

'Look at me, Jesse!' she yells. 'I'm a grown woman, not the innocent child I was when he knew me. I've lost at least two stone since I ran away, cut my hair, dyed it several times, had this, this and this' – she points at her boobs, nose and teeth – 'done, plus we only actually ever met a few times! Usually in the dark, and pretty much all we ever did was shag. He didn't give a shit about me, there's no way he'd have recognized me or possibly even remembered me, for all I know. It made me feel sick to be close to him and to let him touch me before I killed him, but it was nothing he hadn't done before and it's not like I'm exactly fussy about who I go with anyway thanks to how he used me back then, it's just sex after all, and it was worth it as a means to an end . . .'

She is sobbing so hard now I can barely hear what she's saying. I give her a hug. She is trembling. 'But I still don't understand why you didn't ask me to help you?' I say softly. 'Or why you went through the whole thing of—'

She pushes me away. 'Aren't you listening? I already told you why! There's no way you'd have gone along with it. I wanted to do it so that I could get rid of him without casting suspicion on myself. If I am in theory dead, that means I can't be a suspect! Don't you see? It's perfect. And you wouldn't have helped me kill him, I knew that. You'd have talked me out of it. But this way we can have it all. And seeing how weird you're being about it even now it's done and you can't do anything about it, I can see I was right not to tell you from the start.'

She is screaming and crying now and part of me wants to leave her to it because I still can't believe she killed someone, and it feels like she is angry at me because she knows I wouldn't have done it for her. But then I think about what he put her through, how he used her all those years ago and all my anger is directed towards him instead.

How dare he hurt her like that! How fucking dare he! She was right to kill him.

'It's OK, Lola,' I soothe. 'It's all going to be OK. I'm going to help you.'

PART NINE

60

Alice

28 January 2022, 12:00
The Caribbean

Someone is stealing food from the fridge. When the guests are on board, the food stores are very carefully regulated and detailed inventories kept – it's the only way you can operate when you have to prepare several thousand meals a day for around six thousand guests, and that's before you're even thinking about the crew.

But with so few of us here right now, while I need to make sure there are enough supplies to keep us going until the next bunkering, it's not necessary to be so exact about it all. However, I like to think that I keep everyone pretty well-fed on the limited budget available, and there should be no reason for anyone to go hungry. There are 24-hour snack stations for the crew so they can help themselves to things like fruit and crisps. There's no reason for people to be in my fridges and store cupboards, but it seems that someone has been. Whereas many of the kitchens are staffed almost 24/7 during a cruise, to provide a constant flow of delicious offerings for our gluttonous clients, on a lay-up, crew meals are served at set times only. This means there are large tranches of the day when the kitchens are deserted.

Some of the things that have disappeared are a bit strange, not the kind of thing someone would steal just because they've got midnight munchies. Entire roast chickens have gone missing several times. Bags of uncooked potatoes. Enormous tubs of mayonnaise. Butter and cream. It's a pain for me as I have meal plans and suddenly I have to think of something else if I don't have enough ingredients, though I am used to being flexible. But the bigger worry is that whoever has been taking things clearly doesn't know how to operate the fridge door properly and keeps leaving it so that it swings open, which could be disastrous. The last thing we want on board is food which isn't properly stored and a bout of food poisoning. I know this better than anyone, and so I'm particularly paranoid about it.

I asked Bill if I could have a look at the CCTV to see what was happening but it's not running everywhere because they're in the process of installing a new system. But he said he could switch on some relevant cameras and keep an eye. Meantime I have stuck a passive-aggressive note on the fridge door saying *Please do not take food without permission* and another which says *Please keep the door closed at all times on pain of death*. I could go to Leo but I don't really want to get anyone in trouble unnecessarily. I just want them to stop taking my stuff.

61

Antonio

5 February 2022, 12:00
The Caribbean

Doctor Stuart has asked me to come and see him. His is far and away the nicest doctor's surgery I've ever been in.

Both the chairs we are sitting in are Eames, or at least, Eames-style – I wouldn't know the difference. Seeing a doctor on board is a very different experience to seeing a doctor on the NHS. Passengers pay for the privilege, emergency or not, so I guess Heracles provides luxe surroundings to help justify the no doubt huge charges passengers pay for their consultations. Behind Stuart there is a view of the sea through a huge window and on the walls, several prints of Damien Hirst's diamond-encrusted skull and a poster depicting his famous *Pharmacy* installation, as well as various similarly themed posters which look as though they're by the same artist.

I had assumed Stuart simply wanted to ask me how I was feeling after my last visit to his surgery, and had prepared answers accordingly, so I wouldn't panic and say something I shouldn't. I was planning to say I was feeling much better now, I'd been doing some meditation and practising mindfulness, coming to terms with life without Lola and that there wasn't anything I needed to talk to anyone about.

But as it turns out, that isn't what he wants. 'I had the DNA test results back from the lab,' he says.

'OK,' I say. What is he telling me this for? I'd pretty much forgotten the tests had even happened. 'And was there anything conclusive?'

He looks down at a sheaf of papers on his desk. 'Not exactly conclusive, no. But there was something surprising, and I wanted to talk to you about it before I go to Leo.' He pauses. 'Or to the police.'

My heart starts beating faster as in a flash I realize what it is he's going to say. 'Oh yes?' I ask, my voice a little higher than it would usually be.

'Yes. I don't know the ins and outs of who greased whose palm, but Nico managed to acquire the results from the search of Rick's room for me to send off with the DNA samples which were taken here to see if any kind of match could be found. I don't think Nico felt the police were sufficiently bothered about the case.'

He pauses. 'There were hairs found in Rick's room which, when compared against the samples taken from the crew, don't seem to belong to anyone on board. Now,

311

of course there are some possibilities – that the room hasn't been cleaned to Heracles' scrupulously high standards and that they were left over from a previous guest, or someone who has left since the lay-up began – not that there have been many.'

'OK,' I prompt. My palms are sweating and I surreptitiously wipe them on my trousers.

'But what's even more surprising about it,' he continues, 'is that while the DNA is not a match for you, it *is* a match for someone who would appear to be a close relative of yours. A cousin, maybe. Or a sibling.'

He narrows his eyes at me. 'Any idea how that might have happened?' he asks.

'No!' I yelp. 'It must be a mistake. It's not possible. Lola is the only family I had left and now she's dead.' My voice catches in my throat at the mere idea of her lifeless body, even though I know she's alive. 'I don't know where my dad is – he left when I was a child. Mum died a few years ago – she had cancer,' I add pointlessly. 'And that's it. There's no other close family anymore.'

What is he intimating? That he knows Lola was in that room? That he knows she's alive? That he knows she killed Rick? But how could he know? *Can* he know? Shit, shit, shit.

Stuart sits back in his chair. 'Lab mistakes and mix-ups are possible, but they don't happen often. I will get it checked again, of course, but in the meantime if there's anything you want to tell me, now is the time.'

My heart is beating so hard I'm surprised he can't hear it. I shake my head. 'Nothing to tell.' I need to sort this. He knows something. Or at least suspects. He does, I'm sure of it. I need to do something. Need to help Lola.

'Actually, there is something,' I gabble, remembering the clothes Lola left for me, and her reasons for it. Wow. She really was planning ahead – thinking of everything.

I take a deep breath. 'I've got some of Lola's clothes. Jumpers. A few scarves. Sometimes when I miss her, I wear them. It makes me feel like she's still close. They smell of her.'

Tears start to fall – I'm terrified and I don't know what to do – but Stuart thankfully interprets my reaction as grief. His expression changes to one of sympathy and he pushes a box of tissues towards me. I take one and blow my nose.

'That's entirely understandable,' he says. 'But it doesn't explain why you were in Rick's room.'

He doesn't believe me. I can tell. He knows Lola is alive. He suspects that she killed Rick. He's waiting for me to tell him. It's all going to be over. 'He's a mate,' I mutter hoarsely. 'I wanted to talk. About Lola.'

Stuart nods again, but I can see in his expression that he knows I'm lying. Maybe he thinks I swing both ways as Rick was rumoured to do and that we were lovers. But more likely, he knows that I'm covering up for Lola. What the fuck are we going to do? However I've fudged it just now, what it boils down to is that he's got evidence that someone related to me not only killed Rick, but, in all likelihood, must be on this ship. He doesn't believe my excuse about the clothes, I can tell. It's only a matter of time until Lola gets found out, I know it is. I think Stuart already knows. I rub my forehead. Shit, shit, shit.

313

'Antonio, I hope you don't mind me saying this,' Stuart continues, 'but while initially I thought you were doing OK, I don't think you're coping with Lola's . . . disappearance very well. Not only from our conversation today, but from having seen you around the ship over the last couple of weeks – you seem to be finding things increasingly difficult. I'd like you to consider taking some anti-anxiety medication. I think it may help you. You don't have to take them for long, they're not addictive and, for most people, don't have side effects.'

He is still talking but I'm not listening, my mind whirring. What is he going to do now? Will he show the DNA results to Leo? Then the police? What will they do? Will they question me again? Can they find out that Lola is alive now that they have her DNA? Will they be able to tell it didn't come from a jumper and that it's more recent? Did Lola factor that into her plans? This is all going wrong. She's going to get caught and go to prison and she won't cope and she will kill herself because I have let her down again just like before and then I will surely die too.

'OK,' I squeak, not sure exactly what I've agreed to because I'm not listening.

'Good. I'll give you some pills to take, which will hopefully make you feel calmer and sleep better, and then a script for some more for when you're back on land.'

Oh God. At this rate, as soon as I'm back on land, I'm going to prison. As is Lola. Unless I'm taken away before then and she's left to starve to death in the crew area of the ship or has to give herself up because . . . oh God oh God oh God.

As he turns round to get the pills from his cupboard, in the throes of panic I pick up a bronze statuette of an elephant and smash him over the head with it. Then I grab the form he's holding, my DNA results, along with the pile of papers on the desk, which I assume are the other results.

But I can't leave him here! What if someone comes in and finds him? I haven't been to the medical centre much since I joined the ship, so I don't know my way around. I run out of the consulting room to see what else I can find – a waiting room, several other consulting rooms, loads of locked cupboards. I shove some of the pills from the medicine cupboard he'd opened into my pockets – I don't know what they are but they might come in handy, you never know, and carry on looking.

Using my access-all-areas key which I have for the cleaning, I open an unmarked door at the end of the corridor. And there is exactly what I need; no one will come in here.

The mortuary. I go back to the consulting room and putting my hands under Stuart's armpits, I pull him along the corridor and manage to manhandle him into one of the mortuary drawers.

I'm too agitated to tell if he's even dead. I think he is, but I'm not sure. At least he's out of the way. I need to find Lola and sort this out.

Oh God. She's going to be livid. This was not part of her plan. But I did this for her. She'll understand that. Won't she?

62

Lola

5 February 2022, 12:30
The Caribbean

'You did what?' I cry.

Jesse is shaking and snivelling and really pissing me off. 'I know, Lola, I'm sorry, I panicked. When he said that there was DNA of a relative of mine, I was so scared he knew you were here, still alive, and that you killed Rick and . . .'

'For God's sake!' I shout. 'I left you the jumpers for that very reason as a precaution – I knew the police would be involved at some point. I didn't expect all this stupid crew DNA testing though! And it sounds like Stuart was more worried about your mental health than about whether I might have come back from the dead! And quite rightly so, given what you've done! What the fuck did you have to brain him for?'

'I know – I'm sorry . . .'

'And now we've got a dead body on our hands! God, Jesse, you've completely fucked this up. Can you see why I didn't tell you what I was doing from the outset? I'm starting to regret involving you. I should have found someone I could rely on properly.' I am utterly fuming. I can barely see straight, I'm so angry. This was definitely not part of my plan. It was all perfectly arranged and now Jesse's gone and messed it all up.

He grabs my hand, but I snatch it away. 'Please Lola, don't be like that. I can fix it. I know I can. He might not even be dead . . .'

What? 'Don't you see?' I interrupt. 'If he's not dead that's even worse. Then you'd have to come up with an explanation for why you battered him over the head for no reason!'

'I can . . . I can say . . .' he stutters.

'Stop it, Jesse, I need to think,' I snap. 'You need to go back and check if he's dead. Right now. If he's not, you need to finish him off. That's the only way out of this. And then either way, you need to get rid of the body. This risks messing up everything – you do realize that, don't you?'

'I know,' he mutters. I see tears coming to his eyes. He needs to hold it together. I can't have him spoiling everything, not when I've come this far. 'Oh God, Lola, I don't think I can do it,' he whines. 'Can you come with me? I've never seen a dead body before.'

'Stop being so pathetic!' I yell, confident in the knowledge that there are several decks between us and anyone else. 'Be a man about it for once in your life. Get up there before he wakes up, if he's going to, or before someone goes to try

317

and find him for some of his pills or help with their stupid injuries. You need to do this NOW. I can't come, I can't be seen. You know that. Your mess, you sort it out.'

Suddenly it comes to me what we can do. I click my fingers. 'I know. You're a cleaner now. Take one of the cleaning trollies. Those are massive. Load him into that.'

'And then what? Where will I take him? Throw him overboard?'

Fucking hell, this is such a nightmare. 'No. That's a terrible idea. From what you say, it will be obvious he's been killed if his body's found as you've helpfully smashed his skull in,' I say sarcastically. 'If we do that, he might wash up somewhere. The last thing we want is more police sniffing around.'

It's clearly going to be down to me to sort this out as usual – I can't rely on Jesse to come up with any sort of sensible plan. Then I have an idea. It's gruesome, but it's the best I can think of at short notice. 'Put him in the macerator,' I say.

Jesse's mouth falls open. 'Seriously?'

'Yes! He's dead – or he will be by the time he goes in! What difference does it make? He's not going to care by then, is he?' Fuck's sake. I've spent literally years planning this and Jesse goes and ruins it just like that with his flailing and panicking.

He bites his lip and looks at the floor.

'I don't think I can,' he says, so quietly I can barely hear him.

I nod tersely. 'Right. So you'd prefer to go to prison, would you? And leave me to die of starvation down here on my own or have to admit to faking my own death? Do you want me to rot in jail? All because you fucked up my careful plans? Thanks a lot, Jesse. I thought I could rely on you. Clearly I was wrong.'

As I suspected it would, a wave of panic crosses his face. 'No. There's no way you're going to prison on my account, Lola. I'm sorry. I'm sorry I got us into this mess.'

I force my face into a more sympathetic expression and see him soften. 'That's OK. You were just worrying about me, I know that. It's not the end of the world, it can be sorted. But try to think before you act, next time.' I pause. 'What's done is done. I know it's not nice, but you need to do what I say. Then before anyone notices Stuart's missing, you can start spreading a rumour that he'd said he'd had enough of being stuck on ship and was going to go for a swim, forbidden or not. Tell Mara – that way it'll be sure to get around quickly.'

He nods. 'OK.' There is a pause. 'But what if he's not dead?'

I sigh. Fuck's sake. Do I really have to spoon-feed him everything?

'Then you'll simply have to hit him again until he is.'

63

Antonio

5 February 2022, 13:00
The Caribbean

I pull on latex gloves, grab a trolley from the storeroom and head back to the medical centre. My legs are wobbly and my stomach is churning.

I've never seen Lola so cold and it scared me. But she is right, I have messed up badly. It was stupid to hit Stuart. All he said was that the hair found was from a relative of mine – it didn't mean it was Lola! It could have been from some half-brother I never knew I had or something – you hear stories like that all the time. I did the wrong thing, and I owe it to Lola to sort this out. I am not going to let her down again.

On the long walk down the corridor I pray that Stuart is already dead. I don't want to have to hit him again. Then I feel tears rising because I have either become someone who is wishing an innocent man dead, or someone who is planning to commit a murder. Either is awful, and makes me not the kind of person I'd ever have thought I'd be. A killer.

For a second, I wonder if I am looking at this the wrong way. Is my loyalty in the wrong place? Am I going to kill someone just because Lola told me to? Is it really OK to take someone's life to protect her? Should I 'fess up, tell Leo that Lola's alive, tell him what she did and that I killed Stuart because of her? In the long run, would that be better? For both of us? Have we got any chance at all of getting away with what we're doing? What we've done?

I take a deep breath and push the thoughts away. No. I need to stick to Lola's plan. She didn't kill Stuart – I did. She didn't make me do it – I panicked and did it myself. I messed up her plan. And whether I like it or not, I am as guilty as her now. If I confess, we both go to prison, for murder and probably other things as well, perverting the course of justice or something like that. If I get on with things and do as she has asked, 'man up' or whatever it was she said, everything will turn out OK.

Won't it?

Taking a deep breath, I use my key card to open the surgery door. 'Hello?' I call gingerly, listening intently in case I can hear Stuart banging or shouting from inside the mortuary drawer, but thankfully, all is quiet. Would he suffocate in one of those drawers? Surely not so quickly. Are they refrigerated when the mortuary is, officially, not in use? I've got no idea. But even if they are, I doubt being inside one would kill someone in such a short amount of time. Would it?

Taking the trolley with me so I don't have to drag the body any further than necessary, I pick up the elephant statue I hit Stuart with before in case I need it again and head to the mortuary. Inside, it is still quiet as the grave, I think to myself, inappropriately, and stifle a nervous laugh. What is wrong with me? A man is dead, or I am about to kill him. This is hardly a time for levity.

I lift the elephant high above my head and in one quick movement, open the drawer.

It's empty.

64

Alice

5 February 2022, 13:30
The Caribbean

So I found out who is stealing the food using the footage from Bill's cameras – Antonio. It's so strange. He's always seemed so straight and normal – until recently.

I think he must blame himself for Lola's suicide, after the row they had and him hitting her like that. And while she was always great fun to spend time with, there was definitely a dark side to her, a more troubled side. She was never the most stable of people, so I wonder if their row was the final straw for her.

Poor Lola. I really miss her. But she is gone, and I can't do anything about that, sadly. However, what I can do is prevent the crew in my culinary care getting food poisoning.

I doubt Antonio knows how serious leaving a fridge door open can be. My mind rushes back to that awful time when I managed to pass the buck over a bout of food poisoning in one of my restaurants by blaming a dodgy supplier when it was actually a faulty fridge which I should have been on top of. I got away with it, but it was a close-run thing and, a large part of the reason why I felt I needed to take a break.

None of us is perfect. But I like to think I learn from my mistakes, at least, and I'm not going to let it happen again.

65

Antonio

5 February 2022, 13:30
The Caribbean

My head swims and for a couple of seconds my vision blurs
and I think I might pass out. I take a deep breath and swallow
down the rising bile. Where is he? I wasn't gone long – how
did he get out? I look at the huge, stainless-steel body-sized
drawers – surely you can't open them from the inside? Is
there a safety latch in there in case someone is put in by
accident and they're not dead after all?

The room seems to tilt and I put a hand out to steady
myself. I take another deep breath, counting like I was taught
to years back as a way of dealing with my catastrophizing
when I used to regularly have panic attacks. In, one two three.
Out, one two three. In one two three. Out, one two three.

Better. Calm down, I tell myself, and force myself to look at the drawer again. There's no way he could have opened that himself from the inside. Momentarily I feel better but then the thought strikes me like a thunderbolt that if he didn't let himself out, someone else must have helped him out. Someone must have found him. Heard him shouting, maybe. And that is SO much worse.

I let out a cry of anguish as I picture Stuart limping along the corridor, clutching his head and aided by his rescuer as he tells them what I did. Who rescued him? Where are they going? Probably to Leo, who will call the police and then they'll come and arrest me and they'll know that I must be hiding something otherwise I wouldn't have hit Stuart and they'll work out that Lola must be alive and they'll search the ship for her and they'll find her and she'll go to prison too and she will kill herself in prison because she could never cope with something like that and I will have let her down again and it will all be my fault and I would want to die too.

I hit the stainless-steel wall in frustration and then something occurs to me. I pull open the other drawers in a frenzy and – oh God – there he is. I actually laugh out loud. I just got the wrong drawer.

A wave of shame washes over me because I am laughing again and quite clearly a man is dead. Stuart's eyes are open and glassy. I swallow down another wave of nausea. I brush my hand over his face to close his eyelids like I've seen them do in films, reassuring myself that I am already wearing gloves but then I think about what I've got to do next and realize that it's not going to matter whether I'm wearing gloves or not. No one is going to be able to take fingerprints

326

or any other evidence from Stuart once he's been through where I'm going to put him. This time vomit actually rises into my mouth but I swallow it back – I cannot throw up in here. Not now.

I need to be quick. I pull Stuart out of the drawer and he falls awkwardly onto the ground. He is not a large man but he seems to weigh a ton. The phrase 'dead weight' springs into my mind and I see now what it means.

I push the thought away. This is not the time to be thinking about stuff like that, for fuck's sake. Concentrate. I take the sheets out of the base of the trolley – I only put a couple in before I brought it out from the store cupboard – and drag Stuart's torso in. I then gather up his arms and legs, bending and twisting him until he's all in. It's all so undignified. Poor Stuart. He doesn't deserve any of this. And yet, I did this to him. It's my fault.

The realization hits me once again that I have murdered this man and I wonder whether I should give myself up. I'm not sure I can live with this. I can go to Leo now, tell him that Stuart and I had a fight, maybe because he said something bad about Lola, maybe that he'd had sex with her (he probably has, I don't know) and then treated her badly or something and that I accidentally killed him during our fight. That kind of thing happens, doesn't it? Maybe I could confess to killing Stuart without needing to involve Lola at all. It would be easy enough to give myself a few fake injuries here and now. I'm not afraid of pain.

No one would need to know that Lola is still alive – I can stick to the story I told Stuart about me wearing her clothes. That would work, wouldn't it?

I look down at Stuart, twisted up in the bottom of the trolley. Yes, giving myself up now would be the better option, I decide. I can argue diminished responsibility, grieving for Lola. She can still live her life, albeit without the life insurance, which I don't imagine I'd manage to share with her while I'm in prison. Can prisoners even inherit money? I have no idea. I doubt it.

I wouldn't get off scot-free, I know that. But a sentence for manslaughter would be much less than for murder, surely? I could be out in a few years. It wouldn't be so bad.

But then I realize I can't do that. I can't spend years without her with no idea what Lola's doing. She wouldn't manage without me – she needs me there to prop her up when she falls down, to help her through her latest crisis. There have been many before, there are no doubt still many to come. Who would help her get through next time she's in despair?

I shake myself mentally. Giving myself up is a stupid idea, even if I could do it without dropping Lola in the shit too. Quite apart from anything else, in the short term Lola needs someone to bring her food while she hides out on the ship. Without me she would starve, or have to reveal that she's faked her own death, with all the repercussions that would have. Either scenario is unthinkable.

I make sure Stuart's hands and feet are inside the trolley, cover him with sheets and a pile of towels, and wheel him out into the corridor.

66

Alice

5 February 2022, 13:40
The Caribbean

I'm on my way to find Antonio to talk to him about the food when I bump into him near the medical centre.

'Antonio, I was looking for you. Can I have a word?'

He gives me a startled look as if I've already accused him of something. I wonder, not for the first time, if he suspects that Lola told me he hit her.

'Um, can it wait? I'm a bit busy right now. Can I come and see you when I've finished my rounds?'

He indicates the cleaning trolley he's pushing.

Why is he being so shifty and weird? 'Won't take long,' I say, because how urgent can cleaning an almost-empty ship be? I'd rather get this out the way. 'Look, I don't know how to say this so I'll just come out with it: I know you've been stealing food and I'd like you to stop.'

He looks at me. He's very pale and his eyes are red. I wonder if he's been crying. 'Stealing food?' he repeats.

'Yes. Don't try to deny it – I know it was you – I saw you on CCTV. It's not a biggie in the scheme of things but it's a hassle for me for many reasons if the stocks aren't quite what I expect.'

He nods, but he's fidgeting and looking over my shoulder and I get the impression he's not really listening.

'I think I keep you all pretty well fed and as you know, there are always snack stations but if you need more, that's OK, I don't want anyone to go hungry, but please ask next time. Don't just take. Quite apart from the stock-taking, there are health and safety reasons why I can't have unauthorized people going in the stores, especially as you didn't always close the door properly. My reputation is at stake here,' I add stiffly. I'm not going to go into the details of what happened before. 'I can't risk a shipful of passengers getting ill because someone had midnight munchies and left the fridge door open.'

Antonio shifts awkwardly and nods. 'Got it. Sorry.' He's still not looking at me.

'In all honesty, I find it hard to understand why you're taking some of the things you've been taking,' I add. He looks so stressed. I wonder if he's on the verge of a breakdown. Lola going missing has obviously hit him hard.

And even though I know he pissed Lola off, I'm now wondering if it was actually true that he hit her. Would he do that? Apart from that one day, they seemed about as close as any siblings I've ever met. But then again, why would she make it up? I push the thought away. My loyalty here should be with poor, dead Lola, not with possibly-violent-but-certainly-overprotective Antonio.

'Sometimes I prefer to eat away from everyone else,' he says hoarsely. 'What with everything that's happened. I'm not up to making small talk.'

I see a tear roll down his cheek. I can't have upset him that much, can I? He really does seem on edge. 'That's OK,' I say. 'I know you're going through a lot. But ask next time, OK?'

He nods.

'Don't worry,' I add. I suddenly feel sorry for him. Whatever he did or didn't do, his sister and, as I understand it, last remaining living relative is dead, and he is clearly suffering now. 'Leo doesn't need to know. I can sort the stock sheets. No real harm done.' I notice he is shaking. 'Antonio, maybe you should see if Stuart can sort you out with something if you're finding it hard to cope? It's none of my business, but I know that Lola would want you to look after yourself.'

He nods and wipes away a tear. 'Thanks,' he says. 'I appreciate your concern. I won't take any more of your food. But I have to get on now.'

67

Antonio

5 February 2022, 14:00
The Caribbean

I've never seen the macerator before. I don't know anything about it, I don't know how it works and until today, I didn't even know that it existed. I'd never thought about what happens to the food waste on the ship. Lola told me where it was – she's had a lot of time on her hands lately and has apparently been spending some of it looking at plans of the ship.

The macerator is a huge, terrifying-looking stainless-steel machine with a hopper-style thing on top. The room it's in, which is on an even lower deck than the crew area, is cavernous and full of metal pipes. It's totally silent bar the squeak of the trolley as I push it across the floor, and my footsteps, the sound of which seems to ricochet around the room as if I was wearing tap shoes rather than trainers.

I step onto the metal platform with the trolley at ground level and press a button. There is a low rumble as the machine fires up which echoes round the room. I press another, smaller button with an 'up' arrow on and the platform slowly starts to rise. It judders to a stop at the top when the floor is at the same level as the top of the hopper. I roll Stuart out of the trolley and onto the platform. Moving the trolley out of the way, I give Stuart a shove and he topples into the machine. There is a grinding sound and this time I can't keep the vomit down as Stuart is turned into fish food which will be spat out into the ocean. I throw the DNA results I snatched from his surgery in with him, though I know it's nothing but a short stopgap – I'm sure the results must be somewhere on his computer too. I'm not a religious man, but I can't help but pray silently for forgiveness as I wipe my mouth with my sleeve, swipe my tears away and press the down arrow to get me back to ground level.

I wait at the bottom for a couple of minutes before switching off the machine to make sure it's finished whatever it needed to do. I try not to think about what I've just done, but it's impossible. It's hard to believe I will ever feel normal again. Surely the image of Stuart in the mortuary drawer will be there every time I close my eyes. And I'm convinced I'm never going to be able to forget the sound of his bones crunching in this awful machine.

When I was in Stuart's surgery, I felt that doing this was worth it to make it up to Lola. Make amends for not protecting her when she was a child. Helping her to have

333

the life she's always wanted, the life she deserves. But right this minute, I'm not so sure. She will be expecting me to go and see her, to confirm that I've done what she asked.

But I don't want to see her right now so I go back to my suite instead. I think it's the first time I've ever felt so negatively about her. I strip off my clothes, run a bath as hot as I can stand and stay in it until the water has almost turned cold, drinking neat vodka from a bottle and trying to blot what I've done from my mind.

Right now, I'm not sure I'm doing the right thing.

68

Alice

7 February 2022, 12:00
The Caribbean

I can't find Stuart, and I'm worried.

He and I have fallen into a routine of staying together most nights now. With Lola and Rick both gone, who were really my only friends on board, it gets pretty lonely. So when I don't see or hear from Stuart for two nights in a row, at first I wonder if I've done something to upset him and he's ignoring me, but that doesn't seem like something he'd do. I try texting, and go to his surgery, which is all closed up, but I can't find him anywhere. I ask around. No one seems to have seen him lately.

Even though we're pretty casual, I have started to feel quite fond of him and not knowing where he is makes me uneasy, especially with everything else that has been going on. I've already lost Lola and Rick. The thought of losing yet another of my friends is untenable. The ship is big, admittedly, but there aren't many of us here and normally you'd see people around even if you weren't specifically looking for them.

'No, luvvie,' Mara says. 'I haven't seen him. But I heard a few people saying that he was talking about going swimming.'

The pools aren't in use at the moment so swimming can only mean one thing – in the ocean – and it's strictly forbidden. It doesn't sound like something Stuart would do. Would he?

'Swimming?' I repeat. 'Are you sure?'

Unless he meant it as some terrible, dark euphemism. But he seemed fine last time I saw him. Still a little cagey about his past, yes, but no more so than usual. Certainly not on the verge of killing himself.

But then again, I didn't think Lola was either, so who am I to judge?

Mara shrugs. 'I'm not sure. I'm just repeating what I heard.'

'As usual,' I mutter to myself. Mara is the biggest gossip on board.

I go to find Bill, who initially sighs and huffs about me imposing on his time but eventually fiddles with his computer and confirms that Stuart's room key card hasn't been used for a couple of days.

I feel sick. That's not right. 'I'm worried, Bill,' I say. 'He and I, we . . .' I don't want to spell it out, but he clearly gets the gist and rolls his eyes. He presses a button on his desk.

'Doctor Stuart Cummins, please report to the safety office immediately. Repeat, Doctor Stuart Cummins, please report to the safety office immediately.'

'That tannoy goes out all over the ship,' Bill explains, somewhat redundantly. 'That should flush him out.'

'Thanks, Bill. Hope so,' I say. But I've got a bad feeling about this. I'm already pretty sure it won't.

When it becomes clear that Stuart isn't going to turn up after the tannoy, Bill and I go to see Leo. He is frowning over some spreadsheets and clearly not happy to be interrupted.

'What do you mean, missing?' he snaps. 'Fuck's sake. Why can't people just manage themselves and their own business and leave me alone for five minutes? It's a big ship – he's no doubt around somewhere. I'm sure he'll turn up.'

Bill sighs. 'I hope so. A couple of people have been asking for him for various ailments and – you're not going to like this, but there's a rumour going round that he'd had enough of being stuck on board and said he was going to go swimming.'

'Swimming?' Leo splutters. 'I can't see Stuart doing that. He's a sensible chap, isn't he? He's no doubt aware of the dangers and, as far as I know, he tends to follow the rules. Who's saying he said that?'

Bill shrugs. 'Dunno where it came from originally – seems to be common knowledge.'

'Hmm. In my experience, "common knowledge" on board doesn't necessarily mean something is true by any stretch,' Leo says.

I feel a flash of anger; Leo doesn't seem to be taking this very seriously.

'I've been asking around and no one seems to have seen him for the last few days,' I add in a measured tone, as I know Leo doesn't take well to anyone ranting at him. 'And Bill says his room door hasn't been opened for two days, according to the log.'

'As for the surgery, cleaners have been in and out as it's cleaned twice a day but again, it hasn't been opened with his own key card recently either,' Bill adds. 'I tried putting out a tannoy, but no joy.' He pauses. 'With your permission, I'd like to do a muster call, which, as you know, is the best way to be sure whether he's here or not on a ship of this size.'

Leo nods, his expression becoming more serious. About time. 'I see,' he says. I'm under no illusion that he's particularly worried about Stuart – after everything else that's happened, this is probably the last thing he needs – someone else going missing.

'OK. I hear you,' he continues. 'Hopefully it will turn out to be a storm in a teacup, a fuss about nothing. But if you really think there's a danger he's gone missing, then we will do the muster call. In the meantime, let's assume that everything is fine and consider it a routine drill.' He clearly doesn't want anyone to suspect that yet another person has gone missing. And in his place, neither would I. But finding Stuart is what's important here, I don't care about Leo's reputation. 'Did you have a time in mind?' Leo asks.

'I thought 4 p.m. today if that suits,' Bill says. 'Outside

338

of mealtimes, and most people won't be asleep – we'll keep it as low impact as possible. That sound OK?'

Leo sighs. 'Yes. Thank you. We'll do that and go from there.'

69

Antonio

7 February 2022, 16:00
The Caribbean

My heart leaps into my mouth when I hear the muster siren go off. I know what this one is for – it's because someone's noticed Stuart's gone.

It will have been Alice who noticed he was missing. They tried to keep it quiet, but I think they were kind of a couple. I almost died when she stopped me to talk about the food when I had Stuart in the trolley. But she can't have suspected anything. Can she? Even if she does, there's no way I'm telling Lola. Who knows what she might do? She and Alice were friends, but Lola is more ruthless than I'd ever known. If she thinks Alice might stand in the way of her plans, I dread to think what she might do. Or try to make me do.

I've made sure that other people have been cleaning the medical centre lately so that mine won't be the last key card to show up. Crew members are in and out of there all the time so I'm confident there will be enough traces that there'll be no reason for suspicion to come my way. And as Lola suggested, I told a couple of people that Stuart had mentioned he was planning to go swimming. I'd be surprised if the rumour can be traced back to me, it's common knowledge around the ship now. I guess that's one advantage of being somewhere with almost no privacy.

Even though I destroyed the paper copy of my DNA results, I imagine there must also be electronic copies, so it's only a matter of time. Hopefully, if I stick to my story about wearing Lola's jumpers, it should be OK. It holds up. I think. Or does it? I'm so confused.

I feel like time is running out for me and Lola. That the net is closing in, and we need to get off this ship as soon as possible. I'm planning to use this latest incident as my excuse to tell Leo that I'm not coping after losing Lola and I need time away after all. I will tell him I'm going to take a holiday until I feel more able to face the world. Which is kind of the truth.

After having to dispose of Stuart, I left it a couple of days before going to see Lola again – I knew she had enough food and didn't feel quite ready to see her or speak to her yet. Plus I didn't trust myself not to let something slip about Alice bumping into me. It's the first time in my life I've ever felt like that about her and I'm not sure what to think about it.

In the days after I did what I did, I felt like I was going mad. I veered between telling Lola I couldn't cope and was going to give myself up, and despair at the thought that I might go to prison and she'd be alone in the outside world, or that she'd go to prison and I'd have failed her yet again. I briefly considered slipping under the water in the bath and not coming up, just so that I wouldn't have to think about it anymore. To no longer be tormented by the nightmares I'm now having where Stuart looks at me with his glassy, sightless eyes, and instead of his voice, there's only the horrific sound of bones crunching in that machine.

But I got over it. Lola needs me. And I owe her. I can't let her down again.

And now that Alice is on to me stealing food, and possibly even more, I need to be careful. It's another good reason for us to get out of here as soon as possible.

Leo has already said he's open to me taking time off so I don't foresee any issue with that. I can even tell him that before Stuart vanished, he prescribed me pills to help me cope.

I leave my trolley and head to the muster station.

70

Alice

8 February 2022, 10:00
The Caribbean

I don't believe in premonitions or a sixth sense or anything like that, but I'm not surprised when Stuart doesn't turn up for the muster call. I already knew something was badly wrong.

What's happened to him? I'm 99 per cent sure that he wouldn't have done something as stupid as going swimming, and that he wasn't suicidal. Why would he have been?

I barely slept last night. In the early hours of the morning, I even started to wonder if the people going missing could be something to do with me. After all, they were all my friends. Lola, then Rick, then Stuart.

Could someone be hurting people to get at me? But who

would do that, and why? I dismiss the thought. It's ridiculous. I'm being paranoid.

Or is it something to do with Antonio? Why was he stealing food? Why was he so strange when I asked him about it? No. That makes no sense whatsoever. Antonio is behaving strangely because he's grieving for Lola.

Then again, someone must have something to do with Stuart going missing, I'm sure of it. I don't see why he'd leave of his own accord, without a word to me. Someone killed Rick. Maybe Lola too. Something is going on. I just don't understand what or why.

As the person who reported Stuart missing, and who is euphemistically described as the 'closest' person to him on board, I'm summoned to Leo's office, where it seems Nico has been flown in. Again.

My eyes are gritty and red from crying and from lack of sleep and I'm annoyed that Nico's here. His presence has nothing to do with concern for what has happened to Stuart, but rather how his disappearance might reflect on Heracles.

'Right.' Nico is terse. 'So no one has any idea where Stuart is? Or what happened? Or even when, by the sound of it?'

'I, um, saw him four nights ago,' I say, blushing. I don't particularly want to talk about my sex life, but I want to do whatever I can to help Stuart. I have the worst feeling that it's already too late. 'He spent the night with me before I got up early to supervise breakfast.'

'And he was at breakfast three days ago – several people remember that,' Leo says. 'Since then, any possible "sightings" are more vague and less definite, but the records show that his room hasn't been opened except by cleaners since February fifth. So it's likely he went missing that day.'

Nico nods. 'I see. I only met Stuart briefly, but he's been with you for a little while now – does he strike you as the kind of person to simply go missing of his own volition, without a word to anyone? Alice – I believe you – erm – knew him quite well? What do you think?'

'In all honesty, no, he doesn't seem like someone who would do that,' I say truthfully. Don't blame him, I'm saying to myself silently. Someone did this to him. Someone on your precious ship. You allowed it to happen. Do the right thing. Do something about it. Find out who did this.

'There's a rumour circulating that he was planning to go swimming,' Leo interjects, 'but I think that must be a false rumour. I don't really think that's something he would—'

'Swimming!' Nico explodes, his face reddening with anger. 'Christ. I assume your crew know that's strictly forbidden, Leo?'

'They do,' Leo says tersely. 'And they also know that there are serious repercussions for anyone caught doing so. But in spite of all the space and the luxurious suites many of them have bagged for themselves during this lay-up, life on board can get pretty claustrophobia-inducing and that some-times leads people to do things they shouldn't. Especially if it gives them a sense of freedom, as arguably, and of course foolishly, swimming in the sea might do. Perhaps during the next lay-up,' he adds pointedly, 'we could consider leaving one of the swimming pools operational for the crew.'

Nico's face darkens – he didn't like that. 'Yes, we could consider it,' he says, 'though it involves more personnel and more expense. I would hope that, usually, crew members would follow instructions as a matter of course, swimming pool or not.'

I shift awkwardly, literally sitting on my hands. Both men are clearly trying to pass the blame on to each other. *This isn't about you*, I want to shout. *A man is missing. He's probably dead. Do something.*

'There is another possibility,' Leo adds. 'I have been in touch with HR at head office and explained the, erm, situation. It turns out that Stuart had a malpractice suit pending against him so it's possible that . . . well, without putting too fine a point on it, it's possible that it was causing him some stress and he went swimming with the explicit plan of not coming back.'

I try not to let the shock show on my face – I guess Leo assumed I already knew about this. So that was why he never wanted to talk about his past. That was why he was here, getting away from things. 'A young man in his care died,' Leo continues. 'There are no criminal proceedings around it, but the patient's family are apparently campaigning to get the General Medical Council to investigate,' he adds. 'That's all I know, but something like that hanging over you . . . well. You know what I'm saying.'

'He was always a bit cagey about his past,' I say. 'But I don't think he'd have . . . he never gave the impression that . . .'

No. You are not going to do this. You are not going to avoid blame for his death by claiming it was a suicide. It wasn't. I'm sure of it. Something has happened here, I think to myself.

'You think it might have been another suicide, Leo?' Nico asks, completely ignoring what I said. Fuck's sake. 'After that young dancer too? Christ, Leo, what kind of ship do you run here?'

Leo turns puce but he ignores the jibe. 'We've launched two lifeboats to see if there is any sign of him,' he says, 'and have also informed the coastguard.'

Nico looks at him in horror. 'You informed the coastguard? Why?'

'If there is a man overboard, they need to know. I followed procedure, as I would assume you would expect me to do.'

'But we don't KNOW if there's a man overboard,' Nico counters. 'He might have . . . oh I don't know, but it's only a rumour that he went swimming by the sound of it? Ships are always full of rumours which turn out to have no foundation. Maybe he had his own reasons for ignoring the muster call, or he's found his way back to land somehow, just left, I don't know. And quite aside from that, if he has been in the water for three days, there's no way he's still going to be alive now, is there? There was no rush to call the coastguard. I'm in charge, I should have been consulted.'

'I'm the captain of this ship, it's my decision,' Leo says tersely, unable to hide his annoyance.

'Technically, yes,' Nico counters, balling his hands into fists. 'But you must see that two people going missing literally on your watch, within as many months, plus another man being found dead in his room, isn't exactly a good look? That's even before we consider the man who died in the hot tub a couple of years back, and before we even look

347

at the fact that it took three days for you to notice someone was missing this time.'

I've no idea what happened with the man in the hot tub – that would have been before my time. But I wish I'd thought to switch my phone on to record this conversation. It's becoming less and less about Stuart and more and more about blame-apportioning and arse-covering as far as I can see.

Leo takes a deep breath. 'As you well know, I have thirty years of experience and an exemplary record at sea. I assume it was for these reasons that Heracles, and, by extension, you, employed me. We don't know for definite that anything untoward has happened to Stuart. Poor Lola, while the investigation is officially ongoing, almost definitely took her own life. And as for Rick – well, we don't know for sure, but it sounds like that may have simply been a . . . game that got out of control. The head electrician was immediately sacked after the unfortunate hot tub incident, and new measures were put in place to prevent a similar accident ever occurring again.' He pauses. 'Which you approved and signed off, if I remember rightly.'

If the hot tub thing was an accident, why is Nico bringing this up now? What does it have to do with anything?

'I thought we were here to talk about Stuart,' I say pointedly. Both men ignore me.

'If Stuart did go swimming, it's probably because he found it too stressful and boring on board,' Leo continues. 'If that turns out to be the case, it could have been possibly avoided if all the pools hadn't been furloughed to save Heracles a few pennies. If anything needs looking at here, it's Heracles' safety procedures and working conditions, not my leadership skills.'

71

Antonio

8 February 2022, 12:00

'I think you were right about what you said the other day, Captain,' I say to Leo. 'I'm not coping with what happened with Lola, and every day I'm still on board is more and more of a reminder of what happened to her. I have decided that I would like to leave after all. If you're still OK with me doing that.'

I twist my hands nervously in my lap. I'm wearing a hoodie which was quite clearly Lola's – it's too small, pink and says 'Lola' on the back – to add credence to my story that I am on the verge of a breakdown and need to leave the ship. With everything else that's gone on lately, Leo surely can't risk another person going missing in action. Better he lets me leave if I appear like I'm a risk to myself – he will know that. And I want us to leave as soon as possible. The longer Lola and I are on board, the higher the chance of us being found out. I'm sure of it.

'I realize this will cause you staffing problems,' I continue, 'and that it's not easy to get back to land, but I can hang on a few days if you like so you can find someone else to replace me and maybe they can come back on the tender you take me over on? Something like that? I'd rather not wait until the next bunker, if possible. If there is a cost associated with it, I'm very happy for that to be withheld from my wages,' I continue. Now that I've made my decision, in all honesty I can't wait to get back on dry land.

'I've tried to stay,' I continue, 'I thought it would be for the best, staying close to Lola, but it's doing my head in. I feel like I'm going mad. I need to accept that she's gone and move on, but I can't do that here. And what happened to Stuart . . . that was the last straw really. I feel like we're being picked off.'

'Picked off?' Leo repeats. Obviously this is not what I think, but I hope it will make me seem paranoid – like someone who shouldn't be here.

'Yeah,' I add. 'But I know that's stupid. Another, more sensible part of me knows that it's not like there's some kind of psychopathic killer on board. Lola killed herself. Stuart got bored, went swimming, and drowned. Rick probably pissed someone off in some way or other or took one of his kinks too far. That's what happened. Rationally, I know that.'

At least, I hope that's what everyone else thinks. All of these things are the most obvious reasons, and the ones which, so far as I know, seem to be the accepted ones. Though

I'm still worried about whether Alice knows something. She and Lola were friends, but she wouldn't have confided her plans not for something like this. Would she?

I push the thought away. Lola wouldn't double-cross me like that. I'm sure of it.

Leo nods. 'I'm inclined to agree with you, Antonio. All these incidents were both tragic and unfortunate, but, in my opinion, unrelated. Sadly, not everyone is as sensible as you in their thinking.'

'But even so' – I twirl my finger in a circular motion at my temple – 'my mind is going to strange places. That's why I need to get away.'

Leo nods. 'I'm glad you came to talk to me, and I understand. I'll do what I can to assure your job whenever you're ready to come back, but I'm afraid it's now looking increasingly likely that I will no longer be employed by Heracles by the time the boat goes back in service. Nico is, understandably, quite upset about everything that's gone on and seems to be laying at least most of the blame at my feet.'

'You're leaving *Immanis*? Is it . . . because of what's been happening?' I ask. I feel a stab of guilt. Poor Leo. None of this is his fault.

He sighs. 'Let's just say I feel I've reached the end of the road with Heracles. I'm not prepared to be treated like a naughty child or to take the blame for things that are clearly—'

He waves his hand in front of his face, interrupting himself. 'But that is neither here nor there and indeed not something I should be sharing with you anyway. My apologies.'

'I will put in a good word for you and do what I can,' he continues. 'I'm sure HR will understand your reasons for

351

leaving and won't hold it against you. More immediately, I'll see what I can do about arranging a transfer – shall we say in a couple of days? Give you time to get your things together, to say your goodbyes and for me to find a replacement for you.'

'That sounds perfect. I appreciate your help, thank you.'

72

Lola

8 February 2022, 21:00
The Caribbean

'OK, well done,' I say to Jesse when he tells me that Leo is arranging to get him off the boat. Finally he's got something right, thank God. 'I think we need to get away from here as soon as possible. They'll probably dig out the DNA results again at some point and I think it's better that you're not around to have to answer questions about that, given how it went last time.' He is still wearing my jumper, the way I told him to, to back up the theory that that is why my hair was found in Rick's room. The jumper looks totally ridiculous on him but whatever, that only adds to the theory that he's half mad.

Which, to be honest, I'm starting to think he is. Since we

had to get rid of Stuart, Antonio's looked terrible. I've tried to jolly him along as much as I can because I need him to help me get off the boat, quite apart from anything else. It's not something I can do by myself and no one else knows I am here. I can't have him having a crisis of confidence and giving himself up, which I get the impression he's on the verge of doing.

Every time I see him now, I am constantly painting a picture of how perfect life in the Caribbean will be, the beach bar we can buy, or the playboy lifestyle he can live wherever he chooses. But in spite of my efforts, all he keeps going on and on about is how his dreams are messed up with images of Stuart's face staring up at him when he opened that mortuary drawer and the sound he made when he went in the grinder. I hope I can still rely on him, but I'm becoming less and less sure of it. I hope he isn't going to do anything stupid.

'I've still got the bag I used to come on board with Rick,' I tell Jesse, holding up a battered canvas holdall, 'so you can use that to get me off the ship again. The only thing we need to plan carefully is when and how I'm going to sneak into your lovely suite without anyone seeing me. I'm quite excited about spending some time in it while you do your "packing".'

That elicits a small smile. I guess the old Jesse is in there somewhere – I'll have to do all I can to bring him out of himself.

'I can take you up on a cleaning trolley like I did with Stuart,' he says. 'We can cover you in sheets. Better to do it in the daytime as I'd have no reason to be doing my job at night. Hiding in plain sight and all that.'

'Clever Jesse. Yes, that makes sense. Once we know when Leo's arranged your transfer to land, we'll do that.'

His face brightens. 'First day of the rest of our lives and all that.' Though he still doesn't sound convinced.

I wonder again if he is having doubts. I push the thought away. I've done all I can.

73

Antonio

14 February 2022, 21:00
The Caribbean

The crew throw me a leaving party. It's absolutely the last thing I want – I would much rather leave unobtrusively and without anyone asking any more questions, to get away, to lie low for a while.

The party seems so out of step with the current mood of the ship to the point of being entirely inappropriate. But it wasn't my idea – I'm not even sure whose idea it was – so it seems rude not to go along with it.

Rumours are rife, as usual. Some are now saying that Rick and Stuart were a couple and the deaths were some kind of murder-suicide thing. Others are sticking to the original theory put about when Rick was found dead that it was a sex game gone wrong, or that he was a drug dealer who pissed someone off. The more hysterical are suggesting a serial killer and the more superstitious, some kind of demon or curse.

Much to Leo's dismay, I am far from the only one leaving on this tender. The ones who are bailing early no doubt won't be welcome back at Heracles, but they don't seem to care. There are always other cruise lines crying out for experienced staff.

The other rumour going around, which is much more likely to be true than any of the others, is that clients are cancelling trips in their droves. They've heard about what the newspapers have dubbed 'the curse of *Immanis*', and it's been suggested that it won't be going back into service as quickly as was planned.

In spite of all this, Alice is putting on a good spread for us. To mark the occasion, Leo's let her fire up TopSail, the restaurant with the Michelin stars which revolves at the top of the ship. The budget, space and no doubt time available for the prep clearly don't extend to the usual fussy dishes that are served here by obsequious waiters in gloves. Instead we have a buffet, but it's quite a step up from our usual chicken and chips, burgers in buns, pasta, noodles and those kind of things that we've generally had while on lay-up. Today there are fancy starters in what look like shot glasses, fresh fish grilled to order on a *plancha* with several different types of sauces which don't taste like they've come out of a bottle, and there is a chocolate fountain with home-made marshmallows. Someone has even switched on the retro revolving function, which is cute.

I think of Lola, many decks below, nibbling the dry food and meagre snacks I've managed to filch over the last few days, since I've had to be a lot more careful, worried that Alice is on to me. I realize with a pang that while there is no question that I must leave the ships for Lola, I am giving up a lot. We've both been working at sea so long neither of us really knows how to cook properly, and there won't be anyone on hand like Alice to do it for us anymore. No rich clients basically paying our food bill and supporting us with their huge tips. No one will clean our rooms or provide fresh towels – we will have to get used to doing all that ourselves. And while I have a bit of money put aside from Mum's will, most of her money went to the church. I'm not exactly going to be living in the lap of luxury while we wait for Lola's life insurance to come through.

I figure that as the party is being held for me (and notionally the others who are leaving, but none of the others have been on board all that long) I need to make an effort and stay to the end, even though I am desperate to get back to Lola to make our final preparations.

At about 10.30 p.m., Leo dings his glass with a knife and the room falls quiet.

'Don't worry, I'll keep it brief,' he says. 'I wanted to take this opportunity to say thank you to all of you for your hard work during what has been a very trying lay-up for many reasons. And to say goodbye to those who are leaving today – I wish you all the best in your future endeavours.'

'I'd also like to announce that I will also be leaving both *Immanis* and Heracles before the ship resumes its service.

By mutual agreement, myself and management have decided that now is the time for me to go.'

There is a general murmur of mild shock – there had been general rumours that Leo and Nico had had some kind of row, but I had kept it to myself when he told me he was leaving.

'And finally' – he raises his glass – 'to absent friends.'

Everyone raises their glass and murmurs 'to absent friends' and for a moment or two the room is silent as we think of Lola, Rick and Stuart. I feel myself go red and look at the floor. Oh God. I can't wait to get off this ship before someone catches up with us.

74

Lola

15 February 2022, 21:00
The Caribbean

'Lucky you being in this suite all the time while I've been stuck in a manky old windowless cabin,' I say. 'I think it's maybe one of the best on board.' I've seen some of the suites before, during our induction, and the occasional time I've had a dalliance with a rich passenger, much to Jesse's disapproval, of course. Shagging the ship's dancer seemed to be a badge of honour among some of them, and they'd ply me with champagne and even sometimes buy me great presents to make it happen. I wasn't so bothered about any of that, I mainly did it out of boredom. To add a bit of variety and risk into my life. Every day can be the same when you're on ship if you're not careful – I was always looking for ways to shake things up a bit.

Things will be easier on land. More space, less gossip. I don't imagine our accommodation will be as lavish as this though.

'Are you all packed?' I ask Jesse. 'I've put my stuff in this little backpack.' It's a Chanel one given to me by some guest keen to bed me, but I imagine Jesse will assume it's a knock-off. 'My things need to be separate from yours so we can split up as quickly as possible once we're on land. It's vital no one who might recognize me sees me.'

'I've booked my travel and a hotel, using my new ID, for a few days until I can find something more permanent,' I continue. 'The island I've chosen for my eventual destination is perfect – big enough that not everyone knows each other, but not too many tourists, almost none from the UK, no immigration requirements we can't meet and plenty of beaches where I can set up a bar. It will be perfect. You're following up on the insurance claim, aren't you?'

'I am, when I can get the WiFi to work,' I say. 'They're dithering because your body hasn't been found, and that means there are more hoops that have to be jumped through and boxes that have to be ticked. But reading between the lines, I don't think it should be too long.'

'I got a report from Leo which stated that both he and the coastguard were of the firm opinion that you couldn't have survived a fall into the water,' he continues. 'It's lucky that woman saw the dummy you threw – that seems to have helped the case quite considerably.'

75

Antonio

16 February 2022, 06:00
The Caribbean

In the morning Lola folds herself into the holdall and I zip
it up. We are leaving early to fit in with the tides and so
there is no one to bid me goodbye, which suits me fine.

The guy driving the tender appears to speak no English
and neither do the other three passengers, which I'm pleased
about. It's too early to make conversation and I wouldn't
want to chat anyway – it feels too weird knowing Lola is
stowed away in the bag. I'm worried in case she hasn't got
enough air or gets cramp or sneezes or something, but she
assured me she would be fine.

The sea is calm and it is beautiful watching the sun rise
on the half-hour journey. Colourful fish dart about in the

clear blue water and the early morning sun is warm on my face. It feels like a new dawn in so many ways. I nod goodbye to the driver and shake hands with my colleagues who I didn't really know as we dock, and watch as the little boat heads back to sea, dwarfed by the enormous ship we've all come from.

I pick up my two bags and head for the cheap hotel room I've booked. And from there, Lola and I will go our separate ways. For now.

PART TEN

76

Lola

Four years earlier
May 2019
London

'Thank you for coming to see me today, Laura,' Karen rasps. She is painfully thin and looks tiny in her pristine hospital bed. 'I know you don't get much leave from the ship and I appreciate you taking the time to come and see me at my request.'

I take her hand and squeeze it. Our relationship since I was found has been up and down to put it mildly, but this woman, who I have never quite been able to accept as my mother, is dying. The least I can do is try and be pleasant to her during her last days. After all, I haven't exactly made things easy since I arrived back in her life, and have barely bothered to come and see her since I left for the ships, however much Jesse has tried to persuade me. I tagged along with him now and again, but the visits always made me feel uncomfortable so whenever I could, I would make an excuse.

'I know it's been hard for you, being reunited with us out of the blue as you were,' she continues. 'I wish things could have run more smoothly. I know you're not a believer, and I respect that, but I want you to know that every day of your life, I've prayed for you. Since you were born giving thanks, since you went missing for your return, and since your return for guidance as to how I can best help you. And of course, in recent years, for the safety of both you and Jesse while you're at sea.'

'I appreciate that, Karen,' I say. I still can't bring myself to call her Mum. She and Jesse have given up hinting that they would like me to, thankfully. 'And I realize that I have not behaved as well as I could have since I was found.'

She tries to squeeze my hand but I can barely feel it she is so weak. Her skin is papery and her breathing is laboured, in spite of the oxygen mask. 'That's OK, my lovely,' she says. 'I understand that it hasn't been easy for you, coming back into our lives. In retrospect, perhaps we should have done things differently. Taken things more slowly. Allowed you more time to adapt. Perhaps you'd even have been better off with a foster family for a while. But that's all very well with perfect hindsight.'

She pauses as her breathing becomes heavier. I don't say anything.

'I want you to know that your return to us was the best thing that ever happened to me,' she continues. 'When you were taken, it was as if someone had ripped out my heart. When you came back, it allowed me to feel whole again.'

Tears come to my eyes. 'I'm sorry I've been so ungrateful,' I say, as suddenly, I am. I could have been kinder to this woman. I have caused her a lot of pain and none of this was her fault. 'And I'm sorry I worried you so much with my behaviour,' I add. 'The drinking. The . . . parties. Trying to hurt myself. Sometimes I've felt so overwhelmed I haven't known what to do. But none of that was fair on you, I understand that now.'

She tries to squeeze my hand again. 'That's OK. But please promise me you won't do that again. Not for me – I will be gone soon. But for you. And for Jesse. He worries about you so much.'

I pause. 'I can't promise that,' I say, because after all, this is pretty much Karen's death bed and if I can't be honest now, then when? 'But I am feeling much better than I was. Working on the ships suits me. And Jesse is always a huge support when things get difficult, I know I can go to him. I'm learning to cope with being me as I am now. It's just taken a bit of time.'

Karen starts to cough and tears come to her eyes. I help her sit up and take a drink of water. God, I hope she's not going to die right now. Karen specifically asked me to come alone for this visit and Jesse wanted to respect her wishes. But he'd be devastated if she dies and he's not here. And I don't want the responsibility of being the last person she talks to.

'Thank you,' she says. 'Now, the reason I asked you to come here today is that I need to tell you something. I have

369

wrestled with it since you came back, and even for many years before that. In fact even before you were taken.'

Oh God. I'm not sure I'm ready for this. Another declaration of how much I mean to her or something like that. I get it, but it's embarrassing. Awkward.

'Many years ago, I did something terrible, and I can't die with it on my conscience. As you know, I find my religion a great comfort, and I simply can't go to my grave with a secret of this magnitude. I need to meet my Lord with a clean conscience.'

Suddenly I am more interested. My first thought is that she had an affair at some point, and either Jesse or I have a different father. Though as he hasn't been on the scene for many years, I don't see what difference it would make to anything.

'Your – your and Jesse's – father couldn't cope with our secret either. That's why he left. Partly, at least. After what happened, he wanted to come clean, tell someone what had happened. What we did. I said no.' She takes my hand again. 'But it was because I was afraid for you, for you and Jesse. Afraid that I would go to prison and that you would have to grow up without me.'

Prison? So not an affair. A thought strikes me – Jesse says he remembers his father leaving but maybe that's a false memory. Perhaps Karen killed him and lied to Jesse about it? No. Surely not. I can't see she'd have it in her.

She has another coughing fit and this one takes longer to subside. Tears are rolling down her cheeks now – clearly not just from the coughing. She is crying and struggling to speak. 'I always felt that you being taken, and my illness too, were both punishment for what I did.'

370

What is she on about? What can she have done that was so terrible? Punishment for what?

She takes my hand again. 'This is going to be difficult for you to hear, so I want you to prepare yourself.'

Her breathing becomes more laboured as more tears flow.

'About six months before you were snatched, we were driving home from a party. Your father and I were arguing. By that point in our marriage it wasn't unusual. I don't even remember what the argument was originally about now but the upshot was that he wouldn't listen when I told him he was too drunk to drive and demanded to take the wheel. I should have been stronger, insisted, but I didn't. I have regretted that every single day since. Every hour of every day.'

'Our row escalated and I was shouting and screaming at him. You had been asleep in the back of the car but you woke up and started crying. This sent me into more of a rage and I began hitting out at Michael.'

I feel sick. Suddenly I know where this is going. And I don't think I want to hear it.

'Jesse started screaming too and before I knew it he had managed to undo his seatbelt and was standing in the foot-well behind me, trying to stop me hitting his dad. Michael turned round to get him back into his seat and that's when the car lost control, spun across the road and hit a small car which was pulling out of a side road.'

I snatch my hand away from Karen's, staring at her open-mouthed.

'I know,' she forces out. 'I don't expect you to forgive me. But telling you is the only way I can even start to forgive

371

myself, or hope that my God will forgive me, wherever I am going next. That car we hit was driven by a young woman and she had her little girl in the back.'

My hand flies to my mouth. She doesn't need to spell it out. It's already obvious to me who they were, otherwise why would she be telling me? They were Dad's girlfriend and child.

'The only comfort I can give you is that they were killed immediately. They wouldn't have suffered and they wouldn't have known anything about it.'

'But . . . why didn't you go to prison?' I ask.

'Because we lied,' she forces out. 'We told the police that I was driving because I was sober. That the other driver was careless, we weren't to blame and that it couldn't have been avoided.'

I stare at her, open-mouthed. Speechless.

'We told them that Jesse was properly restrained. We didn't tell them we were arguing. We were lucky. There were no witnesses, no cameras, we were out in the countryside. There was an investigation, but I was cleared of any wrongdoing. We weren't speeding and we said the car pulled out without checking or indicating – which it did. It turned out the lady driving the other car was on her phone at the time which added credence to our story. It was ruled an unfortunate accident, helped by the fact that she wasn't fully concentrating at the time, and no charges were brought.'

She has another coughing fit and I stare at her in disbelief.

'The accident may have happened anyway, even if Michael had been sober, even if we hadn't been distracted by our row and by Jesse. Who knows? But whichever way you look at it, we lied, and neither of us ever fully forgave ourselves, or each other. Michael sank into a depression and left. I don't even know where he is now. We cut all ties. I felt it was best for all of us. He felt the same.'

What the fuck?

'And my dad . . . the man who brought me up . . .'

'I can only guess that because we took his daughter from him, he decided to take ours,' she continues. 'The police investigated, of course, when you were taken, but the man you called your dad had disappeared and by then was widely assumed by those who knew him to have killed himself, consumed by grief. Especially when his car was found where it was. As the police lady told you.

'We now know that he had changed his identity and was living with you in the farmhouse in Scotland. But until you came back, and the police mentioned his previous name which they discovered in the documents at your house, I had no idea he took you. No one did, because he was assumed to be dead, so he was never a line of investigation. Everyone thought you had been snatched randomly and that we had simply been deeply, deeply unlucky.'

There is silence, punctuated only by Karen's laboured breathing. Is she really telling me what I think she is?

'So it's your fault my dad died?' I clarify. 'Your fault that his family was killed? It's all down to you that I was taken and have to live with the mental scars? Yours, your husband's and Jesse's.'

'Please, please forgive me,' she rasps, but I am not listening. 'I considered telling you when I made the connection, but I couldn't lose you again! I only wanted . . .'

'Does Jesse know about this?' I snap.

'I told him recently, when I could no longer keep it to myself, but he said that you were too fragile, that telling you would only make things worse and . . .'

'He knew about this?' I shriek. This changes everything. He is not the person I thought he was. He doesn't have my back in the way I thought he did. He doesn't have my back at all.

'We only wanted to do what was best for you, please, my darling, don't blame Jesse, tell me that you'll—'

'You selfish bitch,' I interrupt, standing up and leaving the room, as Karen coughs and pleads at my retreating back. A deafening alarm sounds from one of the monitors she is hitched to and ten seconds later a team of medics crash past me and through her door. I don't look back.

Epilogue

Lola

All things considered, life has been pretty fun since I left the ships. It's kind of interesting pretending to be someone else. And a whole different life to being out at sea. No one to tell me what to do. I love it.

Sometimes I wonder who Daniella du Bois was before I took on her identity. Probably some poor child who died shortly after she was born – as far as I understand, that's often where stolen identities usually come from. I left sorting out that side of things to someone else; I just paid the money, told them what I needed, whoever 'they' were, and that was that. It's amazing what you can buy on the dark net. I felt it was kind of a tribute to my dad. I did the same as he did – exacted revenge and then took a new identity. I hope he'd be proud.

Saint Tibuda is beautiful and exactly what I wanted: a

sparsely populated, not too big and not too small island and with only a few tourists who are more at the backpacker end of the scale than high-rollers. It's not on the cruise-ship circuit and not the kind of place that is ever likely to be, so the chances of me bumping into anyone I've ever worked with are minimal.

And even if I did, they probably wouldn't recognize me. New life, new look. I've reinvented myself before – I can do it again. I've grown my hair, dyed it back to blond and braided it. My boobs have gone up another cup size for no reason other than because I fancied it, and I've even had a bum lift – years of dancing has made me boyish and muscular, and I wanted my curves back. Now that I'm out in the sun all day, I'm more tanned and I don't wear much make-up like I did when I was on the ships. Finally, perhaps for the first time in my life, I am doing something just for myself. Living the way I want to.

My life insurance came through for Jesse about three months after we left the ship. He also inherited the few pounds I'd had from the sale of Karen's house once the church had taken the lion's share, according to her wishes, no doubt trying to buy her way in to heaven after lying about being involved in that crash. I'd already spent most of the money I had left from Dad on cosmetic procedures – obviously I knew I was going to 'die' and as everyone says, you can't take it with you. Better to spend it first.

I kept a bit of money aside to keep me going while I established my new identity, but I needed a new cash injection from somewhere pretty quickly, so it was important the life insurance thing worked out. Apparently, most people of my age don't bother with a will or with insurance – weird, when you think about it. You never know what's round the corner, after all, do you? I mean, look at my life so far. Being abducted – no one could have predicted that. Falling off a ship – no one could have predicted that either. And then coming back as someone else – well, hopefully no one will ever get wind of that. I can't see any reason why they would.

Jesse had always been a sensible accountant-type at heart. I persuaded him away from that path years ago when we boarded the ships because he would have done anything for me, but at his core, that's who he was. He never got over that one throwaway comment his mum made about why he wasn't watching me when I was taken. Since then, he's been trying to make up for 'letting me down'. He did let me down, badly, but not in the way he thinks. He should have told me what Karen and her husband did when he found out. I could never, ever forgive him for not doing that.

Once I was ready, I made Jesse and me a fabulous dinner in the little flat we were living in above the bar on St Tibuda and crushed some pills into his food – enough that I knew they'd definitely do the job. I'd already written his suicide note, in which he confessed to killing both Rick and Stuart to protect his sister from their lecherous ways. He also expressed a wish that the rest of his money came to Daniela. I've no idea yet if it'll be accepted as legally binding. Doesn't really matter though – I made sure that most of the money is in the bar, which is in our joint names. I'll be fine. We only had the bar for a short time, but we had great fun doing it up – it was like playing with a giant dolls' house, like the one Dad made for me when I was small.

Jesse was the last person left who was to blame for what happened. Once Karen told me about the crash, and that Jesse knew about it, I realized what I needed to do. They all played their part, the whole family. I needed to take my revenge on all of them. Not just Rick – I was already planning for that, by then, taking my time, and setting things up.

I went online and tracked down my biological father, Michael. It took a while, but given that he spent half his time online entering competitions from his public Facebook page, in the end it wasn't too hard. While there were no photos of him on display in the house, I managed to find some in the loft when Jesse and I cleared out the house before it was sold, so I knew what he looked like and could be pretty sure I had the right person.

I considered hiring a car, finding where he lived and running him down. It felt like it would be satisfying because it would mirror what he did to Dad's family. But it was clear from his page that he lived a quiet life to the point of almost being a hermit and very rarely went out. Plus, by then I was already working on the ships, I had very little time off and it would be hard to get back to where he lived, and there was also a risk that the 'accident' could get traced to me.

So I needed Michael to come to me. I sent him a message from a fake Facebook account telling him he'd won a competition. A cruise! As I suspected, he entered so many competitions it didn't register that he hadn't actually ever entered this one. Many competitions ask you to 'share' that

378

you've entered, so I knew he was often trying to win holidays from what appeared on his feeds.

I also knew from his competition entries and other posts he was keen on hot tubs. He'd been trying to win one for a while. I timed his 'win' with one of my trips back to the UK and paid for the smallest suite I could find with a hot tub on board *Immanis* with some of my money from Dad. I paid in cash in a high street travel agent which has since closed, as so many have. A cruise doesn't have to cost quite as much as you might imagine if you pick the right time of year and anyway, it was worth it.

Then all it took was a quick google of hot tub safety, taking out a breaker switch and loosening a few of the lights to expose some wires, and the electricity did the rest.

He'd only been on board for a few hours, had seen no one and didn't seem to have any family, having entirely cut himself off from Jesse and Karen. His next of kin was given as his virtually estranged elderly father, who turned out to be in very poor health and living in a nursing home. He was happy to accept the explanation of a tragic freak accident and a compensation payment from Heracles in return for signing an NDA.

Jesse died in his sleep at home while I was out walking my little dog Chi-Chi on St Tibuda's main beach. Everyone knew he was very protective of his sister and that he had been deeply unsettled by her death, so while it was a shock when word of his death filtered back to the people who knew him, it wasn't a surprise. Not that there was anyone very close to him left, except Danielle, of course.

Nothing will bring Dad back. But I've done what I can

to avenge his death, and I've inherited all the money which should have been mine anyway. Dad, you always said I could do anything I want. I hope I've made you proud. I'm living the kind of life I imagine you'd have always hoped for me to have, and I've killed everyone who had a hand in your death.

Rest in Peace.

Acknowledgements

Firstly, many thanks to my agent Gaia Banks for not only taking me on all those years ago but really going beyond the call of duty with this one by taking my fretful plotting calls during your maternity leave. As usual you have been a huge help at all stages of the book and I really appreciate it. Also to my incredible editor Phoebe Morgan for your incredible positivity, patience and generosity with your time, as well as making my books much better than they would have been without your input.

Living on a hill in the middle of nowhere I spend a lot of time online – thanks to all my online friends who find they have to get involved with questions about everything from the use of capital letters to help with character names. Special thanks to Steff Gray for the ship's name, and the people of the Facebook groups Ships in Torbay and Lyme Bay, and Cruise Ships in Torbay and Lyme Bay for their help with various queries and also simply for being such a haven of calm on social media. Life on board *Immanis* is a mix of research and total invention and any anomalies and mistakes are, of course, my own.

Many thanks to my (again mainly online) writer friends (I am SO looking forward to finally meeting some of you this year!) who are such a great support, especially Sarah Clarke for coming up with an idea for a plot point which really helped A LOT. Thank you also to beta readers Hannah Parry, Emma Haughton, Eve Ainsworth, Claire Seeber and Jackie Wesley who read the book at various stages and all helped to shape it in some way or another. I hope you approve of how it turned out!

Thanks to Graham Bartlett @gbpoliceadvisor for reassuring me over another plot panic so quickly and to all the many writers who recommended him when I was having said panic.

Thank you to Stu Cummins, not only for being such as supportive and enthusiastic reader and reviewer, but also for bidding very generously in the Books for Vaccines auction in aid of Care UK to name a character in *The Cruise*. Thank you also for putting up with my over-zealous checking that you didn't mind if he came to a gruesome end!

Thanks as always to Alex for your constant support and doing everything while I get on with the writing, and to Toby and Livi for having grown up into amazing people who make me proud every day.

And thank you to all the readers who have been so supportive of the books so far! I love reading your messages and seeing your pictures on Insta and read and appreciate literally all my reviews.

Finally – a quick word on cruising. This novel was in part inspired by images of the cruise ships laid up off the coast of the UK during Covid, and I'm delighted to see the cruise industry now picking up again. While it is true that occasionally people do go missing from cruise ships, the vast majority of the millions of passengers who cruise each year are delighted with their trips. It remains one of the safest forms of travel and *The Cruise* is not intended to be a realistic depiction of life working on a cruise ship in any way.

If you enjoyed *The Cruise*, don't miss out on Catherine Cooper's other gripping thrillers

Four friends. One luxury getaway. The perfect murder.

French Alps, 1998
Two young men ski into a blizzard . . .
but only one returns.
20 years later
Four people connected to the missing man find themselves
in that same resort. Each has a secret. Two may have
blood on their hands. One is a killer-in-waiting.
Someone knows what really happened that day.
And somebody will pay.

They thought it was perfect. They were wrong . . .

A couple on the brink
A body on the lawn
Welcome to...

THE CHATEAU

CATHERINE COOPER
THE SUNDAY TIMES BESTSELLER

A glamorous chateau

Aura and Nick don't talk about what happened in
England. They've bought a chateau in France to make a
fresh start, and their kids need them to stay together –
whatever it costs.

A couple on the brink

The expat community is welcoming, but when a neigh-
bour is murdered at a lavish party, Aura and Nick don't
know who to trust.

A secret that is bound to come out . . .

Someone knows exactly why they really
came to the chateau. And someone is going
to give them what they deserve.